EDDIE
AND THE
CRUISERS

For James –
in Gambier…
all the best,

P. F. Kluge

Also by P.F. Kluge

The Biggest Elvis

Call From Jersey

Gone Tomorrow

The Master Blaster

EDDIE
AND THE
CRUISERS

P. F. KLUGE

With a new introduction by
Sherman Alexie

THE OVERLOOK PRESS
New York, NY

To Pamela Hollie
and in memory of Denham Sutcliffe

This edition first published in the United States in 2008 by
The Overlook Press, Peter Mayer Publishers, Inc.

141 Wooster Street
New York, NY 10012
www.overlookpress.com
For and special sales, please contact sales@overlookny.com,
or write us at the above address.

Library of Congress Cataloging-in-Publication Data
Kluge, Paul Frederick, 1924–
Eddie and the Cruisers.
I. Title
PZ4.K6775ED   [PS3561.L77]   813'.54   80-14786

ACKNOWLEDGMENTS

Grateful acknowledgment is made to the following for permission to reprint
copyrighted material:

April-Blackwood Music: Portions of lyrics from "My Boyfriend's Back" by
Robert Feldman, Richard Gottehrer, and Gerald Goldstein. Copyright © 1963
by Blackwood Music Inc. All rights reserved. Used by permission.

House of Bryant Publications: Portions of lyrics from "Bird Dog" by Boud-
leaux Bryant. Copyright © 1958 by House of Bryant Publications. All foreign
rights controlled by Acuff-Rose Publishers. International copyright secured.
All right reserves

Manufactured in the United States of America
ISBN 978-1-59020-094-0
10 9 8 7 6 5 4 3 2

"There's not a breathing of the common wind
That will forget thee . . ."

WORDSWORTH,
"To Toussaint L"Ouverture"

Introduction

SHERMAN ALEXIE

Can anybody disappear anymore?

Sure, they can. Think of the airplanes—small, large, jumbo—that have crashed into mountainous forests and have never been found. Think of the children and adults—abducted or misguided or purposefully nomadic—who walked out of their houses and have never been seen again. I remember a special issue of *Sports Illustrated* that asked the existential question, "Where are they now?" The magazine featured a team photo of the Bad News Bears—that group of foul-mouthed, untalented, socially inept, and heroic Little League baseball players of 1970s movie fame—and updated the life stories of all of the kid actors. A few of them had remained in show business, but most of the rest had moved into non-Hollywood lives—nine to five jobs, families, children, and sometimes divorce and early death. But one of the kids—now a man in his mid-forties—could not found. How did *Sports Illustrated* put it? The guy's "whereabouts were unknown." Jesus, if *Sports Illustrated*, a massive journalistic organization, can't find a man—can't find any trace of his current location—it means that man doesn't want to be found.

And what about that other kid actor, the one who starred in a few major 1980s teen movies, then quit show business a few years later and also chose to disappear? I won't use his name because he's hiding in plain sight. Of course, it would be pretty easy to do a Google search and find this guy and his story. I'm sure a few 80's movie fans have already done that, and they would have learned the kid—always a brilliant and eccentric actor—has become a brilliant and eccentric college professor teaching highly esoteric subjects. I found him in seconds. And I've read "Where are they now?" interviews with him where he seems to be both fond and rueful of his Hollywood life. If I were a more aggressive writer (or, frankly, a rude bastard), I'd call up the professor and ask him what it feels like to disappear. I'd ask him if he's ever read P.F. Kluge's novel, *Eddie and the Cruisers*.

And I'm sure he'd tell me that, no, he hasn't read the novel, but he's seen the movie. Or at least heard of the movie. I'm sure the professor would say, "Wasn't that the one about the rock star who disappears? Or drives his car off a bridge and dies? I've seen parts of it on cable, I think." And I'd have to tell him that he's more likely seen parts of *Eddie and the Cruisers 2: Eddie Lives!* And that he shouldn't judge the first film or the novel on the quality of the sequel, which is one of most inert and awful films ever made. But let's not get sidetracked by sequels. Let's focus on the original *Eddie and the Cruisers*, both the film and novel.

The film flopped when it was released into theatres in 1983, but it became one of the first such films to achieve cult status when it was released and "rediscovered" on cable television and home video. I first saw the film on VHS while I was in high school, along with a bunch of my basketball teammates, and most of them hated it. It was too romantic and nostalgic for most teenage boys ("Why would a rock star kill himself? Or even stupider, pretend to kill himself and disappear?"), and the music was too mainstream rock for a bunch of farm kids who either listened entirely to Hank Williams, Jr. and Alabama or to Judas Priest and Black Sabbath. But a few of us quietly loved the flick. My best friend Steve and I became obsessed with it.

First of all, Steve and I had more diverse music tastes than our friends did. We made a point of reading music magazines to search for new bands and to ask music store employees for recommendations. So the New Jersey rock of Eddie and the Cruisers, as performed by John Cafferty and the Beaver Brown Band, was a revelation to us. Of course, Bruce Springsteen is the most famous and talented New Jersey rock star, but he hadn't yet taken over the world when Steve and I first heard Eddie and the Cruisers. In a way, Eddie and the Cruisers was our gateway drug into the three-chord heroin that is Springsteen. And if there is one word to describe Springsteen, Eddie and the Cruisers, and New Jersey rock, it is loneliness. Yes, it's often loneliness that you can dance to, but it's a dance filled with shame, rage, romance, torrid sex, heartbreak, isolation, and the ruined cities of Jersey.

And since Steve and I were also reservation kids, we were well versed in another kind of loneliness, with the genetic dread of being Indian, of being poor, of being forgotten. We were also intimately familiar with suicide and young and tragic death. The fictional rock star, Eddie Wilson, had, in a fit of rage and loneliness and thwarted ambition, had driven his car off a bridge and died. And Steve and I knew a dozen reservation kids who'd also killed themselves, who'd essentially died of broken hearts. I mean, if you've ever been lying in your bed at one in the morning, and heard that tribal 4/4 drum beat ripping through the powwow sky, then you know that Indians were at least partially responsible for inventing the blues.

So, okay, Steve and I were in love with a movie that turned loneliness into a series of Top Forty hits, "On the Dark Side" and "Tender Years" being two of the biggest.

But what about the novel? What about the author, P.F. Kluge?

Well, I'm ashamed to admit that, for many years, I didn't know the movie was based on a book. And though I was a bookish teenager, I'm not sure I would have much cared about reading the novel, especially a "literary" novel that had ambitions and secrets and qualities far beyond that of the mainstream film it inspired. It was only a few years ago, after I had become a successful "literary" writer myself, that I learned the film was based on P.F. Kluge's novel. But it had gone out of print not long after it was published and had never been published in paperback format outside of a special edition printed by Kluge's alma mater and employer, Kenyon College. I am doubly ashamed to admit that I was curious about the novel but had never actively tried to obtain a copy.

Much like its protagonist, Eddie Wilson, the novel had disappeared.

But then, a couple years back, while browsing the shelves of a local used bookstore, I found a battered copy of *Eddie and the Cruisers*. I excitedly bought it, took it home, sat on my couch, and read it straight through in one sitting. I know people say that all the time about great books. But just because it's a cliché doesn't make it any less true. I read the book, happily noticing the plot and character similarities with the movie, but found myself increasingly stunned—more like shattered—by the novel's far darker and disturbing tone.

To get Springsteenian, if the film, *Eddie and the Cruisers*, is an abandoned hotel on the Atlantic City boardwalk, then the novel, *Eddie and the Cruisers*, is that same hotel with a wrecking ball shattering its walls, windows, and foundation.

There is death in this book. Yes, this is a rock and roll novel about death. The death of humans, certainly. But also the death of dreams. The death of ambition. The death of art. The death of hope. Sometimes it feels like P.F. Kluge must have written this while working part-time in an abattoir with a great jukebox. And a great selection or porn. Check out the description of a seminal Eddie and the Cruisers concert:

> "We played for nearly two hours, no breaks, no patter, no tuning or stalling, Eddie rushing from one song to another, and the way he pounced on the songs, the way he explored, prolonged, teased, reprised, exhausted them, you had to think—and I later confirmed this with some other people— that he was fucking the songs."

Or how about this description of why Eddie and the Cruisers, after being off the charts and out of mind for decades, suddenly matter again:

> "Eddie never figured he was writing classics. His songs were the offsprings of moods: a knockout girl in Cape May, a hangover in Absecon. He tossed them off and the met their fates in the most transient of trades, a Number Eight or a Number Eighty. An upward curve and the inevitable downward Fall on the Billboard list. And that was it. Nobody Listened to "golden oldies" back then. We didn't Get nostalgic about dead singers and disbanded Groups. Russ Colombo? Glenn Miller? We looked Ahead, to tonight, this weekend, next summer. Now, Everybody was looking back. Even the kids. That Was the difference between then and now. Something Had changed in the land, and Eddie's music was part Of the change."

Jesus, doesn't that paragraph sound like the mission statement of VH1 and its endless parade of shows featuring washed-up rock stars, actors, and athletes? For a couple of years, VH1 ran a series, *Reunited*, that sought out the members of long-disbanded and formally successful rock bands, like The Motels and ABC and Berlin, and reunited them live and onstage. Last year, I was boggled out of my mind when my fourteen-year-old niece showed up wearing a Ramones T-shirt.

"Do you even know who the Ramones are?" I asked.

"Yeah," she said. "But I like Iggy Pop more."

This is a girl who should be listening to Hannah Montana, and she does and likes it, I think, but she'd much rather dye her hair some strange color and pogo all around an all-ages dance club floor to the roaring (and middle-aged) anarchy of punk.

It would seem that P.F. Kluge was prescient when he wrote *Eddie and the Cruisers* and detailed the ways in which a long-dead rock star can matter more to us—his listeners—than he did when he was alive.

Kurt Cobain, anyone?

Fourteen years after his suicide, he's still a major rock star. Our local alternative radio station, 107.8 THE END, still features Cobain and Nirvana on a nightly basis. And many of the businesses in my neighborhood still feature bounced checks from Courtney Love, Cobain's rock star widow.

And, of course, as with many rock star deaths, there are quite a few conspiracy-minded folks who think Love murdered Cobain, or rather, had him murdered. It's become an important of recent rock and roll mythology (just as it was part of Jim Morrison's supposedly suspicious death). More relevant, there are plenty of folks who think Cobain, Morrison, Jimi Hendrix, and Elvis are still alive and are physically walking the earth.

And in P.F. Kluge's fictional world, there are people who think Eddie Wilson is still alive. Oh, why do they need him to be alive? Because music never dies, and yet there are so many dead men and women's voices roaring, so alive, out of our radios and IPods. It's tough to live with that particular contradiction. We need our dead rock stars to be alive because we want them to create new music.

And there's the thing—the MacGuffin—that motivates and advances this story: it's Eddie Wilson's lost music, the mythical album called *Leaves of Grass*, the title borrowed from Walt Whitman, of course. It's rumored to be a work of genius—an instant classic—that will sell millions of copies and make millions of dollars. And there is somebody—maybe even Eddie Wilson himself or one of his former band mates—who wants possession of that lost music and will do anything—including murder—to obtain it.

But here's the strangest thing about the novel—the most improbable, gorgeous, and mythical part—the album, *Leaves of Grass*, is actually the recording of a legendary studio session featuring Eddie Wilson and—well, I don't want to say too much so let's just say that Walt Whitman would have been extremely excited to be sitting in the recording booth that night.

Okay, so yes, near the end of this introduction, you're probably thinking, "But isn't this just a rock and roll novel? And isn't it an early novel by a young man that is filled with hyperbole, awkward writing, and some poetic pretensions?" And, yes, I'd have to be honest and say, "This novel does have serious problems—foundational issues—but it's also a gorgeous and achingly painful song of the soul. It's not just a rock and roll novel. It is something more."

But, damn it, I have struggled to write more exactly about that "something more." So perhaps I'll let P.F. Kluge do it for me. This is Frank Ridgeway, keyboardist and lyricist for the Cruisers, and English Literature major, describing how he first came to be part of the band:

"Well, there's this phrase that Eddie sings: 'Come on, baby . . . baby, come on!!' Now Sal wanted him to sing it like it was prose, with no break and no emphasis on the repetition. 'Come on, baby, baby, come on.' 'Nice and steady, like it's a damn hula!' Eddie said. Sal pictured dance tunes, and nobody should lose the beat, miss a step. Eddie wanted the pause and he wanted to hit the repetition hard, so that what was first heard as an invitation returned as a . . . scream . . . Then (Eddie) asked me what did I think. Should he sing it straight through, like Sal wanted? Or should he pause? You know what I said? It's embarrassing now. I said, 'I like the caesura.'"

Yes, P.F. Kluge, that brave and crazy bastard, pauses in the middle of a rock and roll novel to invoke that poetic idea, the caesura, which is "a timely pause, a kind of strategic silence. It's not dictated by meter or beat, but by the meaning of what you're trying to get across." But here's the ballsiest thing: After Ridgeway invokes the caesura, Eddie Wilson fucking embraces the concept and makes it his own.

Yes, this is a novel about sex, drugs, rock and roll, murder, and the caesura. How could one not love it?

Writers and would-be writers—I put myself in the second group—are always carrying on about how they need an ideal place to work: a lighthouse, a forester's cottage, a garret or a gatehouse. I'm laboring in much less picturesque surroundings: a rented trailer in a mobile-home park in Melbourne, Florida. I've been here two weeks already, and I'll need at least another month.

It's August down here now, and no matter what you've read about Florida being an all-year vacationland, the airconditioners are running round the clock, the grass—except where the airconditioners drip down—is adobe brown, and the tourists are pointed back to New Jersey, where I belong. Florida, this patch of it, is restored to the senior citizens.

I live a very regulated life. I'm like some of my neighbors, those morbid humorists who call themselves "the purple hearts." A cardiac or two behind them, and not much they can do about the next one but watch their step, save their strength, live carefully to stretch out what little time they have.

The alarm rings at five. I plug in the coffee pot and walk through the trailer camp while it's still dark and cool and safe. If there's a new car parked outside a trailer, or an unfamiliar stranger strolling through the scrub pine, a light on that's usually out, a radio off that's usually on, I notice it. I know who sleeps late and who sleeps light, who gets company and who lives alone, who plays records, who plays cards. I know, approximately, what they've got and how long they have. Like the purple hearts, I want every day to be just like the one before it, no more, no less.

A lot of the old-timers are up at dawn. It's as if, by establishing an early foothold, they improve their chances of lasting through the whole day. It's a sentiment I've come to share, though I'm only in my mid-thirties. So I'm out there first thing, nodding to Walt Schumacher, who likes to walk a little before cooking breakfast for his wife, Minnie, who had a stroke. There's Ed Riley, who goes through life hating the Yankees and that s.o.b. Billy Martin. And Al Ferraro, lame as his dog, Speed, and Martha Darmstadter, who mainly wants to advertise that she's tired of being a widow: "Two Social Security checks can live as cheaply as one." There's not much conversation on the dawn patrol. Evenings are different—nervous, nosey, garrulous.

By nine o'clock, everybody's behind their airconditioners. I stay indoors till dark. I'm either working or napping—restless, unsatisfying naps with all my clothes on, from which I awake feeling smothered and guilty about writing not done.

Early evenings, I've decided, are the time to relax, move around a little, take chances. So, in the hour of barbecues and garden hoses, I emerge with my lies: I am someone named Frank Dayton; I am divorced; I am recovering from an operation which everyone assumes uncovered a hopelessly metastasized cancer. All I had to do was mention the name of the hospital, a famous institution of last resort. Herman Biedermann hinted he could line up laetrile. I asked, instead, for an occasional lift to the I.G.A. store. Since I ditched my car to make my trail harder to follow, Herman is my supermarket connection. He drives, I carry the groceries.

I fit right in here. With remarkably few questions they've accepted me into this melancholy little commune, assuming that I am waiting for the same dread call that they're expecting. In this, of course, they are dead right. No one asks how much time I have, but I know they've discussed it among themselves, and the answer has to be: not much.

1

It began on a Sunday morning.

Not in church. It was at the Safeway supermarket. We do all our food-shopping on Sundays, before the churches let out, and it's become something of a ritual in itself. Bringing home the bacon, bringing in the sheaves.

Do you remember an old daytime TV show called *Supermarket Sweep*? A half-dozen contestants line up at the checkout counter of one of those huge suburban stores where the aisles go on for miles; the cookies alone take up a hundred yards. At the buzzer, the competitors rush out the starting gate and race up and down the aisles, heaving one item after another into their shopping carts. They have five minutes to rampage through the store, and the winner is the one who makes it back to the cash registers with the most expensive load.

That's my family.

While they cruise the aisles, I sit near the door, atop a pile of twenty-five-pound dog-food bags. Sometimes I flip through *People* magazine, or chat with my students' parents, or smile and wave at my family: buy this not that, get the big size not the little.

On other Sundays, bad-mood Sundays, I just think. This was one of those. I watched my wife and two daughters moving around on the other side of the cash registers. I felt like an outsider, a spectator. They weren't mine, they had nothing to do with me. As I watched them proceed from meats to vegetables, I realized for the first time that more than laziness or mere habit kept me from joining them: something inside me was keeping a distance. Something always had.

What would I have made of this, on my own? Probably nothing. I had grown used to being the man I was and had no idea how to go about changing. I'm sure my perching exile atop the dog-food bags would have become just another habit, like my scary little trick of driving with the headlights off on moonlit nights.

That's when it all began.

I heard a radio playing music, rather loud. A group of checkout clerks and bag-boys were standing around somebody's portable radio, listening to music and moving to the beat. They must have liked it. They turned it up again, and this time it was way too loud. The manager popped up behind his glass-walled cubbyhole, cast me an apologetic glance, and shouted for them to turn that damn thing down or they'd have to turn it off. The kids looked over at the manager. They'd heard him, but there was an irritating ten seconds of noncompliance while they waited for the music to end. By the time the manager was ready for a second warning, the song was over.

Doris and the girls reached the cash register just then, so there was nothing I could do right off. But the kid who helped carry our bags to the car—actually, all he did was push the cart through the parking lot and lift the bags into the trunk—had been in the group around the radio. I knew him from school. He was one of my students, a soon-to-be high school graduate who wasn't college material and wasn't worrying about it.

"How are you doing, Anthony?" I asked.

"Fine, Mr. Ridgeway. Could you call me Tony?" He asked politely, but in a way that told me he knew my control over him was ending. He was going to be a high school graduate. Named Tony.

"Sure, Tony. Hey, I wanted to ask you about that song."

"What song?"

"On the radio at the checkout counter. A bunch of you were listening. The manager broke it up."

"Oh yeah . . . that song."

"Yes."

"Well . . . what about it?"

"Is it a new hit?"

"I guess so."

"What's it called?"

"I don't know."

"Who's it by?"

"Got me. Some group. Sounded like a bunch of guys."

"You like that sound?"

"Well . . ." He backed off a little, abashed by the older generation's curiosity. A little annoyed. He'd already spent so many mornings scrambling for answers to my questions, and they were always wrong.

"That music up your alley, Anthony?"

"Yeah," he replied. "Yeah. Suits me fine."

I tipped him fifty cents, slammed the trunk, and watched Tony walk away. No doubt he wondered why his high school teacher couldn't mind his own business. Was I trying to get "with it"? That would be a joke!

But the joke was on you, Anthony. And it was my business. And I was "with it."

I wrote that song.

And I was one of the guys you heard singing.

Long time ago.

The song was no fluke. I kept hearing it. I heard it late that night in my den, while waiting for the late news. I heard it when I drove to school Monday morning: Eddie Wilson and the Parkway Cruisers singing "Far-Away Woman." In the parking lot, the study hall, up and down the corridors, it was in the air, alive and sounding like new.

At first, I was amused. To think that after a dozen years of inflicting great literature on captive juveniles, after all the recitation and discussing and testing—"Thanatopsis" and "Oh Captain, My Captain"—my big breakthrough might be the casual product of a long-ago summer: "Far-Away Woman"! Suddenly, I was part of my students' lives. By accident, I'd connected. Where they drove, or danced, or copulated, my words followed them, my voice singing in the background. And they didn't know it.

That would have meant a lot to me once. I came back to this high school as a teacher just six years after I graduated, and at the start, I was all full of hope of connecting with my students, bartering my reading for their youth. I would help them grow, and they would keep me young. I wanted to be near them, and I hoped they would want to be around me. Not anymore.

I wanted to keep quiet about "Far-Away Woman." What good would it do if people learned that Mr. Ridgeway had once been a Parkway Cruiser? Would my students ask me to emcee talent night? Interview me in the school paper? Spare me that! And spare me the wry wit of my colleagues, who have the minds of clerks and the style of turnkeys. No. I'd had good reasons for never mentioning that summer, and now that this one echo was sounding, my reasons were better than ever. I'd been a teacher for a dozen years; I was a Cruiser for only one. I was—I thought—a good high school teacher, whereas my singing was average, my guitar playing downright bad, and only an odd knack for writing lyrics had persuaded Eddie Wilson to take me into the group. Most important of all: that was then, this was now. The then and the now didn't connect. Not at all. My life as a Cruiser had died on the shoulder of the Garden State Parkway, along with the man who inspired it. When he died, I decided the time of wonder and adventure was over for me. It was time to get to work, to marry, buy a home. When I thought back on that one brief episode, I figured it was gone forever.

So what, I asked myself, if some disc jockey dug into the archives and blew dust off some relic 45 called "Far-Away Woman"? He played it as a whim, a blast from the past, a moldy oldy from the musical groove-yard, gone from the charts but not from our hearts. Who knows how these things happen, these mass-cultural tumults, these vogues and fads and styles? The record draws a response; from way back and far off it reaches out, touches hearts, and triggers memories, and it's all an accident. Before you know it, it's over.

". . . and so I dare to hope
   though changed, no doubt, from what I was when first
   I came among these hills . . ."

You can't ask high school students to read poetry aloud. The tough kids march through it fast, like they were reading out of an auto-parts catalog. The sensitive ones, the college preppies, go overboard: they all sound like Liberace. No matter, one side of the classroom ends up laughing at the other, and the poem gets lost. So I do all the reading, slow, plain, direct, as if we were having an important talk. If my students have to laugh, they have to laugh at me. And they do.

"What's Wordsworth getting at?" I asked, rising from my chair and moving out to the front of the desk. My informal, conversational posture.

"You understand the situation?" I continued. "The poet has returned to a place he loves, a place in the country. He hasn't been back for years. He's looking for changes in the place. But places don't change . . ."

It wasn't working. The plainest, nicest springtime poem in the textbook might have been written in Sanskrit. Some of them were taking notes; at least, they were moving pens across paper. Their yellow magic markers squeaked and left blotches the color of urine stains on public property.

I spoke. They wrote. Truth turned into cliché at the stroke of a pen, filed away and forgotten along with my other senior English themes: "Freedom/Responsibility: go together." "Irony: diff between expect & reality." "Juxtapose: place opposite to show something." And what else? "Ridgeway sucks."

At least the punks didn't pretend industry. They slouched in their chairs and stared out the windows or rooted for the clock on the wall. Give me the punks. Any day.

"Poems don't change. But people do. People change. People change and . . ."

And I despaired. They were too close to graduation. Proms, parties, graduation . . . liberation. The sap rising in dozens of erect, untested penises. Ink drying on a sheaf of birth-control prescriptions. A sense of urgent, straining ripeness. "Far-Away Woman"!

"... or maybe they don't change. What do you think, Mr. Russo?"

"What do *I* think?" Tony leaned back even further in his chair, Gary Gilmore indifferently awaiting the sentence of the court.

"Yes."

"About what?" Such a tone of weariness from him. And why not? Twelve years in this chalky, penal world: cafeteria food, halls that smelled of disinfectant, broken lockers. Twelve years that were almost over, and now I insisted on a reprise of the same old shit. Couldn't I respect the rights of a short-timer?

"About people, Anthony." I relished the "Anthony." I could see he hated it and watched him wondering how he could defy me. He thought about it, taking time to calculate. There was an intelligent man in there someplace.

"What people did you have in mind?"

"Well, take the narrator of the poem. Since that's what we were talking about."

"I wasn't talking," he corrected me.

"Now you are," I snapped. "Read it."

He read aloud, and badly, but I'll say this: everybody listened.

"Well," I pressed, "what do *you* think?"

"He says he's changed. Sh—shoot. What'd you ask me for? It's right there. He's changed. Sure. Know what, Mr. Ridgeway?"

"What?" He was on the attack now. He was going to try to get away with something. And I couldn't stop him. I started it.

"This guy isn't in the hills. He sounds more like he's *over* the hill."

They liked that. The punks laughed first, but the note-takers joined in, once they figured they could get away with it.

"Over the hill, around the bend, washed up. A quart low, minimum."

The bell rang then. Point, game, match . . . and diploma
. . . to Mr. Russo.

I watched them leave and turned back to my desk, gather-
ing up a stack of exams I decided I wouldn't bother grading.
I sat heavily in my chair and swiveled toward the blackboard. It was no good. Why bother? What lived for them was
dead for me. What lived for me was dead to them. Except,
of course, that song—an exception, in this case, which
proved the rule.

No, I'm not such a hot teacher after all, not these days.
Not funny enough to be liked or tough enough to be re-
spected. And the main reason is that I don't much like my
students. It wasn't always that way. My second year, they
voted me most popular faculty member and dedicated the
yearbook to me, complete with an epigraph from Chaucer
that I suggested: "Gladly would he learn, and gladly teach."
Back then, I would've made Tony Russo my personal recla-
mation project. I'd have slapped him with a week of deten-
tion and stayed after school with him, talking late, winning
him over. And if "Far-Away Woman" had popped up then,
you can bet the whole school would've known about it. I'd
have had everybody writing lyrics, and singing them too.

What went wrong? All I can tell you is that, as the years
passed, the gap between me and my students widened. I
thought less and less of the kids who'd inherited my youth.
I resented and envied them. Maybe it's an occupational hazard, inevitable when you see them marching in every September and out every June, year after year, a bountiful
harvest of C's that might as well be F's. Am I putting down
the kids? Well, I guess I am. Were we any different? Yes, I
think we were. Sorry, but I think that things are winding
down in America right now. Perhaps I shouldn't complain—
nobody ever said that things would stay the same forever,
let alone improve, so let's just leave it at this: a dozen years
of seeing what goes in and out of a public high school has
made a pacifist out of me. I pray for peace, peace in these
kids' prime and in my old age, because if these kids ever get

into a war, it'll probably be a wrong war. And, worse yet, I bet they lose.

I got up to leave and saw the guy sitting in the back row, as if I'd kept him after class. Except that he wasn't one of my students. During class I'd barely noticed him because, when it gets close to graduation time, lots of strangers show up: friends, fiancées, relatives. But now he was sitting there alone, and I didn't know why.

He had black curly hair, a thin face, a bit of a beak. Jewish suburban. Not the future doctor-lawyer. More the would-be film critic or musician, the kind of kid who goes into the city on weekends to ride the Staten Island ferry and listen to jazz.

"Are you looking for someone?" I asked.

He was probably in his twenties but dressed like a kid: jeans, running shoes, T-shirt, windbreaker. What's more, he acted like a kid, tense and hyper. It was an effort for him to sit still.

"Yes sir, I am," he replied.

"Who?"

"You. I think."

"You sat all through class?"

"Yes."

"Why?"

"Because I was interested."

"In 'Tintern Abbey'?"

"No sir. That's not the lyric I had in mind."

"What is it then?"

" 'Far-Away Woman.' "

He got up, leaned down, grabbed a knapsack I hadn't noticed, and came toward me, smiling. So I'd been found.

"Let me make sure, first off, that I haven't gotten everything fouled up," he said, with an awkwardness I later realized was cultivated. At the moment it worked.

"You're Frank Ridgeway, Junior. Am I right so far?"

"Yes."

"You live at 232 Old Sawmill Way, in town. Yes?"

"Yes."

"You lived here as a kid, didn't you?"

"Why yes . . . but I don't see how . . ."

"That's how I found you!" he exulted. "Some crummy article from 1958 gave all the Cruisers' hometowns. So when I started this, I hit the phone-book section at the public library. I never figured it would be that simple, and for a while, it wasn't. I mean everybody else has moved. Except Eddie Wilson, of course."

"Yeah," I said. "Eddie's just a memory."

"His parents are still alive, you know. Still living down in Vineland."

"I didn't know," I said. "I'm . . . glad to hear that. Though it seems a little strange."

"Strange? Oh, yeah, I see. The son dead for nearly twenty years and the parents still puttering around." He paused and looked at me as if I, too, would fit in the category strange. "Anyway, I've come to the right place. I mean, just to pin it down, you *are* the same Frank Ridgeway who was with Eddie Wilson and the Parkway Cruisers?"

"Yeah," I said, and began to feel tired.

"That's great!" He looked me up and down, beaming, as if he'd just rescued an endangered species: now, if only it could be persuaded to breed in captivity, the future was bright.

"I'm not sure I'd have spotted you," he said.

"Nobody has."

"I've gone through all the old pictures—magazines and such. What little there was."

"We weren't around that long."

"I've gotten hold of everything there was to get. Pictures you've probably forgotten. I'll make copies. Still . . . it's not that you've gotten real old . . . it's some other kind of change."

"Back then I was a guitar player who bought clothes at the Army-Navy. Now I'm a teacher. I buy suits after Christ-

mas at Herman's on the Highway. 'A little profit on a lot of
suits beats a lot of profit on a few.' "

He kept staring at me and I confess I was beginning to
find this rapt attention flattering, especially after Russo's
triumph of wit. The way he looked at me, you'd have thought
he expected me to break right out into song. I decided I'd
better set him straight.

"Those days I had resin on my fingers," I remarked, clapping my hands together. "These days . . . chalk."

That's when he unzipped his knapsack and I spotted the
tape recorder inside.

"I've got to get this," he said. "Is there an outlet? You
must show movies or something."

"Wait a minute. Haven't you forgotten something?"

"I hope not," he said, still rooting around in the bag. "I
think it's all here, but these contraptions always make me
nervous."

"Like your name. And who you're with. And what you
want."

"Oh! I forgot! I'm sorry. I smuggle myself into your classroom, start interrogating, and you don't even know who I
am."

"Should I?"

"I guess not. Elliot Mannheim. From the City. I'm a free-
lance journalist. I specialize in music writing."

"You write music?"

"About music."

"Who for?"

"*Rolling Stone. Crawdaddy. The Voice.* But I have a
feeling this'll be a book before it's over. A rock-and-roll
version of *The Boys of Summer*. Eddie Wilson and the Parkway Cruisers are going to be very big. You can just feel it
happening, can't you?"

"I can't feel a thing," I answered. I walked over to the
window, where I could see across the lawn and parking lot
to Springfield Avenue and the strange society of past-three-
o'clock hangarounds: library grinds and baseball players,

car thieves and makeouts, clinging to the periphery of a place they seemed so impatient to abandon. Maybe their eagerness to be gone was already infected by nostalgia. No matter. Like it or not, they left, the prodigies and the morons alike. And I stayed.

"Could you please tell me what the hell all this is about?"

"I'm sorry if I—"

"It's nothing you said. I just want to know what's going on."

"You don't know?"

"Not much. An old song on the radio."

"That's it?!"

"Except for that, I'm lost. Look, I'm a thirty-seven-year-old married high school teacher. I've been here for twelve years. It's been that long since I picked up a guitar, or tried a lyric, or stepped inside a music store. I don't go to concerts. I avoid chaperoning dances. And I'm sorry to say that I don't keep up with the publications you mentioned. I don't know anybody who does. So, please . . . enlighten me."

"I never thought you'd be so . . ."

"Out of it?"

"Well, yes . . . unconnected."

"And you're the man who's going to plug me in," I said, plumping myself behind one of the front-row desks. Mannheim responded by leaning against the teacher's desk.

"There's chalk and pointers in the desk, if you need them."

It had started at Christmas, with the incredible success of a British musical group called The Funky Company. I'd never heard of them, but Mannheim assured me they were "humungous." A sold-out coast-to-coast tour, complete with jammed arenas, airport riots, gutted hotel rooms. A quadruple platinum album, or something, and three singles in the top ten. Delinquent bravado and nose-thumbing insolence and yet . . . and yet . . . a curious touch of reverence.

"You had to see it," Mannheim said. "Near the end of

every show. The lights dim and Nick Kapp, the lead singer, just stands in front of the mike, stands and waits till there's not a sound in the arena. Not a cough, not a scream, nothing. Sometimes it takes ten minutes. Then . . . this is incredible . . . he tells the audience there's to be no applause after this next number, and if he hears as much as a hand-clap, it's curtains. No more show, no encores. Can you imagine? He's got thousands of people paralyzed. Then he goes into his rap, low and slow, so the audience is leaning forward to catch every word.

" 'People die,' he says, 'and some die young. Some of them, we remember. Especially the music-makers.' Then he recites a whole list of dead singers, and how they went. Janis Joplin with a needle, Jimi Hendrix choking in his own vomit, Elvis black in the face on his bathroom floor. Eddie Cochran's car crash, Buddy Holly's plane crash and Otis Redding's, and Johnny Ace shooting himself, and Sam Cooke getting shot, and Frankie Lymon overdosing. He goes on and on. It's eerie.

" 'We remember them all,' he says. 'Some more than others. And one group more than most. You make your choice of memories. We've made ours. They paid the dues. We pay the tribute. Ladies and gentlemen, they say we left them down the road. Don't believe it. They're with us tonight. Living fast. Driving hard. Making music. Eddie Wilson and the Parkway Cruisers!' Bedlam! They go right into 'Far-Away Woman,' segue to 'Some Kind of Loving,' and wind up with 'Fast Exit.' '"

After that, it happened fast, Mannheim said. Immediate reissue of "Far-Away Woman," with other songs to follow. Reissue—with sound enhanced for stereo—of the Cruisers' one and only album. And rumors about a movie, *The Eddie Wilson Story.* Everybody loved us. Everybody always had, it seemed.

"That's it," Mannheim concluded. "I still can't believe this is the first you heard of it. No one else has found you?"

"Are they looking?"

"I guess I'm the first," Mannheim said, pleased with himself. "But I'll bet I'm not the last."

He wasn't. I wish he had been.

Elliot Mannheim said he wanted to tape an interview, and I agreed on the condition that the questioning be confined to my experience with Eddie Wilson and the Parkway Cruisers, that my current address and occupation be omitted, and that I receive a copy of the transcript, not for editing or approval but simply for my own records. He agreed.

Janitors start moving through classrooms right after school, emptying baskets and waxing floors, so I suggested we use the teachers' lounge, overlooking the gym. Nominally designated for lesson preparation, it's a sanctuary of intramural backbiting, sports chatter, and, when girls' gym classes romp below, unfettered voyeurism. By late afternoon, it's a sorry sight: Styrofoam cups, discarded newspapers, stale, smoky air.

While Mannheim tested his tape recorder, I paced back and forth among the wreckage. My private joke was over. Things were stirring in my life again.

3

EM: Okay, I'm with Frank Ridgeway, a surviving member of Eddie Wilson and the Parkway Cruisers. He now is a . . .

FR: Skip it. Remember?

EM: Right. He's with me here now. I guess we'll start at the beginning. How and when did you meet the late Eddie Wilson? And how'd you come to join the group?

FR: It was 1957, I met him. By accident. I joined the Cruisers the same way.

EM: Sir?

FR: By accident. A place down the Jersey shore.

EM: Look, this is fine, but do you think you could be a little more expansive. I've got plenty of tape. Take the first meeting with Eddie Wilson, the first time you laid eyes on him. Describe it, as much of it as you can remember.

FR: As much as I remember. (Laugh.) You must think I'm losing my faculties. I remember everything.

EM: Good. That's what I want to hear.

FR: Well, I was . . . what? . . . seventeen? . . . that summer, with one year of college behind me. I'd skipped a couple grades in grammar school, so I got to college early. Too early . . .

Never mind the name of the college—which, in any case, is best known for a literary quarterly it no longer publishes. What happened to me there, on that small, all-male hilltop in Ohio, could have happened anywhere. It wasn't bad grades, or misconduct, or cutting classes. I wish it had been. Then my parents might have understood. No, I was unprepared in other ways, it seemed to me. I'd never worked, or traveled, or slept with a woman. I'd never done anything, and now I was spending what ought to be the best years of my life in musty library carrels and dorms that smelled of masturbation. After one year of college I strained for wildness and adventure and romance without having the vaguest idea where to find them. But I knew they were somewhere else. So I arranged for a perfectly honorable withdrawal before I came home that summer. The result was a family horror show too hackneyed to recount. Hackneyed, but the feelings were real, theirs and mine. So I left home.

With one suitcase and a couple hundred dollars, I considered myself a drifter. Not that I drifted very far. A three-hour bus trip took me from New York to Atlantic City, where the father of a high school friend who'd enlisted owned a bar. I was too young to drink, or serve drinks, or even be on premises, but the Jersey shore got crazy during the summer. A lot of Philadelphia kids drinking a lot of beer. Vince paid me the minimum wage to sweep up after closing, restock coolers, carry out the empties. A "porter"—that's what he said I'd be, and that appealed to me because I recalled the drunken porter from *Macbeth*. Being a porter seemed just fine that summer. I had a cot in the back room —the office-storeroom—and a hot plate. In the morning I could cross the street and swim in the ocean. I was happy being a porter. Nothing exciting had happened, but I was ready, and I was sure I'd recognize adventure when it came along.

EM: A summer job in a bar?
FR: Yes. The sort of odd job they give alcoholics in exchange for free drinks. Thank God, my parents never knew about it.
EM: What was the name of the place?
FR: Vince's Boardwalk Bar.
EM: Does it still exist?
FR: I don't know. I haven't been around there since Eddie died.
EM: It's not far. I don't—
FR: Understand? Why I haven't gone back?
EM: Yes.
FR: I thought you'd have it figured out by now. I'm not the type . . .

. . . who keeps in touch. Why didn't I come right out and say it? I lived my life in compartments, a chapter at a time, with no overlaps, no connections. Remember those special dining plates they made for finicky kids, with little dikes walling off the mashed potatoes from the broccoli, from the meat and gravy? That's how I'd been living my life. That was then, this was now. Well, I was as wrong about life as I was about that plate. Mother was right: it all goes in the same stomach.

EM: I can guess the next part. The bar had a live band, right? Every night, or just weekends?
FR: Every night but Monday. That's the first time I saw them. In June sometime, they came in around closing one Monday night, to set up and practice for the coming week. They could have done the same thing Tuesday morning, I guess, but Eddie always

worked nights. He was a night person, or at least he loved the idea of being a night person. All-nighters and truck stops and crazy ideas at four in the morning. Sudden insights over steak and eggs at a greasy spoon. He got that into a song . . . some of it . . .

EM: "Leaving Town"?

FR: Yeah. Anyway, there they were at two a.m. Vince ran home. He was very into Julius La Rosa. I was supposed to lock up when they finished rehearsing. But they were there to stay, and nothing I could do about it. Remember, I slept in back. I wiped down the bar, cleaned the taps, dusted the liquor bottles, washed the mirrors till Vince's Boardwalk Bar looked like . . . I don't know . . . the Oak Bar at the Plaza. Still, they were barely getting warm. So I opened a beer and came around the front of the bar, watching and listening. I didn't resent being kept up. I wasn't tired. I was just glad to be sitting in a shore bar at three a.m., listening to a bunch of unknowns. Can you beat that?

Can you beat that? I could see that Mannheim wasn't especially impressed. It was no thrill for him, hearing musicians play till dawn. But my life had been lived in daylight. It still was. And, sitting in that tired old teachers' lounge, the memory of a bar at three a.m. was the image of liberty to me.

EM: Yes, well, who was there that night? The names, and maybe you could describe them.

FR: Well, Eddie was there, of course . . .

EM: Yes . . .

FR: I'm sorry. I'm not good at this.

EM: I have the picture on the album cover.

FR: Forget that. They decked us out like a bunch of hoods, put us in a hot rod, and told us to look like James Dean. No . . . Eddie was medium height, on the thin side, black hair that wasn't long—not by current standards—and eyes that were, I guess, green. Not especially handsome or especially tough or artistic-looking. A kid off the streets. Not mean streets. Any streets. Mostly I remember his eyes. Not the color, so much, but the way he used them. The alertness. Never could decide whether he was watching out or just watching.

EM: Good. What about the others?

FR: Well, Sally of course. Long Tall Sally. Sal Amato. He'd known Eddie longest. They'd played Virginia Beach the summer before, and Navy bars in Norfolk during the winter. Just the two of them. The others were newcomers, but Sal and Eddie went back a long ways. You should try to find him.

EM: Do you know where he is?

FR: No.

EM: Well, tell me about Sal.

FR: Loud and lively, in a Philadelphia Italian way. Protective of Eddie, like a big brother.

EM: But little brother was the boss. Was that a problem?

FR: Well, their approaches were different. I could see that right away.

EM: How so?

FR: Most of this you should get from Sal. He could be touchy. Even after this long, I wouldn't want to hit a nerve.

EM: I understand. Is there anything at all you can say?

FR: Just that, yes, they were like brothers. But they came from different places. Sal was a Philadelphia Italian. He joked about it—the same neighborhood that produced Fabian, and Mario Lanza. These days he'd probably add . . . what's his name? . . . In the T-shirt . . . Rocky . . .

EM: Sylvester Stallone.

FR: Yes. That was Sally. Is. I doubt he's changed. His

approach to music was . . . I guess you'd call it conventional, hard-working. Every note he played came with the union label on it. Know what I mean? We'd be playing a club someplace, and if we were going good, Eddie'd never dream of taking a break. But Sally got worried and fidgety, like we were violating some principle of his. There was a meter running inside his head, clicking away like a yellow cab. One night, he approached me. "Working with a break we made seven-fifty an hour. Working without a break knocks us down to four-seventy-five. Jesus, Frank, we get much better, I'll be workin' for nothin'. "

EM: He came to you with this?

FR: Sure. Maybe he was looking for an ally. Or just sympathy. But he never had much to say to the other new guys. And he'd never go directly to Eddie with something like that. Never. Close as they were, Eddie intimidated him. Besides, with new people coming on, Sal was just another one of the guys in the band. The situation was changing, and I guess that worried Sal. I'm sure he had feelings. He always said he did. "I got feelings too, you know."

EM: Okay. I understand where Sal was coming from. What about Eddie?

FR: That's harder . . .

EM: Anything you recall could help. Believe me, he's been dead a long time. After all these years, it's hard to bring him into focus. Back then, there was no serious journalism about rock and roll. I've checked. The clips tell me his favorite color was green, he liked peach ice cream, and he thought he'd like to visit California. Anything you give me has got to be better than that.

FR: I know what you're up against. . . . My problem is different . . . I remember so much.

EM: Just let it flow.

FR: No.

EM: If there's something off-color, personal, illegal, whatever, we can always—

FR: He meant a lot to me.

EM: Maybe if we just talked about his musical approach and put aside the rest.

FR: Okay. That might work. Give me a minute. Turn it off. . . .

Mannheim excused himself and went to the john. It felt good to be alone again, however briefly. Outside, the last rays of sunlight slanted through New Jersey's richly polluted air. I'd be home late. I should have called. Too late now, though. Might as well finish. Wrap it up, shake hands, and drop him at the bus station. Funny, about Eddie, how some people didn't stay dead. Not me. When I died, I'd stay dead forever. . . .

FR: I think I've got it now. Anyway, this will have to do. I hope this . . . revival . . . doesn't get out of hand and turn Eddie Wilson into a James Dean or an Elvis. To me, the wonderful thing about Eddie Wilson, what made me feel so *good* about the guy, was that he was, in so many ways, so typical. Background, taste, outlooks. Check out his parents down in Vineland. His father was a dentist! Typical. That makes it all the more striking that in a few ways—just a few, one or two—he was exceptional. You asked about his music. You've heard the records. The instruments sound ordinary enough, don't they?

EM: Yes.

FR: Feelings. That's what separated Eddie from Sally and from a thousand other guys. He had a knack of catching moods, crystallizing emotions, of . . . realizing life. Sometimes he'd start with the music, some basic rhythm or little riff. Sometimes a word or a phrase. And he'd bring the two together. That's the exceptional thing. Oh, he'd carry us along with him sometimes, but usually he was way out in front, and when he'd found what he wanted, he'd come back to where we were slugging away, and he'd try to make us understand. He wasn't always able to. It drove Sally up the wall, but there was nothing wrong with Sally. He was just like everybody else. Music was work for Sally. A trade. For Eddie it was a voyage. A trip, I guess you'd say. And that's all I'm saying about Eddie right now.

EM: Sure. Fine. Now the others.

FR: Two newcomers. Kenny Hopkins and Wendell Newton. Hopkins was a blond California-lifeguard type. He wasn't really, he was from Westfield, New Jersey, but that's what he was like. I knew him least. But I always had the feeling that this was only an episode for him. Later, he'd pass on to something else. He played okay, but you always felt he was a short-timer. He used to talk about keeping his options open. That was his pet expression. His girls were "options"—but I think he went at everything that way. He was always lining something up. Not like Wendell.

EM: The black piano player.

FR: Eddie shortened it. We called him the Bruiser.

EM: Tough dude?

FR: Wendell?! Hell, no. He was a frail puny kid out of Newark, New Jersey.

EM: And did anyone—

FR: Wait a minute. Something about Wendell Newton. He never said much, always smiled, everything was fine. I thought—still think—he was the best of us all. Personally he was the best. And musically. Eddie had the magic, but when it came to pure music, Wendell ran deep. He played piano mostly, but he did some sax, like the intro to "Far-Away Woman," and he was always experimenting. I even caught him playing a sad, sad flute. Eddie was Eddie. But Wendell was any number of people. If I've wondered about any of them, he's the one. You don't know if he ever did anything else in music?

EM: No.

FR: He never showed up anywhere?

EM: Not by that name. And I think I would have heard. I try to keep in touch. No.

FR: I'm sorry.

EM: How did you shape up as musicians?

FR: Well, I was the worst, hands down. You see, I'd never played.

EM: Never played?

FR: That's right. When Eddie decided he wanted me with the Cruisers, I asked, what for? I can't play. He said, "Give me twenty minutes, I'll teach you. It's easy. Like getting laid." That was a joke, you see, because at that point I knew even less about women than guitars. So he added, "Or riding a bicycle." And he taught me, so at least I could stand up there and not embarrass them. As for the others, Sal was an adequate guitarist, like Eddie, and played piano too, though Wendell handled that. Hopkins was okay. For the most part we were journeymen. All this came later, of course. That first night, I was only a spectator.

EM: No one else was there?

FR: Doc Robbins. I later learned he was the manager. He swept in and out. Flimflam man, barnstorming actor, snake-oil salesman. I'd never met anybody like him. That night, he was there just briefly. And there were a couple girls.

EM: Whose girls?

FR: I forget, if I ever knew. It doesn't matter. . . .

Nothing mattered more! Why is it that the women of that one year are all so vivid? Is it because I was younger? Because I was a virgin, and everyone I saw might be my first? Maybe so. I was so alive, waiting for my life to begin! How many women did I have during that year as a Parkway Cruiser? Two dozen? And yet the most vivid of all was Eddie's girl, Joann. She was there that first night.

The very thought of her disturbed me. I could tell myself it was a long time ago. But just then, when she walked out of the background of the scene I was describing to Elliot Mannheim, she took my breath away. It was like something suddenly stirred in my chest, breaking inward compartments, breaching walls, mixing together what the years had sorted out.

Joann and the other girl came over to the bar where I'd been sitting with the one book that I carried that summer, a Louis Untermeyer poetry anthology. I'm not sure I'd actually been reading it, but the idea of reading poetry in a bar before dawn mattered a lot to me. God! What a pompous little phony! And she knew it. She sniffed out the vulnerability, the virginity, and everything. She did nothing but smile a little at me, and we both knew she had my number.

EM: So they took you on? A nonmusician? Why?
FR: I'm still not sure. Oh, I know it was Eddie's decision. Hopkins took it as a joke. Wendell was puzzled, though too polite to say anything. Sal beefed about how my coming on cut down on his piece of the pie. So it was Eddie. All I can tell you was how it happened. . . .

It started that first night, though the summer was nearly over before I got onstage. The rehearsal wasn't going well. Even I could see it. There had been problems adding two new men to what had been a duo, and Sally wasn't making it any easier. He threw off a lot of stubborn, literal-minded, exasperating questions. Sally didn't like new ideas, not if the old ones still paid a living wage. Before long they were shouting at each other, and Eddie called for a break. He came over to the bar where the girls were sitting and I was supposedly reading poetry. And he talked about the problem they were having. It was such a small thing! . . .

FR: There's a minor song we did—"Down on My Knees." Have you heard it?

EM: Sure.

FR: Well, there's this phrase that Eddie sings: "Come on, baby . . . baby, come on!!" Now Sally wanted him to sing it like it was prose, with no break and no emphasis on the repetition. "Come on, baby, baby come on." "Nice and steady, like it's a damn hula!" Eddie said. Sally pictured dance tunes, and nobody should lose the beat, miss a step. Eddie wanted the pause and he wanted to hit the repetition hard, so that what was first heard as an invitation returned as a . . . scream. Are you with me?

EM: What happened?

FR: He told the girls what was happening. He spoke real low. Things were tense. Then he asked me what did I think. Should he sing it straight through, like Sally wanted? Or should he pause? You know what I said? It's embarrassing now. I said, "I like the caesura."

EM: Caesura?

FR: He didn't know what it was either. He got this incredulous expression on his face, and he started laughing. . . .

"What did you say?"

"Caesura. It's a—"

"No, wait a minute." He put one hand on my shoulder and

motioned Sally over with the other. "Hey, you big dumb guinea."

Sally stalked over, looking as if he'd already lost the argument. It was always that way. When they were both shouting angrily, there was a chance Sal would prevail. But when Eddie came out with that amazed, boyish, tickled-to-death laugh, it was over.

"Who's he?" Sally asked.

"I'm the porter. I work—"

"An expert," Eddie interrupted, pointing at the poetry anthology on the bar. "College professor. Now what did you say about 'come on, baby . . . baby, come on'?"

"I said I liked the caesura."

"See, Sally. My way. With the Caesarean."

"What's a—"

"Tell him. What's your name?"

"Frank."

"Tell him, Frankie."

"It's a phrase used in poetry criticism. A caesura. It's a timely pause, a kind of strategic silence. It's not dictated by meter or beat, but by the meaning of what you're trying to get across."

"That's just exactly right," Eddie said, sounding as if he were prepared to correct me if I slipped. "Now show this man one of those things. Give him a for-instance."

"Well . . . there's Milton." I thumbed desperately through the paperback.

"Yeah, Milton'll do fine," Eddie approved. "Take your time, Frankie."

At last, I found it.

"This is from the opening of *Paradise Lost*. I'll read it without the caesura, then I'll read it with. I think you'll hear the difference. Here goes. 'Of man's first disobedience and the fruit of that forbidden tree, sing heavenly muse.' "

It came out prosaic, singsongy. Sally never had a chance.

"Sounds like shit," Eddie said. "Now let's hear it the other way."

" 'Of man's first disobedience and the fruit of that forbidden tree . . . sing heavenly muse!' "

"Now *that* has got a little class!" Eddie said. "Sally, am I right?"

Poor Sal shrugged and walked back to the bandstand. Eddie followed, but he turned to me before he left the bar. "Good. You can stay."

FR: . . . that's how it started. Eddie got in the habit of dropping by the bar and talking. When they performed, he'd stop in the storeroom between sets. We talked.

EM: But that made you a member?

FR: I was the Wordman. Don't you see? It's the only thing that my life now has in common with my life then. Words. Eddie started using me as a critic, a sounding board, a tryout. By the end of summer, he decided he wanted me to come along, and that was all right with me. So I became a Cruiser. There you have it.

No, he didn't have it. And neither did I . . . quite yet. As I spoke to Mannheim I sensed vast gaps opening up in the story I was telling. So many things I was leaving out, things hardly remembered, things I couldn't say: how I watched the Cruisers from behind the bar, the way they joked and played, the things they cared about, and the things that concerned them not at all. I came from a good family that lived orderly lives, that planned and saved, piling day on day, as if building a wall around a property they'd barely taken time to contemplate, saving their enjoyment for when the work was done. And here were the Cruisers, throwing themselves into each day as if it were the first and last. They blew me away, every one of them. There wasn't one I didn't envy, wouldn't have traded places with. For how long? Maybe not forever. But for a while! For now! For as long as I could feel the way that they felt, every day.

Joann noticed me first, I'm sure. She'd catch me staring at the stage while the Cruisers played, or singing crazy little bathroom falsettos while I restocked the coolers in the morning, doo-wops and sh-bops that nobody was supposed to hear. I think it amused her to see me change, see me drawn into Eddie's world.

Dancing was part of it. My repertory began and ended with the box step. I was only a few years away from dances where all the boys threw one of their shoes in the center of the gymnasium and the girls got to dance with the guy whose shoe they picked off the floor. I figured I was awkward, and thinking made me so. I compensated, though. It suited me just fine, leaning against Vince's bar, making devastating comments about the action on the dance floor. It was a perfect perch for the chicken-hearted. I got to be pretty funny. At that time, the Cruisers were doing mostly covers of other people's songs. And I tossed off on-the-spot parodies, especially when Joann was there to hear them. I even adopted the old Steve Allen routine of reading lyrics deadpan, as if they were serious verse. All things considered, it served me right, one Friday night when I was being very droll that Joann simply yanked me out from behind the bar and forced me onto the floor. We danced. And to my great amazement, nobody laughed at me or even noticed I was there. Was I good? Hardly. But I was no worse than all the rest. I was part of the crowd, and that felt good.

From then on, it was just a matter of time. Eddie started taking an interest in me. He got in the habit of hanging around the back room, which he called his office or his studio. First he called me "kid," and then "kid four-eyes," from the glasses I needed for reading. That lasted till the afternoon he named me—crowned me—"Wordman."

I came in from my morning swim and found him waiting for me there, sitting on my couch. I was surprised to see him. Nobody else was there yet, not even Vince.

"How come," Eddie asked, "I never notice how this place smells at night?"

"What smell?" I asked, switching on my hot plate to boil water for coffee.

"Beer, man," he said, gesturing at the cases of empties stacked against the wall. "Don't you smell it? Warm, stale beer. The dregs. Last night's beer, and the night before's."

"Oh yeah." I shrugged. "I guess I like it. Beer is summer to me . . . and . . ."

"What else?" Eddie asked. I thought he might be laughing at me, the way Sally and the others laughed when I got a little too thoughtful.

"I don't know. It's masculine and it's organic. It's the memory of good times. And a way of measuring them. I just look up from my bed, and I know how well we did the night before."

"Holee shit!" Eddie said, laughing softly.

"Okay, okay, I know what Sally would say." Sally had a way of pretending he was playing a violin and asking sarcastically, "Could we put this to music?"

"That's why I'm here, kid," Eddie said. "And for Christ's sake, don't tell Sally."

"What do you want, Eddie?"

"Words," he said. "For songs."

"Lyrics?"

"Yeah. I want songs for the Cruisers. Our own stuff."

"Eddie, I'm no songwriter. That's a profession. People spend years—"

"What am I gonna do?" he asked impatiently. "Call up the union and tell them to send somebody over? Like it's some busted plumbing? You're here now. Whatever we got right now, you're part of. So write. Instead of those smart-ass takeoffs I been hearin' about."

"But what do you want? I need something to go on."

"I want songs that nobody else is singing," Eddie said, getting up. To him, asking me for songs was a casual errand, like ordering a pizza to go. "Something a little distinctive, you know? That people are gonna remember? Like your damn beer bottles. Jesus, I got to get out of here."

Those were my instructions. Except that I'll always remember the look he gave me as he turned in the doorway on his way out. The way his eyes enlisted me. And his smile goaded us all.

"And, Wordman? Don't tell Sally. He'll think I'm aimin' to put us on the 'Voice of Firestone.'"

I realized that it was up to me to end the interview with Mannheim. He'd sit forever, changing tapes. Everything I had, he wanted. But there was too much that I wasn't ready to give. I thought I'd said enough. And besides, I told him, it was getting late.

That upset him. We'd barely begun, he said. There was so much more to talk about.

Like what? I asked.

Everything.

What about what I'd already told him? Was that nothing?

Oh, that was fine, but there was so much more. He seemed almost angry, as if I'd been cheating him. He wanted to know about the development of each song, how the words and music came together. And everything that happened after the summer: the tour, clubs, concerts, the sessions down at Lakehurst, and the accident that ended everything.

That settled it. . . .

"Mannheim, there's no way on earth I can go through that accident story tonight."

"I'm not sure you realize the importance of the information you have," he answered firmly. The nervous petitioner had been replaced by a young man who knew exactly what he wanted. And who hadn't gotten it yet.

"Maybe I do know the importance," I countered. "Maybe it's so important to me that I can't go through it all tonight. I want to think about it. Eddie's dead and you're alive, but he was my friend. . . . I just met you."

He backed off immediately. "Hey, I'm sorry. I was out of line. I was so excited at finding you. I wanted to get it all."

"You got plenty."

"And good stuff. I'm grateful. But look . . . there is more. Do you think I could call you again?"

"Again? Did you call this time?"

"I mean . . . well, next time I'll call and we'll set it up . . . at your convenience."

"Call the school. The office. Don't call my home."

I drove him to the bus stop, with five minutes to spare before the last bus back to New York. If I hadn't ended the taping, I'd have been stuck with him for the night. Maybe he hadn't thought about that, or maybe he didn't care. It's hard to be sure about someone like Mannheim.

"I hope you find the others," I said, as we drove through town.

"I've got some leads. I'll let you know when I get back to you, how I made out."

"I'd appreciate that."

"Any messages? If I get lucky."

"No. Just tell them Wordman says hello."

"Anything else?"

"Tell—if you find Wendell—tell him that life is turning out to be longer than expected."

"What's it mean?"

"He'll understand."

When we reached the bus stop, Mannheim grabbed his bag and opened the door.

"Thanks again," he said, "and I'm sorry if I got pushy."

"Forget it," I said. I offered him my hand. He took it, shifting into the thumb-grasping handshake some of my students used.

"I don't mind telling you, this is going to be some kind of story," Mannheim said. "It could do a lot for both of us."

"You sure?"

"What I mean is . . ." There it was again, the pause that suggested he was searching for the right way of putting things. Would you call it a caesura? "I'd like us to work together on this. I want you to be candid with me. There'll be other people coming to you, wanting to talk, and I can't tell you not to. I wouldn't dream of it. But if our story works . . ."

"You want me to play hard-to-get? Is that it?"

"Well, yes. You talk to everybody and the story deflates. If you keep it exclusive . . . we'll do better."

"Right," I said. It was odd, having this kid lecture me on how business worked in the real world. Like that, I was his partner. Junior partner. "Our story."

"Well, I'll look forward to working with you some more," Mannheim said as the bus rolled in. "I guess my questions took you back a-ways."

"They did," I said, nodding good-bye. Half a lifetime, I thought, as I drove home. And half to go. That was amazing. It's what I'd meant in my message to Wendell about life turning out to be longer than expected. It wasn't that Eddie had died so young so much as that the rest of us had gone on living for so long.

Last night, Herman Biedermann and I made our weekly trip to the I.G.A. store. While he gathered groceries, I called home. I spoke to the kids first—they think I'm taking a refresher course at Penn State. I'm glad I got done with them before Doris came on the line. Her news was unsettling. Someone called her. A Mr. Slocum. Slow-come? Said he was a lawyer. Said he needed to talk to me immediately about a—get this—property settlement. An estate in which I had a "vital" interest. Where could I be reached? Doris had followed my instructions. I was traveling, she said, but I called home from time to time, and if Mr. Slocum cared to leave his number, she'd see that I got his message. Mr. Slocum hung up.

So now I know they've narrowed it down to me. I don't suppose I've got much longer down here. It might take some time, but they've found everyone they've looked for so far, and there's no reason to think that I'll escape. What's more, I'm not sure I want to. I'm afraid, but there are things I have to know.

· · ·

Mannheim's visit changed things in a way that both pleased and disconcerted me. My day-to-day life, though superficially the same, was filled with echoes, resonances, connections. Memories. Things that I thought were dead were only sleeping.

I confess that in dealing with Mannheim, I had exaggerated my distance from the year I spent with Eddie and the Cruisers. Even before "Far-Away Woman" surfaced, I had sometimes been captured by fragments of the past.

Those old songs die hard, I used to think. I thought so every year around New Year's, when radio stations dipped into their archives and played "blasts from the past" and I'd hear us all singing again. It made me sad to know that yet another year had wedged itself between then and now. I thought about it watching television late at night, when some mail-order record house would flog an anthology of golden oldies from the rockin' fifties. There we'd be, among a dozen others, $5.98 for a three-record set, not for sale in stores, operators waiting for your call. I wondered whether anyone else in the audience could be as moved, or hurt, as I was.

Maybe the Cruisers. I wondered about them too. I mused about where they were now, how they'd turned out, whether they might be sitting in front of a TV, calling out, "Hey, look, I'm on the tube again!"

Mostly, though, I thought about Eddie Wilson. That was different. I wondered how he would have aged, what he would have made of the things that happened since he died: the Beatles, the Stones, Isaac Hayes, Woodstock. I wanted him around. I missed his instincts, his emotional outreach, his sense of adventure. The last time I'd heard live music, or closed a bar, or written a line I cared about was when Eddie was alive. So I missed him both for himself and for what he might have brought out in me. He and the person I might have been had died together. The bottom line was sadness.

"Far-Away Woman" changed that now. I kept my eyes open and saw things I normally would have missed. I listened more often to the radio, I eavesdropped on my students, I read carefully some of the magazines that Mannheim had mentioned. I sensed a quickening, a sharpening of all my faculties. And little by little, it paid off.

One noontime, I crossed Springfield Avenue to buy a newspaper at Dom's place, a student hangout. Since I was there already, I sat down for a cheeseburger and a cup of coffee.

I heard "Far-Away Woman" three times during lunch. Every time it started, with Wendell's sax sounding like a signal from some distant, foggy island, I tensed and broke out sweating, like a ghost was about to tap me on the shoulder. And I waited for someone to make a remark: Get that dusty piece of shit off the machine! What is it, a 78 or something? But no, they couldn't tell, or they didn't care, that it was nearly twenty years since Wendell's lips touched that sax and Eddie Wilson sang the words that he and I had worked out in the beery back room of Vince's Boardwalk Bar.

> "Far-away woman
> Passing out of sight,
> Which way you moving
> Into the night?
> Comin' toward me,
> Or runnin' away . . ."

"Got somethin' for me, Wordman?"

Eddie jumped on top of an empty keg of draft and waited for me to begin.

"I don't know about the music, Eddie. Whether it's a fast song or a slow one . . ."

"We got musicians," Eddie said. "Wendell—he'll turn it into blues and Sally'll make it a cha-cha. Hopkins'll beat the shit out of it any which way. You just leave that to me."

"All I did was try to write a song about a woman, about—"

"Hey, Wordman! What say you just read the damn thing to me? Then I'll know what it's about."

I read it, just the first six lines, which was all I had. All the rest—the false starts, broken rhymes, the self-indulgence and pretentiousness—was under my bed. I read it and waited for Eddie to crack up, or call Sally in to witness my goofiest moment yet.

"So where's the rest of it?" Eddie asked, like I'd served him a bun without a hamburger in the middle.

"I haven't—"

"Well, finish it."

"You want me to continue?"

"Might as well." He was already leaving. I knew that Eddie wasn't much of a talker. Except for occasional outbursts which were practically soliloquies, he relied on nods, gestures, shrugs—on his body, his eyes. But this was one time I wouldn't let him get away.

"Just a damn minute!" I shouted so loud he stopped in his tracks. "What did I do? I'm working the bar. Your garden-variety college dropout. You come to me and you say, hey kid—since you're here—while you're resting—why not write me some songs. Something special, just for the Cruisers. That's not much to go on, you know? But I like you guys. I sit down and I put out. I really try. And I don't care if this is the worst thing you've heard since the 'Ballad of Davy Crockett.' I want some feedback. I want to know what you want from me!"

At the start Eddie was surprised. Then I thought I saw anger. And discomfort. The way he came at me across the room, I thought he might slug me. But he put a hand on each shoulder and pushed me back down onto the keg he'd occupied. Then he hunkered down on the floor in front of me. Then he laughed.

"Holee shit!" he said. "The things she gets me into. First time outta the gate, I got me a prima donna Wordman!"

"*She* got you? . . ."

"Just be quiet, Wordman." He put a finger over his mouth to show me what quiet meant. "We've got this mutual friend who thinks you could be good. She told me to try you. I listened to her. Now don't start asking me what I want from you. I don't know yet. The question is . . . what do you have to give? So let's find out. Now let me tell you something else. About the Cruisers. What I want for the Cruisers. Every night I'm up there working, three, four sets a night, and I look down at people dancing and drinking, which is fine by me. But what I want is . . ."

He stopped. He stared down at the floor.

". . . is songs that echo. We play and sing all right, but that's just the beginning of it. I want more. Most of the stuff we're singing now, they're like the sheets in somebody's bed. Spread 'em and soil 'em and ship 'em out to the laundry. You know? But our songs—I want us to be able to fold ourselves up in them forever."

He stayed a moment longer, crouching on the floor, head down. It felt like a confessional. And it embarrassed both of us.

"That's as much as you're gonna get out of me, Wordman," Eddie said. "Ever." That night I got back to work.

Sitting in Dom's Varsity Luncheonette, the record sounded incredibly old to me; a Caruso aria couldn't have seemed more out of place. But the kids liked it fine. Why? Was Eddie so good that he could jump the years and come out sounding like new? Or were the kids such indiscriminate consumers, so beyond critical thought that they gobbled up songs like so much junk food? There were dozens of other songs on that jukebox, lots of buttons to push, yet they chose Eddie Wilson and the Parkway Cruisers again and again! Why?! For the thousandth time I wished I could get inside their heads. Usually I felt that way in class, when I was angry or frustrated, when I didn't know what it took to get through to them. But this time it was different. I looked at them while

Eddie was singing, looked at this generation of T-shirts and cheeseburgers, and wondered.

Maybe it was time to let go of the deal I'd wanted to make with them a dozen years before. If I couldn't make peace, at least I should call a truce. They couldn't keep me young or make me happy, and I couldn't make them wise. My life mattered more to me than theirs. And my youth, so far behind, was more important to me than theirs. Maybe there'd come a time when the kids and I could work it out. Not now. Not when I felt so incomplete. My life was fragments. I needed to pull it together, form a whole—all the way from then till now.

Eddie Wilson and the Parkway Cruisers' "Far-Away Woman" was Number Three that week, and "Down on My Knees" was climbing the charts. The first time around, "Far-Away Woman" had barely cracked the Top Ten, and that was about the biggest hit we ever had. "Down on My Knees" had missed the Top Forty altogether. It was pretty ironic, and I wondered if anyone else felt the same way. They did.

DEAD SINCE '58
JERSEY'S EDDIE WILSON
FOCUS OF MUSIC REVIVAL

Two decades after his death in a car crash on the Garden State Parkway, Vineland-born musician Eddie Wilson is finally where he'd always dreamed he would be—near the top of the nation's list of top-selling records.

"Far-Away Woman," recorded by Wilson and the Parkway Cruisers, was Number Three and climbing last week, *Billboard* magazine states. Other Wilson songs are also coming to the fore.

"There have been posthumous hits before," declared New York-based film and music critic Jay Whitehead. "But usually, they came right after the singer's death, right on the heels of the tragedy, as in the case of Sam

Cooke ('A Change Is Gonna Come'), Otis Redding ('Dock of the Bay'), and Jim Croce ('I Got a Name'). I don't think there's ever been such a surge of interest in a musician who's been dead twenty years."

Wilson recorded a dozen songs in the year preceding his death. His songs were "moderately successful," and this success sent the Wilson group on an East Coast tour that was cut short by his death, near Asbury Park, New Jersey, on June 8, 1958. Wilson's group disbanded soon afterward.

The "Wilson Renaissance"—that's what insiders are calling it—was spurred by tributes from British groups who say they were influenced by Wilson's records. Now, however, the phenomenon has a momentum of its own, with original Wilson 45's bringing up to a hundred dollars from "oldies but goodies" collectors.

"We're sorry Eddie couldn't live to see all this," the late singer's 70-year-old father, Harding Wilson of Vineland, told the *Press-Courier*. "But his mom and I are glad that we're still here. And we want to thank all Eddie's fans—the old ones and the new ones."

The senior Wilsons aren't the only ones elated by the revival. One of Wilson's busiest new fans is a Patterson-based entrepreneur who purchased rights to Wilson's records "for a song" from the now-defunct firm which originally released them.

"Don't call it a business, call it a hobby," cautions Lewis Eisen, president of bustling Ekko Records. "It's like mining stocks, these old copyrights and records. You assume they're worthless. That's the safe bet. But sometimes you're wrong. It's nice being wrong."

That same week, a newsmagazine placed us among their "best bets for summer."

SOLID GOLD: Eddie Wilson and the Parkway Cruisers were a small-time New Jersey-based rock 'n' roll group of the late fifties. Disbanded and forgotten after Wilson's death in a car crash, the group's sole album is the surprise find of the summer. Though technically primitive, the Cruisers' songs bristle with a vitality and feeling rare in today's discs. Indeed, the music's curiously dated quality is among its most appealing traits. "Far-Away Woman" pulsates with a Gatsby-like romanticism. "On the Dark Side" signals an early white fascination with black music and culture. "Blue Lady," "Call on Me," "Down on My Knees," indeed, all the tiny Wilson repertory brims with a special sense of time and place. The Cruisers' album will carry you back. Don't miss it.

The call came late Friday morning, a week after Mannheim's first visit. The assistant principal's secretary came into my third-period study hall with a message to return a long-distance phone call. I didn't recognize the area code—it wasn't New York City's 212—and I assumed that Mannheim must have unearthed another aging Cruiser. Maybe he was with one of them right now, waiting for me to call.

I left a frightened secretary in charge of the study hall and rushed to the bank of pay phones in the main lobby. I'd begun to look forward to my next session with Mannheim.

"KCGM."

"I'm sorry. Is this 511–274–5486?"

"That's right. Voice of the Poconos. Who do you want, please?"

"I don't know. My name's Frank Ridgeway, and I'm returning a call. I think it's from Elliot Mannheim."

"No Mannheim here. Hang on a minute, I'll ask around." I heard someone shouting my name and, from somewhere, a muffled reply.

"Where are you calling from?"

"A phone booth." I gave the number.

"Stay there for five minutes. He's on the air now. He'll call back."

For five minutes I waited obediently, reading graffiti that were scratched and penciled onto the walls. An overrated genre, crudely obscene when not self-consciously clever.

The phone rang.

"Hello, Wordman."

It gave me a chill, hearing my old Cruiser nickname again. I felt like some deep-cover spy, settled down happily in a foreign country, suddenly receiving the code word that meant it was time to rise and strike.

"Who is this?"

"You get one clue," the caller said.

There followed a few seconds of silence.

"Ready, Wordman?"

"Yes."

"This is the night-stalker, the blues-talker, the water-walker, bringing you his special magic from the land of doo-wap-de-wap. Lord of tides, taker of sides, master of time and rhyme, hold onto your heart, little girl, I'll make it mine, 'cause I'm comin' on strong, stayin' long, talkin' loud and drawin' a crowd, and hey there, Wordman, say there, Wordman, what ever happened to you?"

Now I knew. How many times had I listened to his doggerel raps, part Walt Whitman and part Wolfman Jack? In bars and truck stops, while we set up and packed up, all along the road, all that year, there was no one else quite like him. Even now, miraculously, I could still remember the reply.

"Master of voices, maker of choices, unmoved mover, and man of the hour. Whatever happened to you, Doc?"

"I'm a disc jockey, Wordman. I play beautiful music for beautiful losers. Voice of the Poconos. Say, what'd you tell the squirt?"

"The squirt?"

"Mannheim. He was out here yesterday. He should have saved the bus fare. With what I gave him and a nickel, he could weigh himself. How about you?"

"He wanted to know how I joined the Cruisers, what they were like."

"Yeah, sure. He was jerking you off, but good."

"He said he wanted another session. When I got your message, I thought it was him calling."

"And you were ready and willing, right? Like he's Ralph Edwards and *This Is Your Life.*"

"Not my life. Eddie's. And I don't see the harm in it."

"No, Wordman, I'm sure you don't."

"Look, if there's something I should know . . ."

"Tell me this, Wordman, this Mannheim, after he got done asking you about what came first, words or music, and who taught you how to play the guitar, and how did you join the group, he didn't just happen to inquire about those Lakehurst sessions, did he? Did he mention Lakehurst?"

"Yes, he did, but only in passing. It was one of the topics we were going to cover next time."

"He had you right where he wanted you, hot to give him everything for nothing. For Eddie, right? You were doing it for Eddie. I knew I better call. Look, when can you get over here. How soon?"

"Why?"

"You need me, Wordman. You need me fast and you need me bad."

"Why?"

"Just trust me! You trusted that creep kid with the tape recorder, so trust your old coach."

"Where are you?"

"Just across the border."

"Canada?!"

"Pennsylvania. Stroudsburg."

I beat my students out of the high school parking lot that afternoon, and I didn't call home until I stopped for gas at Flemington.

Everybody knows at least one person like Doc Robbins. One's usually all you can take. He's the sort who breaks into your life, challenging, disrupting, changing, and as soon as you count on him, he's gone. No explanations. Weeks can pass, or years. Then, one day, he's back. Don't expect an apology: he doesn't seem to realize how long he's been away. He makes it sound like he was with you all along, in constant touch, and it was your fault if you didn't notice.

"Never bullshit a bullshitter"—his slogan, coda, credo, all in one. That was Doc. He mastered every game he joined, and then, just when he might start winning, he walked away. He never found the hustle that was worth his full time. That included Eddie Wilson and the Parkway Cruisers. Oh, I'm sure we were near the top of Doc's list that year, along with an Orange Julius franchise in the Virgin Islands and a dog track down in Florida. With Doc, there was always a list, and it changed as quickly as the Top Ten.

That summer, he swept in and out of Vince's Boardwalk a couple times a week. After a few hours of shouting and whispering, phone calls and handshakes, a flurry of jokes and drinks on the house, he'd be gone. Maybe Eddie had some way of reaching him in an emergency, but he seemed as surprised as anybody at Doc's comings and goings.

It wasn't a bad setup, though. Doc would take care of business—sign paychecks, pay bills—and then he'd vanish. Anybody pressed us, we'd tell them they'd have to talk to Doc. Then we'd be left alone. "Get on with the music," as Eddie would say.

Doc was the first real "character" I'd ever met, and I spent as much time with him as I could. I rode with him, drank with him, shagged phone calls for him. Whenever he was with us on the road, we'd split a room and trade jokes and bits all night. I guess I thought there was a mystery about him and that I was the man to solve it. Maybe I was kidding myself and there was nothing to discover. Anyway, he eluded me. I never figured out whether we were something special or just another deal. I thought for sure I'd find out the morning they buried Eddie Wilson down in Vineland. Nothing doing. They said he visited the parents the night before. By morning he was gone.

· · ·

"Barry Manilow spent a weekend in New England a while
ago, and from the sound of this record, he's been moping
around ever since. Tell the folks about it, Barry."

He lifted the needle onto the record, switched off the studio mike, and motioned me over toward where he was sitting
at the console.

"Howdy, Wordman. Long time."

"Doc. How have you been?"

"The hits just keep on coming," he shrugged. For once,
there was nothing to joke about. The radio station was desperately small-time, just a cut above the places that sell live
chickens and Jesus pictures over the air. Office, transmitter,
studio, and all, it sat off the highway on a weed-and-gravel
lot, flanked by a drive-in movie and a finish-it-yourself furniture place.

"You haven't changed a hell of a lot, Wordman," Doc said,
and that surprised me. I thought I'd changed a lot. "Still a
kid. And don't bother returning the compliment."

It hadn't occurred to me. Doc was a mess: overweight,
pale, and wearing a toupee that even I could spot. He
coughed incessantly, a nasty smoker's hack that he dis-
charged into Styrofoam cups full of cold carry-out coffee.
When he was on the air, he somehow mustered his resources
and sounded a little like the man I used to know, but even
then it was just a sour echo of the old Big Bopper.

"Okay, you near-beer fans. Remember Mock-*bird*-ing-
bird? Charley and Inez Foxx, summer of sixty-three? Do
you remember? James Taylor and Carly Simon are betting
that you don't . . ."

He snapped off the mike.

"Shit like this could get a man in trouble. Say, we got some
catching up to do."

I guess I didn't respond as readily as he'd hoped. I still
wondered why he'd contacted me, why I needed him. He
didn't look like a man who could help anybody.

"Okay. I'll start off. My turn to curtsy, your turn to bow.
After Eddie died. I sat on my ass in Central America for half

a year. I ran a radio station in Puerto Rico. I guess I was married a little down there. Later, I handled press relations for an Arizona congressman, and I had a piece of a music magazine that never got off the ground and a bowling alley in Roselle Park, and somewhere along the way I kind of remember a small problem trafficking in drugs. There's some episodes I forget, but you get the general idea. I've been in this dump for two years. Okay? Your turn, Wordman."

He put on something by a group he called "the Squeegees." Then he leaned back in his chair and waited for me to begin.

"So?"

"Nothing quite so checkered, Doc. When Eddie died, that was it for me. I got out of music. Not that I was ever that far in. I haven't looked back much. I finished college, put in a year of graduate school, and . . ."

Doc waved his hand in front of a huge yawn, and I recognized the beginning of one of his old bits.

". . . obtained a position teaching English at a regional high school in northern New Jersey. The same place I graduated from. I've been there a dozen years and . . ."

Now he slumped forward onto the desk, like he was nodding off on me.

"Stop it!" I raced along while he snored. "I'm married and I have two kids, girls, and a house I own, and next year we're going to rent a camper and drive across—oh, you asshole!"

He'd fallen out of his chair and curled up on the floor in a fetal position.

"I still don't know why you wanted to see me," I said, a little annoyed.

"Calm down," he said as he arose. "I've got your best interests at heart. Wait a second."

He stacked up some 45's.

"Back-to-back sounds coming up now. Something for the armchair traveler. From the land of cottonmouths and bayous, Linda Ronstadt down on 'Blue Bayou,' copying an old

Roy Orbison song. From there, we take you to the land of Coors beer and condominia with a young fellow who's high on life, Mr. John Denver, and no matter what you hear, John Denver isn't Alfred E. Neuman in disguise."

He turned toward me when he was done. "This isn't as bad as it looks. There's a state college in town and the kids like my irreverent wit. They tell me I'm a cult figure in the dorms. Time and again they invite me out to concerts and stuff."

"Sure, Doc."

"Pay's not bad and its a cheap place to live. Clean air. Friendly. And not all that far from New York. You can make it in a coupla hours."

"Do you ever go?"

"No reason to go . . . but I could."

"I guess that's something . . . just the access and knowing that if you had to go you could be there. . . ."

"Oh, screw it, kid. You have eyes. Draw your own conclusions. You wouldn't bullshit me. I can't bullshit you. Anyway, I wanted you to realize where I'm at. The way I see it, Eddie is my ticket out. And yours."

"Eddie? Ticket to where?"

"Wherever you want to go. He's gonna be big. Bigger than ever."

"He's dead."

"Doesn't matter. This is larger than life."

"A handful of records from the fifties? Sorry, Doc, I can't see it."

"Just listen. Hear me out. I'm gonna put on an album. Donna Summer. They'll be humping all over the Poconos. When the album's done, I'll be finished, and you can do whatever you want. It's your decision. You don't owe me anything. Could be, you owe yourself a little. But that's for you to decide. You talked to the creep, so I guess you know what's been happening with Eddie Wilson and the Parkway Cruisers lately."

"I don't know why, though."

"I do. It's not so hard to figure out. I'll get to that. Anyway you know the reissued records are hot stuff and the originals are collector's items. You've probably seen some newspaper articles too, and that's only the beginning. I've had half a dozen calls since the creep called. And you've heard about the movie, right? *The Eddie Wilson Story.* You with me so far?"

I nodded. So far. But from the way Doc stirred around in his chair, from the look in his eyes and the tone of his voice, spitting and coughing as he raced along, I sensed that from here on out we were headed toward craziness: a broken-down disc jockey spinning fantasies to a Donna Summer beat.

"I know you, kid. That is, I knew you once, and I don't figure people change. I know what you think. You think it's nice, right? Nice for Eddie, nice for Eddie's parents, and just plain nice. And I'll bet that's the end of it. Let me ask you, you ever told anybody you were a Parkway Cruiser?"

"No."

"Not your kids, even?"

"No."

"Your wife?"

"No."

"It's like I figured. You're just sitting on it, letting it happen. Well, not me. My mind doesn't work that way. Now listen carefully. What I'm telling you is between us, no matter what you decide. Promise?"

"Sure, Doc." I did my best not to laugh at him. No doubt about it, Doc Robbins was a deep-dish eccentric, the small-town inventor who spends his life raging about how the corporate biggies screwed him out of his million-dollar patent.

"Now we can't do much about the records. The oldies are all gone. And the reissues, well, we took a fucking there, and it's my fault. Right after Eddie died, I sold all the rights to this highway Jew, Eisen, and now he's sitting on the mother lode. Shit, I could kick myself. But there's nothing I can do about it now.

"This movie deal is something else again. I'm looking into it. The way I see it, they need help. They gotta have a story, right, some kind of script, and locations, and period stuff. That's where we come in. Technical consultants, source material. They got to come to us. Who else they got? Eddie's parents? Not unless they need a cast dentist. That's another thing. There ought to be a part for both of us. Not that we should necessarily play ourselves, but they could fit us in around the edges. It's money in the bank. Like I told you, I'm not pushing. Just a coupla phone calls. I'll wait for them to come to us."

"What if they don't come?" I couldn't help asking. "Suppose they fake it. Set it in California, turn us into a surfer group."

"Let 'em try! Beautiful! Let 'em try. They'll get a screwing they're not gonna believe. We'll sue—libel, invasion of privacy, abuse of copyright. We'll get a lawyer."

"They've got lawyers too," I said, but Doc wasn't listening to me.

"We'll wait until they're about half done with the filming, when the money's committed and everybody's working, and then we'll jump. It'll never go to court. They'll settle."

Suddenly, I didn't want to see Doc Robbins anymore. I wanted out and home and back to being myself. I wouldn't help him in any of his conspiracies, but I wouldn't hurt him either. If he failed, it was too bad, and if he prospered, fine, but either way I wanted out.

"It sounds like you can't miss," I said. "I wish you all the luck in the world."

"You don't see it my way, do you, kid?" he said. "You figure they'll do what they want, and there's no way we can stop 'em?"

"Since you asked me . . . yes."

He started coughing then, spitting and wiping, but he kept his back to me and put his hands at the side of his head, like he was afraid of losing his toupee. When he calmed down some, he lit another cigarette. The match fizzed inside the Styrofoam cup. He made a half-hearted effort to straighten his desk.

"I've lost my touch for sure," he said finally, laughing bitterly. "If I can't convince *you*, who can I convince?"

I felt guilty about turning Doc down. Sometimes at the Safeway, there's some eager, sad lady passing out free samples of a new product—cheese or cookies or clam dip. I take some and it tastes terrible and I walk on, feeling like a shit for not having bought anything. That's the way Doc Robbins made me feel. He was peddling nonsense, but I wished that I could make a small purchase on my way out the door.

"You never know . . . the movie people . . . they might be interested."

"Sure, kid." Doc wasn't taking charity. It was all or nothing. "A trip to the Coast and a chance to meet the stars. Thanks a lot. Thanks for dropping by. I knew you would. You were always a decent kid. Even if you couldn't play worth a damn. How about a lift home? It's not far."

"Sure, Doc." I felt like a hospital visitor searching for a graceful exit, anxious to kill time with petty errands and small favors.

"And now darkness settles over the land of ooh-baa-dee and the Voice of the Poconos sinks below the level of a lover's whisper. Are you listening? Till rosy-fingered aurora streaks the morning sky, this is Doc Robbins sneaking into the night, with a smile on my face and a dollar in my wallet and a song in my heart. The Captain and Tennille, children: 'Love Will Keep Us Together.'"

"Serves 'em right," Doc said. "Let's blow."

5

I unlocked the car door and threw my dog's collar and my wife's checkbook into the glove compartment. Meanwhile, Doc stood watching the screen of the drive-in movie: a bunch of police cars racing down an interstate.

"*Vigilante Force,*" he said. "You seen it?"

"No."

"You should go, really. You might not feel so bad about Eddie dying young. It could've been worse. He could've grown up to be Kris Kristofferson."

"I don't kid about Eddie."

"Neither do I," Doc said. "Ah, don't mind me, kid. I'm just a jerkwater deejay with big ideas. And no takers. Just drive on down the highway."

He grinned and patted my shoulder.

"Make like a Cruiser."

I drove as fast as I could, badly wanting this visit to be over. On my way to see Doc, I'd been convinced that for once I should trust my instincts, follow out the feelings that led back into the past. It wasn't my style. The Word-man, they'd called me, and I guess they meant it as a compliment. Turning feelings into words had been my bit of alchemy among Eddie and the Cruisers. But when it came to pure feelings, I was lost. Look where my feelings had landed me now.

Emotions are risky, I realized. For a solid week memories of that Cruiser year had me in turmoil. As if some underground main had broken, the memories came welling to the surface with a freshness and clarity that shocked me. They'd convinced me that there was something important down there, something that had been buried for years but was still alive, begging to be unearthed, a spring and not a broken pipe.

Now I knew better. Nostalgia was the impurest form of memory. Selecting and sentimentalizing, first you victimized yourself. And then, if you acted on your feelings, you entered a world of tacky souvenirs, cheap rituals, monuments to nothing. A world of ghouls, catered by morbid hucksters like Doc Robbins. If I hadn't come to Stroudsburg, I'd remember him as a fabulous character, a roadside original. But I'd come back, and the price of the trip was that I now saw him as he was, a penny-ante predator, a dollar short and a day late.

"Make like a Cruiser." Sure, Doc. Grease is the word. How about digging up some Eddie Wilson imitators. A lookalike talent hunt. Hasn't that occurred to you? Or why not do a James Dean? Hit the junkyards and blowtorch the car he died in into little pieces for the tourist trade. Pass the word: he's still alive, he had plastic surgery. He froze himself. He cloned. Only leave me out of it.

"Make like a Cruiser." Already, it sounded like a slogan lettered on a T-shirt. When Eddie came up with the name, he made it sound like a password for adventure, straight out of Kerouac—endless trips across the country, explorations and discoveries along the way. There'd be no catching us when we hit the road. A good thing he didn't live to see the junk that lined the highway, to sense the flattening of the land-scape, the pointlessness of the trip.

"Know what I was wondering?" Doc asked. "It's just an idea, I know you're gonna hate it."

"What is it?"

"I was thinking about bringing the group back together. You and Wendell and Kenny and Sal. 'Eddie Wilson's Original Parkway Cruisers.' What do you think?"

"What the hell do you think I think?" I snapped.

"I think you hate it," he replied immediately. "You don't want any part of it, and you don't want any part of anyone who does. Including me. Especially me."

"Doc, you're a mind-reader. Only, if you read my mind so well, why'd you even bother asking?"

"It's my nature. Oh shit, kid, I'm sorry."

"Okay."

Like that, it was over—his hustling and my anger—and we both relaxed. When Doc finished pitching, he was good company again. You just had to get past his hustles.

"Remember those quotes you used to give me?" he asked. "That real good stuff?"

"I remember digging things up . . . but what, exactly, I can't—"

"Sure you can. I'd rush into Vince's with a lot of hot talk. A tip here, a piece of the action there, getting in on the ground floor someplace else. And I'd have 'em all snowed. Eddie'd be worrying he couldn't afford me. Sally wanted me to invest his life savings. Kenny went 'oh wow, oh wow,' and Wendell just sat there smiling, like we were all gonna be rich that afternoon. Everybody but you, sitting at the bar, you little prig, and as soon as I stopped for breath you'd let me have it. 'Doctor, behind every great fortune lies a great crime.' Or, 'Doctor, Disraeli would say you're climbing the greasy pole of success.' Or, 'worshipping Mammon.' I re-member. 'What's it all mean, Doc, the getting and the spend-ing?' Smart-ass kid! One time, I came in wearing some threads that had a little flash, and you did twenty minutes on 'conspicuous consumption.' I acted pissed, but no kidding, you cracked me up, no lie. I still use some of that good stuff. Remember this one?

> 'Placed on this isthmus of a middle state,
> A being darkly wise and rudely great;
> With too much knowledge for the Sceptic side,
> With too much weakness for the Stoic's pride,
> He hangs between . . .'

Who was that? I forget the name."

"Alexander Pope," I replied, ashamed of myself. I remembered the name. But I'd forgotten the lines.

"Yeah, Pope. I use his stuff for a sign-off now and then. Some of these kids, they think I made it up myself. He dead?"

"Pope? Yes."

"A long time? More than twenty-seven years?"

"A lot longer."

"Nobody's gonna sue me then. Public domain. Knocks 'em out, these apple-knockers. Hey, how about . . .

> 'Great lord of all things, yet a prey to all;
> Sole judge of truth, in endless error hurled;
> The glory, jest, and riddle of the world.'

Same guy, isn't it? Pope?"

"Yes."

"I figured it was. Slow down, kid. It's on the right, just past the welding-supplies place."

The highway and the motel Doc lived in had grown old together, bypassed by better roads and newer lodgings. It was a cabin court, a sad little place with individual bungalows and empty garages to collect last year's leaves and a "Vacancy" sign they didn't even bother turning on.

"They may look like shacks on the outside," Doc said, as he motioned me through the door and reached for the light switch, "but you'd be surprised at the interior."

It was a total, wall-to-wall trashing. Everything that could be lifted was upside down: chairs, lamps, desk, table. Everything that could be cut was slashed: pillows, cushions, clothing, suitcases. What they couldn't toss or cut, they'd smashed: alarm clock, radio, plates and glasses, cups and saucers. They'd turned on the water in the kitchen and bathroom, started fires in the living room and bedroom, and left without sticking around to see which one won.

"Maid's day off," Doc said.

"What happened?"

"Last night. When I got home from the studio. I wanted you to see what they did. See, kid, it's like the punch line to the old joke. 'I might be paranoid, but that doesn't mean they're not after me.' "

"Who's after you?"

"Music lovers!"

"Why?"

"They think I'm into something. They think I have something they want. Too bad you weren't around last night. You could have told them I'm a worthless crock of shit."

"Is there anything I can do?"

"Don't extend yourself. No need to clean up. I'll just move over to another cabin. There's nine of 'em, all empty. Anyway, they'll keep comin' back at me till they get what they want. Beer okay?"

Without waiting for an answer, he disappeared inside. I heard him moving through the puddles in the kitchen. I sat outside in one of two metal garden chairs that had escaped the holocaust.

"It's warm. Sorry." He came back out and sat next to me. When he snapped open the can, it spurted out onto his shirt and pants.

"I wondered why they left the beer." He handed me the

open can after it stopped foaming and opened the second one more carefully, holding it out in front of him till it calmed down. Then he drained it in a swallow.

"You still haven't figured it out, have you?" he said.

"No."

"Try. Think about it. What could they be after? What do I have that's worth stealing? Was it my Sony radio? My Robert Hall suit? My Wilkinson blades?"

"Doc, I can't . . ."

"Don't give up yet. I'll give you a clue. Two clues. This radio station I work for is—what would you say?—obscure? rustic? But my name does show up in various broadcasting directories. And on the union rolls. That's one clue. And I'll remind you that I was manager of Eddie Wilson and the Parkway Cruisers, and every record you guys ever made had my name on it as producer. In short, I'm not hard to find, if you want to find me. And someone obviously does. What I want you to tell me is . . . why?"

I sat there for a while, trying to look thoughtful, but I didn't have the faintest idea. There were, of course, any number of reasons why someone might be after Doc Robbins.

"I know what you're thinking. A guy like Doc, no telling how many trash cans he's knocked over in his time. Bad checks, bogus contracts, broken promises, it could be anything. And it sure as hell could be. Except they called me at the studio last night, from here, just when they were leaving. They told me what they wanted. I told them I didn't have it. They were not convinced. And it has to do with Eddie and the Cruisers, all right. It has to do with *you*. They can't get it from me, they could come looking for you."

"Doc, for Christ's sake, what are they after?"

"The tapes."

"What tapes?"

"From Lakehurst."

· · ·

It's halfway between New York and Atlantic City. When we were there, the Lakewood area was already on the skids. I remembered Hasidic Jews with pale skins and dark suits, cautiously sunning on the verandahs of ancient kosher hotels that were subject to suspicious fires in the off-season. I remembered blacks, a generation away from tenant farming, who crowded into frame houses on the edge of town and sold tomatoes and peaches along the highway. I only saw them: in those days, James Brown was a secret they were keeping to themselves.

The month in nearby Lakehurst was Eddie's idea. First he called it a vacation, but we saw through that. What Eddie wanted was some time off to work with Wendell.

"A month in the studio!" Sally jeered. "Just when we were gettin' hot. A month to ... compose? Who pays you for being creative?!"

Hopkins went back to Westfield. I retired to the back room at Vince's. And Sally returned home to Philadelphia. He was the one who hurt the most. I remember the morning we dropped Wendell and Eddie off at the studio Doc had found for them, a place whose acoustics, he claimed, "couldn't be duplicated for a million bucks."

"Huck and Jim in New Jersey," I joked, as we drove down a winding dirt road through the pine barrens. Wendell and Eddie sat quietly in back. I was up front with Sally. Hopkins had already split.

"Hey, Eddie," Sally heckled, "what say you write a song about how them big Jewish hotels burn down in the winters. Insurance fires. You call it 'Jewish Lightning.' Can't miss!"

Sally hooted when he saw what Doc had rented: a forlorn quonset at the end of the road. While I helped Eddie and Wendell unpack their gear, Sally worked himself into a manic fit. First he theorized that the hut was a Nazi headquarters; he knew that the Hindenburg had crashed and burned just two miles away. Or maybe it was a storage deposit for cigarettes and firecrackers bootlegged up from

Carolina. To Wendell, he hinted that it had to be a Klan headquarters: that combination of sandy soil and pine trees was just what they loved. But as soon as we left, Sally fell silent and stayed that way, the whole ride to Atlantic City.

The month passed. We hit the road again. Nothing was said about how the experiment turned out. If there was new material, I never heard it. Of course, it's not likely that I would have. A week after leaving Lakehurst, Eddie was dead.

"Me and my big mouth," Doc was saying. "I brought it on myself."

"Brought what on, Doc?"

"This craziness. See, kid, for years I been wondering what Eddie was up to out in the woods."

"Did you ever ask him?"

"Sure I did, right after we hit the road again. We were headed to the state fairgrounds at Flemington, him and me and that Joann girl in the car. I figured I was the manager, you know? But he was acting funny around then, so I worked up to it real careful. So how was Lakehurst? Were the acoustics okay? Have everything you need? Enough tape? I told him I figured it was a real step up, moving into a studio, since I got a double hernia from carrying recording equipment into Vince's Bar. Believe me, Wordman, I wasn't pushy. I wanted to know, I figured I had a right, but I was gonna let him tell me in his own way."

"And?"

" 'I've got something like nothing you've ever heard,' he says. I didn't know how to take it, whether or not he was putting me on. About once a week for the rest of my life I've been replaying that sentence, trying to decide whether he was jerking me off. Did I say once a week?"

"Yes."

"Not lately. Lately it's been once a day. So a coupla weeks ago, there's this tri-state broadcasters' convention up at Great Gorge, and I run into a guy on one of the trade papers.

I decide, what's to lose? Why not write a note, put it in a bottle, toss it in the ocean, and see where it floats. Here."

LOST CHORDS?
FORMER MANAGER HINTS AT
EDDIE WILSON CACHE

Surprise best-seller Eddie Wilson may have left behind a legacy of unreleased tunes. That's the hopeful theory of the late rock and roller's one-time manager, Earl "Doc" Robbins, now a KCGM (Stroudsburg) deejay.

"Just before Eddie died, I set him up in a recording studio," says Robbins. "He had a full month of work. Nobody distracted him, not even me. And the results were dynamite. Eddie told me so himself."

Robbins concedes he never heard the tapes and doesn't know anybody who has. Their current whereabouts is equally a mystery.

"Eddie was keeping them to himself until he had everything just right," says Robbins. "After he died, I looked around, but they weren't to be found."

If located, the Wilson tunes could extend an already unprecedented revival. Based on only 12 known cuts—all contained on a single l.p.—the Cruiser craze is bound to run out of gas. The new material could be priceless.

"It's not the money," protests Robbins. "It's the music. Eddie gave it all he had. His new audience deserves to hear it all."

"So that's what did it," Doc resumed. "Somebody read that thing and figured I was just bullshitting—that I had the tapes myself and was fixing to make a big deal out of rediscovering them. Not a bad idea. But, fact is, I don't have 'em."

"Would you tell me if you did?"

"Hell, no! You'da never heard from me again!" Doc laughed. "But I don't have 'em. So the question doesn't come up. Do you have 'em?"

"No."

"I didn't think so. But that won't help much."

"What do you mean?"

"I mean, when they come looking for you. This is a treasure hunt. They'll come after you. You got the same name you always had, the same face. You live in the same town. You're not much of a mover. Unless they find them someplace else first, they'll come at you. I guarantee you."

"But, Doc . . . who are they?"

"Where you been, Wordman? You think there's a shortage of crooks in the world?"

"Don't condescend to me, Doc."

"Okay, okay. You want to know what I think? I think it's the squirt. Your little pen pal."

"Mannheim?"

"His tender years don't disqualify him. They help him get past the likes of you."

"You think he totaled your place?"

"Maybe not him personally. But I bet he had a little to do with it. Look, it's just a hunch. He showed up at the station with a tape recorder, I thought he might be all right. I wasn't gonna give him nothin', but I guess he looked legit. Anxious, awkward, all those words. But you know what? After he left, I left. I didn't follow him. But I go home past the shopping center down the road, and there he is, making a long-distance phone call . . ."

"He could have been—"

"Calling mother? Sure. But our boy is driving a vintage M.G., which was remarkable considering he told me he came out on the bus. And the vintage M.G. has a little fuckie doll in the front seat."

"So he's a rich kid."

"Sure. You could say that. He's a kid who's rich. And if he packed a gun, you'd say he's just a rich kid who happens to like guns. And if he has a stiff in the trunk, you'd say he's a rich kid who likes guns who's studying to be a mortician Sure, Wordman. Keep on giving him the benefit of the doubt."

"Okay, but if they found the tapes, they'd be trading in—'

"Stolen goods? Absolutely. Pirates do. And they could go the pirate route, peddling under the table. Or they'll set up a half-dozen dummy companies, here and in Europe and on some islands you never heard of, and finally make a sale to a legit distributor, and we can spend the rest of our lives trying to get what's rightfully ours. And it is ours! That's what gripes me. Waiting twenty years to get hosed."

Doc fell silent then, and so did I. We watched the traffic on the highway like a pair of unlucky hitchhikers. We belonged together. We were both losers. Doc's defeats were many and varied—close to the surface and easy to spot. My defeats went deeper.

"What are we gonna do about it?" he asked.

"Do we have a choice?" Spoken like a true loser.

"I don't. Kid, I'm broke. I barely beat the checks to the bank, every week. And I can't move around like I used to. I need you."

"Me?"

"You. You got two legs. You got a car and a little money put aside. You got a summer vacation coming up. What were you gonna do this summer, anyway?"

"Teach summer school."

"Don't. Give this a shot."

"How?"

"Go around to the Cruisers, whoever you can find, and see if you can get a line on the tapes."

"The article says you asked around back then and that you couldn't find anything. Why should I be any luckier now?"

"That's bullshit. I never asked. How was I to know what was gonna happen? Besides, the group was kind of uptight after Lakehurst. Sally and I never got along anyway. I never said much to Wendell. And that Hopkins kid, I never trusted. He was too cute by half. But hell, I just didn't think those tapes would be worth a dime."

"So it's not just the music, is it? It's the money."

"Yeah, sure. But I . . . it's more than the money. . . . Once in my life, I'd like to bring home a winner. You believe me?"

"I don't know."

"You asked me why all this was happening. Why are Eddie Wilson and the Parkway Cruisers so hot? You want me to tell you? You think you can handle it?"

"Try me."

"You were great."

"You mean Eddie was great."

"I mean you were all great. You were great together. I'm not saying I knew it at the time. But I can hear it now. Along with a million other people. I play a lot of records. You guys had something they don't have now. And they know it. This generation ain't worth shit. Look at their music. Their movies. If it's not a remake, it's a sequel. You guys were originals. They don't make 'em anymore."

"But Eddie—"

"—was the key, the spark. Sure. But you were all part of it. Eddie needed Sally 'cause Sally was steady, regular, solid. Wendell was a wizard, so he needed him. And he needed Hopkins because Hopkins believed in nothing but fun, and if it wasn't fun, he wouldn't do it, and Eddie didn't want the fun to go out of his music. And he needed you, Wordman. Because you were our touch of class."

"Come off it, Doc," I protested. "Eddie just took me along for the ride. Like Sally used to say—they kidnapped me off a bookmobile."

"Eddie had his reasons," Doc responded. "And charity wasn't one of them. You think I didn't brace him about it, when he said you were gonna be a Cruiser? The bookworm? The egghead? Joe College? You know what he told me?"

"No," I said. It made me uncomfortable, knowing that I was going to learn something new about what had ended long ago. My memories of that time were firm and set and familiar. I was their proprietor and manager. Receiving new information upset me. And Doc sensed my weakness. The old pitchman leaned forward so his eyes stared straight into mine, and his hand touched my knee.

"I wasn't in your corner, Wordman. I can remember it like

yesterday. I found Eddie in the back room at Vince's, him and that girl, and I said, 'Eddie, who needs this kid? What you want him for? A pen pal? If it's free tickets, I can handle it. He wants to tag along, that's fine. But put him up on stage? Sounds to me like you're trying to carry six pounds of shit in a five-pound bag.' Know what he said?"

"No," I answered in a whisper, abashed at the thought that I was going to hear Eddie's voice all over again, Eddie talking about me.

"He said, 'I want the kid along, Doc. There's something he's got, we need.' 'Like what?' I ask. And for a minute there, I figure I stumped him. He ran his hands through his hair like he always did when he didn't know what to say, and he turns away and I'm thinking, well I guess that's settled, and then, damn it, Eddie faces me and starts in again. 'The way he reacts. The words he uses. The way he comes at songs, like they're not dance music, they're lyrics.' 'He can't dance worth a damn, that's for sure,' I said, 'but come on, Eddie, what's with you, you fixing to write an opera?' He says, 'Words and music, Doc, words and music.' And he crossed his fingers, showing how they go together."

He rested in his chair and waited for the story to take effect. He already had me where he wanted me, but he finished me off anyway, crossing his fingers just like Eddie had.

"Words and music. You and Eddie. That's how much he thought of you. So do Eddie a favor. Check around. See what's left of Eddie out there."

"I wouldn't know where to start."

"I can point you in the right direction, for Sally anyway. From there on out, you follow your nose."

"I don't know, Doc."

"Yes you do. Give it a shot. What's to lose? Summer school? What's that? I went once. You got brown-nosers in front of the room and future criminals in back. Besides, you got twenty years of summer school in front of you."

He had me there.

That night, driving back to New Jersey, I wondered how to tell Doris about my decision to spend the summer on the road, hunting down old Cruisers. I thought we'd go into the breakfast-nook with a pot of coffee, and I'd start from that first night at Vince's.

Our heart-to-heart talk didn't come off. When I got home, the house was empty—Doris, kids, and all. I moved from room to room feeling like a burglar, till the phone rang.

"You're home," she said. "Where have you been?"

"Pennsylvania. Stroudsburg. Looking up an old friend who called me at school."

"From college days?"

"Yes, kind of. Where are you?"

"At my parents. The kids finished school today. Remember?"

"High school doesn't end till Monday," I answered lamely. "How are they?"

"Riding horses and watching television. Fine. Why not ask how I am?"

"That was next. How are you?"

"Not so good, Frank. Look, if there's one thing we can agree on, it's that we can't go on the way we have been. Agreed?"

"If you say so."

"If *I* say so . . . are you putting it on me?"

"What do you want, Doris? A unanimous vote?"

"I want a talk."

"That's what I was hoping for tonight," I said. "I know you couldn't have guessed. Look, after Monday, I'd like to hit the road a while, just sorting things out. Travels with Charley, minus dog. After that, I think we can . . settle things. Okay?"

"I don't mind."

"Anybody asks, tell them I'm taking a summer refresher course someplace. Penn State, say . . . just don't tell them where I am."

"All right."

We talked a while longer, about kids and bills and relatives. We talked amicably, the same way people separate amicably, a normal-sounding conversation hollowed out by the knowledge of what was happening to us.

You know how, when they bury someone, they pile the dirt high, leaving behind a mound of soil and flowers? And how, with time and rain and frost, that mound dwindles down to flat earth? And how, later on, you find a hole in the ground, or maybe a puddle, deepening as walls collapse and cave in down below? Our marriage was something like that: it just settled into the ground.

Oh, I can show that Doris was the first to flirt, the first to stray, the first to fall. But that's just for-the-record. Down deep, I know that it was mostly my fault. She had a way of leaping into the future, planning, anticipating, pressing forward. What's that TV serial called—*Search for Tomorrow*? That could be her slogan, and for years she tried to make it mine. She cared about where I taught, how much I made, whether I'd get to be an assistant principal or maybe move over to the local prep. She cared about where we lived, about trading up into bigger homes and better neighborhoods. In short, she cared about our advancement through life.

Only I wasn't coming along. Her discontent led her to look ahead. And so, while I kept waiting for the life I led to feel right, she drifted off. And I couldn't blame her. I couldn't imagine anyone coming home to watch me brood.

Where would she be tonight? A seminar for real estate agents? Having coffee with a college friend? Heaving her flanks in a motel? No matter. No fault. We were headed in different directions. Doris rushed into the future. And I pointed my car west along the turnpike, headed into the past.

Two days later, I found Sally.

Months before, Doc Robbins had clipped an advertisement in a music trade magazine.

**EDDIE WILSON'S ORIGINAL
PARKWAY CRUISERS**

with Sal Amato

"Let the Good Times Roll"

523-681-4285

"Don't be so surprised," Doc had said. "We got guys calling themselves Drifters, Platters, Coasters. Sometimes they got one or two original members, sometimes uncles and cousins, and sometimes they're all a bunch of stand-ins. Happens all the time on the oldies-but-goodies circuit."

I checked into a Holiday Inn outside Columbus, Ohio, in the late afternoon. I took supper down the road, not wanting to risk an encounter with Sally before I'd seen the show. It was dark when I came back to the motel, driving past a sign that made me wince. At the bottom it read: "Original Cruisers—Tonight." Up top, in much larger letters, "CONGRATS TO JUNE GRADS."

There were shows at eight and eleven, with disco tapes in between. I lingered in my room, reading through the visitors' guide to the capital of the Buckeye State, killing time as nervously as if I were appearing on stage myself. I bet Sally wasn't nervous. How could he be, doing two or three shows a night for half his lifetime? And I'll bet he didn't brag about every show being new and different. Not Sally. He'd boast about their sameness, about keeping standards up, quality control. No, Sally wouldn't be jittery—does an assembly-line worker fidget when the next car comes down the line? He was probably piling away a mountain of Italian food this minute: soup, pasta, meat and vegetables, dessert and coffee. I remembered that no matter where we were, no matter how rushed for time, Sally always ordered a hot meal.

We'd gotten along okay. Of course he resented me, but no more than he resented everybody else. Like the other newcomers, I diluted his partnership with Eddie and his paycheck, and what the hell was this paint-by-numbers guitar player doing onstage anyway? But as Eddie drifted off, Sally came to need me. He needed someone to listen to him. Life for Sally was a series of beefs, blowups, bum raps. Sally thought he was the quiet strong man of the Cruisers, the team-player, sacrificing himself so that Eddie could look good. And what did he get for it? Nothing but dumped on! His counsel was ignored, his warnings went unheeded, his reasonable requests shunted aside. Mind you, he wasn't the kind of guy who went around saying "I told you so," but, "Jeez, if that Eddie would only listen once in a while, life would be so much easier!" Sally lived for the day that Eddie would come to his oldest partner and his best friend (whether he knew it or not) and, having grown tired of "freaks and jerkoffs," he'd say, "Okay, Sally, you were right, we'll do it your way for a while." Sally prayed for that day and prepared himself and, well, you know what happened. Ninety miles an hour on a wet road, the cops said.

Sally! The last time I'd seen him had been the worst day of his life, till then. In the morning we'd buried his best friend in Vineland. And in the afternoon we all died a little.

The Cruisers attended Eddie's last rites as a group. We called at the parents' house, went to the church and the cemetery together, and left in Sally's car. I supposed that he'd drop us off at the bus station or something, and we'd all go our separate ways, trading addresses and phone numbers and promises to keep in touch. But Sally had other plans.

"Need a drink, damn it," he burst out after we'd driven twenty mournful miles. He turned into a roadside restaurant that just happened to be named Amato's Villa Napoli. That's when I knew. "On me, you guys," Sally said.

It was all on Sally, of course, or on Sally's uncle, who owned the place. Everything on the house—nothing too good for Sally's best friends. They'd set the table in the back room. I can still see it: a godawful room-length mural of the bay of Naples, a tiny bandstand with an accordion on a chair, and a couple of chubby naked statues that pissed whiskey sours at sixty bucks an hour during big weddings.

Before we knew what was happening, they were bringing out the food: trays of hot and cold antipasto, soup, pasta, veal, and chicken.

"Hey, let's eat, you guys," Sally urged, as he stuffed a napkin into his shirt front. "Chow down. Anything you need that ain't here, just ask. They'll make it special. These are my people. But remember, leave room for dessert."

Sally attacked the food, hearty and jovial.

"Hey, Wendell," he called out. "Guinea soul food! Bet you never seen the likes of this in Newark!"

"Nope," Wendell answered, staring at an artichoke.

"The best in the world," Sally said. "I grew up on this stuff. Now you see why I get homesick in some place like Ohio. Hey, dig in, everybody. You leave anything, these Italians take it personal. Kenny, you better watch out for the garlic. It's an aphrodisiac."

"Thanks, Sally," Kenny responded. He tried to be decent. "Like they say, 'Close your eyes and you're eating in Italy.'"

That's how it went for an hour and a half: heavy food and Sally's jokes to match. I never was less hungry than when I sat down that day at the Villa Napoli, and I'm sure the others felt the same. Sally had miscalculated disastrously. Still, we tried our best. I guess we knew what Sally was trying to accomplish. And we knew it was doomed. That didn't help our appetites.

I prayed. Over anisette and tortoni, I prayed that the meal would end quietly. Hit the road. Meet again someday, okay?

"Okay," Sally began. "Let's talk. This morning we put Eddie in the ground. He was your friend and my friend. Mine first. I got nothing to prove in that department. Understand me? My thoughts and feelings inside? Anybody got any doubts along those lines, say so, and we'll clear it up right now."

He was like a plucky kid daring anyone to invade his territory. The territory was Eddie.

"The question is . . . and Eddie would want us to ask it, with no delay and no screwin' around . . . what next for us? The question is . . ."

No, don't say it, Sally, I pleaded as I stared at an unfinished piece of veal.

". . . what would Eddie want us to do?"

He glanced around the table, as if he wanted to allow time for the question to sink in. And to let us appreciate the fact that he was already planning for the future.

"Okay," he said. "We got a good basic group, but we're gonna need a lead singer. I say, let's not rush it. We'll bring in guests and give 'em a shot. Candidates. No permanent replacement till we find somebody who's good. Somebody enough like Eddie so's we hold onto the old crowd. But different, too, so's we can build on what we had."

"What's Doc think?" Kenny asked.

"Doc who?!" Sally retorted. "The show-biz whiz who booked us into an amateur night in Newark? Doc, who put his name on our records as producer because he went out and rented some tape recorders? That Doc? The Doc who missed Eddie's funeral this morning? Is that the Doc you mean? Listen, I'll do everything he did and more and I'll do it for free! I got better connections, anyway. What would you guys say if I told you I was already in contact with the number-one supper club in Cherry Hill, New Jersey? Or that I had conversations with Claude Richards about a television spot whenever we're ready? And how about a solid month's work in the Catskills, right up to Labor Day? How's that sound?"

Again, he waited, clearly wanting us to be impressed by what he'd done for us. But no one said a word.

"I'm telling you guys, we got to move now!" he insisted. "We can't just . . . die. We got to take our shot now, before they forget us. They forget fast, you better believe me. So what do you say? Do we get on with the music?"

I'll never forget that moment. I sneaked a glance around the table, and every one of us was sitting with his head bowed, like students who didn't want to be called on.

"I don't believe this!" Sally shouted, slamming the table so the dishes rattled. "It's like I'm pullin' your fuckin' teeth. Do I get a response from you guys? What d'ya say? A little table talk? Dinner conversation? You, Hopkins. How about it?"

If anyone had to go first, I'd just as soon that it was Kenny. Still, I felt for him.

"No, Sal," Kenny answered softly.

"Beg your pardon," Sally fired back, mockingly cupping his hand to his ear. "Could you speak a little louder, please? These drum solos you been playin' must be going to my brains."

"Sal, I said no," Hopkins replied, holding his ground. "I hope you heard me."

"Sure I did, but could you—"

"I've made other plans, is all."

"Other plans, huh? That's nice. You mind telling me? In

case somebody asks me what ever happened to you, I don't want to look any dumber than I have to."

"Doc arranged it for me," Kenny said. "During Lakehurst. I mean, Eddie was looking out for himself. Why shouldn't I?"

"Sure," Sally said. "Why the hell not? I'll bet the good doctor found you something choice."

"A cruise ship. Caribbean. They need a musician. It sounded like fun."

"Count on Doc to—"

"Just remember that I set this up before Eddie died. It's a decision that has nothing to do with you, Sal. Understand? I was just waiting for a chance to tell Eddie."

"Wow, I feel better already," Sally said. Irony wasn't his style. It came out nasty, and it hurt him about twice as much as his intended target. "Well, Wendell, my man, your turn at bat. Want to tell me what ship you're shippin' out on?"

The silence was painful. Even Sally felt it. When he spoke to Wendell again, he was patient, almost gentle.

"Hey, Wendell? You know I ride you. I crack Amos and Andy jokes. I tell stories about Rastus and Lorenzo. I drive through Newark, I drive fast, with the doors locked and the windows up. Because that's how they do where I come from. But, no lie, I really want to know which way you're headed."

"I always liked you, Sally," Wendell said. "And thanks for the meal."

"It was nothin'," Sally said.

"I'm gonna have nice memories of you guys," Wendell said. "And of Eddie."

"Which means?"

"Thanks," said Wendell. "And so long."

"But, Wendell," Sally persisted. I think he was more curious than hurt. "Where *you* gonna go? How many mixed groups are there? I mean, there's us and the Del Vikings and who else?"

"There's black groups," Wendell said. Sally seemed sur-

prised that Wendell would even consider them. It was like
moving from Short Hills back into Newark.

"How about you?" Sally said to me. "Mr. Entomologist."

"Sally, I keep telling you. Entomologist is a Bugman
Etymologist is a Wordman."

"Words—bugs—who cares? I don't suppose you'd care to
spend the summer in the Catskills."

"No thanks. There's too much I'd miss."

Sally nodded, understanding me to mean that I'd be miss
ing Eddie, which was just as well. Had I gone I would have
missed him, even though, just then, I was wondering about
Joann Carlino and how she was spending this funeral after
noon.

That's how the Cruisers disbanded. Sally delivered the
valedictory, pushing his plate away from him, planting his
elbows on the table, putting his hands over his face, just like
he was about to say grace for us.

"You fuckin' guys," he said. "You clowns. You piss me
off."

He covered his eyes. He was crying.

"Looks like an eat-and-run situation, don't it? Well, no
body ain't gonna keep you where you don't wanna be. I ain't
beggin'. Unless this was beggin'. Which it was."

He pushed a napkin around his eyes and stared at us, as
if he wanted to remember what we were like.

"Nobody asked what am I gonna do."

"Your turn, Sally," I said.

"I'm gonna miss you guys. But do me one little favor,
okay? Don't come back at me a month or a year from now
There's gonna be some kind of a band called the Cruisers.
And I'm gonna be the leader of that half-assed outfit. And
I'm gonna give it my best shot. So I'm askin' you nice to stay
away. Okay? No droppin' by to say hello, no old-timers day
or auld lang syne. Because I'm not too sure I could handle
that. Deal?"

We all agreed. And I guessed we kept our word.

· · ·

I sat in the lobby of the Holiday Inn, just outside the lounge, waiting for the lights to dim so I could enter unobtrusively. Posted on the wall was a glossy picture of the Cruisers: Sally and four white kids who didn't look like anybody.

"Trying to spot which one is you?"

Elliot Mannheim, equipped with tape recorder and girlfriend, was preparing to catch the show. He seemed glad to see me. And his girlfriend seemed impressed. Susan Foley wasn't the Mannheim type. He was intense, urban, Jewish. She was the sort of tall, full blonde who might be from Wisconsin, California-bound.

"You were an original Cruiser?" she asked.

"From beginning to end—right, Mr. Ridgeway?"

"I'm not so sure," I answered, pointing to the lounge. "I guess it hasn't ended. I was a Cruiser for one year. There's a man in there who's been one for nearly twenty."

"What brings you out?" Mannheim asked.

"Same as you. Curiosity."

"We're sitting ringside," Mannheim said. He peeked inside. "Not hard to arrange. But we'd love to have you join us. It would add a dimension."

"Please come," the girl said.

"Not now," I answered, with a twinge of regret. It had been a while since a young woman had found me interesting. But she probably wanted to talk about the Cruisers, about what Eddie was like or, God forbid, the details of the crash.

"Sally doesn't know I'm here," I told them. "If he spots me it could be disconcerting for both of us. And he's just crazy enough to call me up onstage. So I think I'll just sit at the bar."

"You're not going to leave without saying hello, are you?" Mannheim asked.

"No . . . I guess not."

"Then we'll see you in Mr. Amato's room, after the show.

It's two-oh-three, in back. I'll be taping an interview. Be great if you could join in, have a dialogue with him. A Cruiser reunion after twenty years!"

"I don't know about that."

"Well, drop by anyway. I'll tell him you're coming."

"No, please. Don't."

"Okay," Mannheim conceded. "It'll be a surprise."

"But you will drop in," the girl insisted. Oh hell, I thought, for sure she's writing an Ohio State thesis on music of the 1950's.

"Sure," I relented. "I'll be there. See you later."

I waited a moment more after they left. The lounge was darker now, and some guitars were being tuned. The microphone growled and squeaked like a metal pig being forced down a slaughterhouse chute.

"Ladies and gentlemen, Holiday Inn is proud to present a group that's been bringing us hits for twenty years. A big hand, please, for some Jersey boys who made good. Eddie Wilson's Original Parkway Cruisers!"

I stepped inside and headed straight for the bar, like a salesman who badly needed a drink. Oh? Live music tonight? I really hadn't noticed. What's on draft? I had a beer in one hand and a bunch of peanuts in the other before I faced the music.

Sally was sitting behind the piano on a stage that was maybe a foot above a tiny dance floor. To his left, a drummer. To his right, two guitarists. He was heavier, for sure, and his hair looked like it had been combed to cover thin spots, Bill Haley–style, but he was still Sally. Steady work, food that stuck between the ribs, and no fuckin' around.

The Cruisers were dressed in the kind of dark, formal suits that would be Sally's idea of class. Sal had an added touch: a white linen scarf around his neck.

I didn't recognize the first tune: a busy little warmup instrumental that musicians use when they've come on-stage. It was the kind of tune you just break even on. The audience applauded politely, neither disappointed nor especially pleased. The next was different.

> "Shadows are longer now
> Where I go
> Sun is falling
> Down bloody and low . . ."

It wasn't Sally's voice. It was Eddie's. It came from the drummer, a gawky, nondescript kid who gave me a tingly thrilling sensation I hadn't known for years. Close my eyes and it could have been Eddie, singing "On the Dark Side."

> "Step to the dark side . . .
> Who needs light?
> Gonna *feel* my way, baby
> And it's gonna feel right . . ."

Eddie Wilson didn't have a great voice. He used to kid about it—"Well, I'm no Frankie Laine." And then he'd do a marvelous thing: a slow, smoky version of "Moonlight Gambler." He treated it the way Ray Charles would have, turning a slap-happy anthem into—what?—a menacing invitation. When Eddie sang it, you knew that bad things could happen in the moonlight. No, you wouldn't mix him up with Frankie Laine, but he had a voice that was his own. And like many such voices, once you heard it, you could imitate it. We all did passable Eddie imitations. But this kid had Eddie down cold.

The audience loved him. There was a sprinkling of kids, but most looked old enough to have caught Eddie the first time around. That didn't make them old, but they weren't young either. Their bodies hinted of children at home.

> "Gonna feel for the dark side
> Don't care what I find,

My love's gonna guide me,
Gonna help me go blind. . . ."

They cheered wildly for the kid, who bowed awkwardly
when he was done, cast a guilty look at Sally, and ducked
back behind the drums. Sally had the kid under tight con-
trols, I saw, an Eddie puppet he dangled in front of the
audience.

"That's the memory-lane voice of Eddie Wilson," Sally
said from behind the piano. He didn't introduce the kid. "The
original sound of the Parkway Cruisers."

The very name brought some cheers. They were ready to
sing along, clap hands, dance, turn back the clock.

"We were a bunch of kids from the Jersey shore. Any
Jersey people here tonight?" (Hurray.) "You remember the
feeling of the fifties? Sand in your shoes, ants in your pants,
and a secret weapon in your wallet? Am I right? You made
the babies, we made the hits. We're gonna play 'em all for
you."

More cheers. Requests. "Far-Away Woman." "Down on
My Knees."

"You'll get 'em all," Sally promised. "But you know, we're
Cruisers. And Cruisers don't stand still. Gotta keep movin'
down that road, knocking off the miles."

He held up an album.

"*The Cruisers Now!* Our latest. We're still moving. At
your record stores. In the lobby. Under your windshield
wipers. You don't buy it, we'll cop your hubcaps. Like to
do a few cuts for you. This next one I wrote myself.
'Disco Boardwalk.' Like to see some dancers in front of
me."

Nobody danced. Nobody moved. Hardly anybody applauded. Not for "Disco Boardwalk," or for Sally's soon-to-
be-released novelty tune about joggers, or for his impres-
sions of Little Richard, Fats Domino, and Chuck Berry.
Sally's act didn't fall into the toilet: it dove in and stayed

there and pretended it was an Olympic-size swimming pool. It laughed and splashed and shouted, "Come on in, the water's fine."

You could see the audience turn old and sour and disapproving. One moment they were young again; the next minute they were worried about their babysitters. "Uh . . . this was a mistake . . . not what we thought." "Honey . . . it's late . . . the kids."

I was into my fourth beer. There were moments when going back to check out the Cruisers seemed absolutely right. It wasn't the tapes. It was the idea of getting in touch with a time when I'd been part of something good.

Now, once again, the pendulum had swung to the other side. I saw an aging audience out for cheap thrills and a pathetically out-of-step musician who refused to provide them. I felt terrible just then. It was too bad for everybody: for dead Eddie and misfit Sally, for the ripped-off audience and the cuckold English teacher at the bar.

I checked out Mannheim's table, wondering about how to break my promise to show up in Sally's room. I ran straight into a stare and a sad smile from the girl. Susan Foley understands, I thought. I shrugged and waved good-bye. She shook her head. No, don't leave yet. I know it's awful, of course, but don't go. So I stayed.

Sally was in the middle of more "new material" when the audience got out of hand. I think he was doing something inspired by *Star Wars,* with lots of flashing lights and weird notes and clanging sounds. It reminded me of a Spike Jones routine, it was that bad.

"Just play the hits," a man shouted. "Fuck the kid stuff!"

"Oldies but goodies," cried a woman, and before long they took up the chant, stomping their feet and clapping their hands in unison. "Oldies but goodies! Oldies but goodies!"

Sally tried finishing the space number, but it was hopeless. He motioned for the others to stop playing. Then he turned

on his piano stool and faced the still-chanting audience, waiting for them to quiet down.

"You been a great audience," he said, and I hoped I was
the only one who knew him well enough to spot the hate in
his eyes.

"Okay music lovers. Get on with the music! Time to rock
and roll! Eddie Wilson time! Wendell Newton, Kenny Hopkins, Frank Ridgeway, and yours truly, keeping faith on the
piano. Are you ready?"

The audience loved him now, knowing they'd won.

The Cruisers broke into a fast, angry version of "Down on
My Knees," with Sally singing lead.

> "Saying to you baby, baby please,
> What else you want
> When I'm down on my knees?"

There were a dozen cuts on our one and only l.p., and
Sally went through all of them. In order. On the demand-
ing tunes like "Leavin' Town" and "It'll Happen Tonight," he called on the drummer, but otherwise he took
the lead himself, pounding out the songs with an angry
competence that the audience mistook for conviction.
How many times has Little Richard keened "Long Tall
Sally"? Or Jerry Lee Lewis slugged his way through
"Whole Lotta Shakin' Goin' On"? That many times and
more, Sally had worked his way through Eddie's dozen
songs. And, to judge from his new material, the future
held nothing but more of the same. Twenty years from
now, he'd be held over in Sun City and St. Pete. They'd
need a doctor in attendance.

At last the customers were getting what they'd paid for,
drinking hard, crowding the dance floor. The whole room felt
like a high school reunion, with everyone out to demonstrate
that they were still young.

"Hold on, everybody," Sally shouted when he'd almost

worked his way through the album. "Time to light a candle."

Some dancers stayed on the floor, leaning against each other. Some retreated to their tables, holding hands. The Cruisers began playing "Those Oldies But Goodies Remind Me of You," very slow and melancholy.

"I wanna say a word about the past," Sally intoned. "The past isn't gone." (Cheers for the past.) "The past's not dead!" ("You bet your ass it ain't!" someone shouted.) "Not as long as we carry the music in our hearts. Not as long as we remember the good things. I wanna tell you about one of the good things that happened to me."

A hush fell over the Holiday Inn. A few gasps. A reaching for handkerchiefs. They knew they were being set up. And they loved it.

"You'd think it'd be hard to remember someone who's been gone for twenty years," Sally said. "Well, I got news. Not Eddie Wilson. He's part of yesterday, sure. But he's part of today, too, you'd better believe. And tomorrow . . . never doubt it."

Now the Cruisers were singing "Those Oldies But Goodies . . ." and Sally's monologue sounded like one of those spoken passages that turn up in the middle of country-and-western records.

"He was a kid, like any other kid. Like you and me used to be. . . . He was one of us, always, and that's how come he wrote songs that reached out and touched us, touched us where we live. . . .

"People ask me, how come this group is still called Eddie Wilson's Original Parkway Cruisers. Is it for the money? Publicity? Let 'em think what they want, because down deep I've settled that one for myself. Because Eddie Wilson is as much a part of this group as I am. We're still together, him and me. Never a day passes, I don't think he's around somewhere. Down the road a ways. Around a corner. In the neighborhood. Not far away at all. . . ."

You can guess what happened next: a sudden silence, a dimming of the lights, and the sound of Wendell Newton's sax leading into "Far-Away Woman."

No point in calling for an encore. "Far-Away Woman" ended the show like an anthem or a hymn. There was nothing left for Sally to play and nothing for the audience to do but head home.

I took time finishing my beer. I needed time to calm down. Granted, there was an integral sleaziness in Sally's act. It reminded me of a show we'd seen at Disney World, where they have moving, talking, life-sized replicas of U.S. presidents onstage, and Abe Lincoln delivers a snatch of the Gettysburg oldie-but-goodie. That's the kind of act that Sally had. I didn't envy him. He shared the stage with robots, a ventriloquist upstaged by his dummies. He invoked Eddie's ghost and made a living out of it, but he was that ghost's dependent. The least stir of independence and his audience was gone.

And yet, how could you account for the overwhelming magic of those songs? The singer was dead, and the songs were two decades old. But look at what had happened tonight! The songs were part of people's lives, milestones and measuring sticks. They turned people into dancers, brought tears, evoked memories, made them young again. Where books and movies didn't reach, Eddie's songs arrived so effortlessly, riveted in time and place and yet . . . transcendent. I could see him now, lifting his hands, an amazed look on his face, just like after I'd dug out a poem he liked: "Holee shit!"

Eddie never figured he was writing classics. His songs were the offspring of moods: a knockout girl in Cape May, a hangover in Absecon. He tossed them off and they met their fates in the most transient of trades, a Number Eight or a Number Eighty. An upward curve and an inevitable downward fall on the *Billboard* list. And that was it. Nobody listened to "golden oldies" back then. We didn't get nostalgic about dead singers and disbanded groups. Russ Colombo? Glenn Miller? We looked ahead, to tonight, this weekend, next summer. Now, everybody was looking back. Even the kids. That was the difference between then and now. Something had changed in the land, and Eddie's music was part of the change.

"You're coming, aren't you?"

Mannheim had sent Susan Foley to fetch me.

"Yeah. I'll be there."

"How'd you like the show?" she asked.

"Mixed emotions."

"I could see them on your face."

"What about you?"

"I was glad I saw it," she said. "But I wouldn't come back."

"Do you think I could buy you a drink before we go?"

I was ready to step over to a table, but she hopped right up on a bar stool and seemed perfectly at home.

"What are you doing here?" I asked. "I mean, I was a Cruiser. A historic Parkway Cruiser. That's my excuse."

"I need an excuse?"

"Excuse me. But I'm still curious. Is it Mannheim? Or the music?"

"School's out."

"I wasn't sure of that. I pegged you as a graduate student in . . . I don't know . . . sociology or American studies. 'A Typical Musical Group of the Nineteen-Fifties.' Another writer, like your boyfriend."

"I'm not a writer."

"And?"

"He's not my boyfriend. We went to college together, back East. I'm a graduate student now. And my thesis has nothing to do with the Cruisers. Unless you sang about martial law in the Philippines."

"Political science?"

"Law."

"I'm sorry. I ask a lot of awkward questions. That is, I ask them awkwardly."

I'm not sure my apology was needed. Susan Foley seemed more amused than offended. My clumsiness amused her.

"What were they doing when you left?" I asked.

"Elliot had started taping. Your name popped up, by the way."

"Mannheim didn't tell Sally?"

"No. He didn't say you were coming. He asked him to appraise the musical talent of the original Cruisers. He mentioned you first, like you were the easiest to dispose of. 'Well, there was that Ridgeway kid on guitar. A José Feliciano, he wasn't. He could make a guitar sound like a ukulele!' "

I laughed at that, and she did too.

"Maybe we better head over there," I said, "and save my reputation."

We walked out of the lounge together. She was good-looking enough to turn some heads, I saw, and nice enough to take my arm.

"That's not all Sal said," she told me as we passed the deserted swimming pool.

"Oh no. Let's hear it. Count on Sally to get in with the low blows."

"This wasn't. He said you were quote some kind of genius with words, a regular whiz kid, close quote. He said you helped Eddie Wilson write a lot of the songs. Like 'Far-Away Woman' and 'On the Dark Side.' Is that true?"

"I helped. Eddie had the ideas and some of the words. But they took a lot of organizing and smoothing out. That was my job."

"It sounded like a lot more than that. And those are great songs. I'm no nostalgia buff, but I know when a song gets under my skin. Those are great. Did you ever follow up?"

"Follow up?"

"After Eddie Wilson died. Didn't you write any more songs?"

"No."

"Or poems or books?"

"No."

"What did you get into?"

"Teachers' college."

"That's not what I meant."

"I'm sorry." I paused, sensing that she was waiting for an explanation, but there wasn't much I could add. "That part of my life stopped dead when Eddie died."

"So then—pardon me—but why are *you* here?" I guessed she had me there: a solitary thirty-seven-year-old man who drove six hundred miles to catch a lounge act at a motel in Ohio. For what?

She persisted. "You said that part of your life had stopped dead. So what's *your* excuse?"

"I wanted to see how things turned out for some old friends of mine," I said.

"That's all?"

"No. . . ." The next part came hard. It was the first time I'd put it into words. "I wanted to see how things . . . how things might have turned out for me."

"Son of a bitch!" Sal shouted. "Look what comes walkin' through the door. Wordman himself!"

I offered him a hand, but Sally wouldn't settle for anything less than a bear hug and a spin around the room. He smelled of beer and pizza and cigars. He always smelled like that. Pot wasn't his style: it made you do crazy things and maybe miss work.

"What'd I tell you?" he shouted to Mannheim, who was sitting on a couch with his tape recorder on the coffee table. "When you're hot, you're hot! You know who this guy is?"

I didn't have time to tell him Mannheim and I were introduced. Mannheim didn't try to clue him in either.

"It's the Wordman! Frank Ridgeway! One of the *original* Original Cruisers!"

He turned to me in a mock aside.

"See that kid in the corner? He's a writer for *Rolling* fucking *Stone*! Came out to interview me!"

"We were talking about the old days," Mannheim said.

"Maybe you'd like to join in, Mr. Ridgeway, since you were part of it."

I wondered why Mannheim kept acting like this was our first meeting. I guessed maybe he was protecting Sally's feelings, pretending that his first priority was talking to the Cruisers' current leader. So I played along.

"I was just a go-fer," I said. "Hot coffee and cold beer. Sal here knew Eddie way before I did. He goes back to the beginning."

"The old days!" Sal exclaimed, throwing himself into his chair. "All he wants to talk about is ancient history. Kid acts like he just opened up a grave. I keep telling him I got an act that's ready to move. The best of the old days and the best of the new."

"I was getting to that, Mr. Amato," Mannheim said. "I want to hear about your plans. But I thought we'd start from the beginning."

"Sure. Humor the old man. Three reels of tape for what's dead and a half a reel for what's alive." He sat there stubbornly, swigging his beer. But the moment of rebellion was brief. Sal knew he was a prisoner of the past. "Okay, junior, where were we?"

"We were up to the time Eddie went to Lakehurst."

"Where'd you hear about Lakehurst?"

"I did some homework, checked your bookings. There's a month off. No club dates, no nothing. That's all I know. A vacation?"

"You got it. Eddie had himself a terrific vacation on the shore. He went to mattresses in Kosherville. Right, Wordman?"

I stayed out of it.

"That's all it was? All play, no work?"

"Chicken soup and brisket of beef. Not my speed, kid. I was in Philadelphia."

"I heard the Cruisers rented a recording studio down in Lakehurst."

"What kind of homework you been doin'?"

"I should have mentioned it before. I contacted your former manager. Earl Robbins."

"Where'd you dredge him up. Outa what sewer?"

"He's a disc jockey now. Eastern Pennsylvania."

"Yeah? You think you might be in touch with him again?"

"Maybe."

"Give him a message. Remind him I got the name Eddie Wilson and the Original Parkway Cruisers sewed up tight. Copyrighted and paid for. I hear he's screwin' around—it's his ass. You tell him that."

"I don't want to involve—"

"Tell him I'm still waitin' for him to show up at Eddie's funeral. Put that in your interview."

"About Lakehurst . . ."

"So?"

"The studio. What happened there?"

"Studio? You call it a studio? Doc called it a studio. I call it a rusty, dusty piece of crap."

"But what happened there?"

"What makes you think anything happened? Eddie messed around with some new material, him and Wendell . . ."

I could see that Sal was still hurting, after all the years.

"They went out into the woods and had a séance. Or a beer party. I don't know. I wasn't invited. . . . Say, Wordman . . ."

He was still pained and angry. I could see old wounds reopening, poisons seeping out through cracking scars.

". . . should I tell him how Eddie got you laid the first time? I mean, if we're gonna list all our great accomplishments, that's the match of anything that came out of Lakehurst."

"I don't think that's what this man's after," I said, my ears burning in embarrassment. Susan Foley was smoking a cigarette quietly and looking through the visitors' guide. That meant she hadn't missed a thing.

"I don't know much about Lakehurst," I said. "I wasn't

around much either." I spoke to Mannheim but my words were meant for Sally, to calm him down and make him hurt less. "Eddie and I had our ups and downs. Toward the end it was a down. We'd played a college not long before and ... something happened ... that strained our relationship. Nothing permanent. Except that he died. That made it permanent. Anyway, I draw a blank on Lakehurst."

"We were all go-fers near the end," Sally said. "Except for Wendell. Him and Eddie were a regular Huck and Jim. Ah, the hell with it. What did you want to know?"

"Those studio sessions."

"What Wordman says goes double for me. My wife's been getting calls every day back home. No tapes. No unreleased masterpieces. Anybody asks you, tell him to stay outa my attic."

I watched Mannheim pause and decide to give it one more try.

"Some things you've said lead me to believe maybe the Cruisers weren't as tight as they used to be near the end. Like maybe Eddie Wilson was getting ready to cut out on his own, or reconstitute the group. Could it be he was jamming with new people out in the woods? Presley was on the East Coast that spring, and Buddy Holly . . ."

Sally was due to explode, I thought, and this time I wouldn't try to stop him. Mannheim combined obsequiousness and arrogance: he kissed ass for what he wanted, and he sneered at what he didn't need.

But Sally surprised me, leaning back in his chair, closing his eyes, smiling wearily like he'd heard it all before.

"Who knows what was on Eddie's mind at the end?" he asked with a shrug. "Do you know, Wordman?"

"No," I said. "Eddie was hard to figure, toward the end."

"We were tight for years," Sally said. "Ain't nobody was tighter than Eddie and me. Nobody. That the truth, Wordman?"

"Yeah, Sal."

"But at the end?"

"At the end? At the end they buried him. I was there at the end. And I'll tell you one thing, kid. I didn't see no Elvis Presley pull up at the funeral. Nor no Buddy Holly. Wasn't nobody famous there that I remember. Now was there anything else you needed?"

There wasn't really. I was sure of that. But Mannheim was smooth. He wasted an hour of tape feigning an interest in the post-Eddie Wilson Parkway Cruisers. He wanted to know all about how gallant Sal held the group together, kept the name alive, loyally waited for the predestined rediscovery. He asked about Sal's new material, his future plans. And, sad to say, it seemed to work. Starved for credit and attention, Sal poured out all his plans—an original score for *The Eddie Wilson Story,* a Cruiser festival on the Jersey shore, and so on. By the time they finished, he was full of enthusiasm. Seeing Mannheim and Susan Foley out the door, he said how he'd always tried to do what Eddie would have done so that, in a sense, Sally was living for both of them. As long as he survived, Eddie's life continued.

"If he was around today, he'd be on the road with me now," Sally assured him. "And we'd never run outa gas."

"Nice kid," Sally said.

"The hell he is," I answered.

"All right, he's a piece of shit. So what? A little ink never hurt the bookings."

"Don't get me wrong, Sally. Whatever's coming to you, you deserve it."

"Beer?"

"Sure."

"I deserve one myself," Sally said. "A small beer. What'd you say it was? Small beer? You told me once. The way you were always coming up with stuff."

"Small beer? The second or third batch. Weaker than the first."

"Penny-ante, second-rate—right? Bottoms up." He swallowed and belched. "Tastes okay. Light beer. That's what they call it these days. Half the calories. So I drink twice as much. Progress! Where you been hidin', Wordman?"

"High school teaching in northern New Jersey. Same place ever since I got out of college."

"No lie! I used to wonder about you. I figured you moved to California, maybe. Writin' for movies under an assumed name or something."

"No, I never left the Garden State."

"I been playing the shore spots pretty regular through the years. How come you never stopped in?"

"I don't get down there much anymore."

"Yeah, it's changed, it's gettin' built up now," Sal conceded, as if new construction were what had kept us from running into each other for fifteen years.

"You hear? Vince died. Prostate cancer. Damn thing, it's like walkin' around with a time bomb up your ass. But you look okay, Wordman."

"You too."

"I got a place in Haven Beach, right on Barnegat. Come down in the summer, we'll go crabbing."

"Thanks, Sally, I'll do that."

That's when it happened. Sally noticed that I didn't ask for his phone number or address. And I noticed that he hadn't offered it. And the awkwardness cracked us up.

"Ridgeway, I don't want to meet your lovely wife and kids," he said. "I really don't."

"I don't want to sample your polluted crabs."

"So what brings you out here? Or are you gonna tell me you were drivin' along the highway, saw my name on the marquee, and decided to say hello for old time's sake?"

"Not exactly."

"You want something, don't you? You don't want a job. You don't write songs for a living. You're not gonna touch me for a loan. And I guess you already seen the show. Beats me, Wordman. I got nothing you want."

No, he didn't. He had little enough for himself but a dozen

songs to recycle forever, like one of those roadhouse juke-
boxes where they never change the records.

"It's this Eddie revival. Caught me at a funny time. I'm
tired of my job. My wife's tired of me. And all of a sudden,
I'm hearing 'Far-Away Woman' on every corner, and I start
thinking about the old days. This Mannheim finds me, and all
of a sudden it's all I care about."

"Mannheim came to *you* first?"

"Yes."

"How come he didn't say so?"

"Sally, he's an operator."

"So what's your operation? How come you didn't clue me
in when you came in here? What makes you so all-of-a-
sudden cute?"

"Sally, what difference does it make?"

"I feel like I'm being double-teamed. That's the difference."

"I'm not working with him, Sally. He came to me first
because I live close to New York. Okay?"

"And then after he sees you, you decide to stroll down
Memory Lane. That it?"

"That's not all. You might as well know. I heard from Doc
Robbins."

"Now we hit bottom."

"I know you never liked him . . ."

"I had eyes and ears. And a nose. A nose was all you
needed."

"He's hard up these days, Sally. You saw him, you'd have
pity."

"When he's dead, I'll pity him. Remember the funeral?"

"Sally, he was full of gimmicks. Then and now. He wants
to revive the Cruisers—"

"Revive?! He'll need reviving . . ."

"He talked about the movie too."

"That figures!"

"All that's between you and him. You guys fight it out, I
don't care. But there was something else. Somebody

wrecked Doc's place. I saw it. They were after the Lakehurst tapes!"

"Lakehurst tapes?"

"Doc thinks—and I guess some people agree with him—that Eddie was up to something big that month."

Without warning, Sally reached out, picked up the coffee table, and heaved it across the room. Empty beer cans and newspapers crashed against the floor. I jumped up while Sally collapsed back onto the sofa, laughing or crying, I couldn't tell. He was like one of those stretched-out incredible faces you see in newspapers, mouth twisted, tears pouring, and you have to read the caption before you know whether you're at an earthquake or a circus.

Sally gestured me back to my chair and slowly settled down.

"My Rod Stewart imitation," he said, and then he cried, or laughed, some more. "Lakehurst tapes, huh? Something Eddie put aside for posterity. That what they're lookin' around for?"

"Yes."

"It's amazin', Wordman. It cracks me up, it truly does."

"What does?"

"They started playin' our stuff again, and I really believed that this time, after twenty years of just makin' it, it was *my* turn. I figured, well, Eddie had his shot, now this is mine. It's me they'll come to. What a fuckin' dummy I must be!"

"Ah, Sally . . ."

"No, don't 'ah, Sally' me. I get the picture now. It's still Eddie, isn't it? Nothin's changed. They couldn't care less for me. It's more Eddie they want."

"Even if it doesn't exist?"

"Yeah, that's funny too. What was it you used to say, Wordman? About proving that something hadn't happened. You remember?"

"I said it's hard to prove a negative. I get you. The tapes are like that."

"Hard to prove a negative," Sally repeated. "It sure as hell is. Especially when the negative ain't true."

"What?"

"I'm telling you: the negative is positive."

"You told Mannheim . . ."

"A lie. There's tapes."

Sally went crazy in Philadelphia, knowing that Eddie and Wendell were exploring new territory in Lakehurst while he sat around his home, driving his uncle's bakery truck around a neighborhood that hadn't changed in years. Before a week went by, he tried calling Eddie, but there was no phone at the quonset, and Eddie was rarely at the motel Doc had mentioned to him.

"I tried for days. Finally I got through, at six in the morning. I guess I woke him up. I told him I wanted to be with him, the way I'd always been. Hey, I was no chump. I had ideas! And Eddie, he says, sure, he'd like to hear them. I start pitchin' over the phone, anything I could think of, and he says, 'Yeah, Sally, sounds great. We got to talk sometime soon.' And then, you know, that was it. Time to hang up. 'This phone call must be costing you a fortune.' Hell, after that I knew what I had to do. Have it out with Eddie. I'd crash his private party."

Sally prepared himself for a final scene, marshaling arguments for a speech that he forgot as soon as he arrived. But twenty years later he remembered his speech: how they'd started together, a pair of buddies out for loose change, how they'd worked hard and played hard. "In my family, they say, 'Don't do business with friends,' " Sal was going to tell him, " 'but who the hell else you want to do business with?' "

Now he was ready to chuck it. To hell with business, to hell with friends. He arrived late at night—the radio station was playing the national anthem, he recalled—but there were a couple cars tucked between the pines, big-assed cars with New York and Pennsylvania plates, and chauffeurs waiting quietly inside. He knocked on the door, scared as a guy who interrupts a Mafia sitdown, and no one answered. He pounded away, furious at the lockout.

"That Joann chick finally opened up. Eddie's chick. You remember that lalapalooza?"

"Yes."

"She acted nonchalant. 'Oh, hi Sally.' I pushed past her. 'Where is he? I got to see him now!' Know what it was like in there? Ever walk into an all-black place by mistake, just needing a beer? Everything stops all of a sudden?"

"Like that?"

"Exactly."

"Who were they?"

"You don't understand. I just told you. It was a room full of niggers. South Philly, wall-to-wall. And booze and food and chicks and bodyguards and instruments. Jesus Christ!"

"Who were they?"

"How the hell should I know? They didn't exactly form a receiving line so I could be properly introduced. I saw some of 'em turn their backs and slide into corners, like they was worried I was takin' names. I spotted Eddie and went to where he was, next to Wendell. Wendell smiles hello and moves off, but before I could say a word, some overdressed spade moves in, lays a look on me, and says to Eddie, 'You promised everything would be secret.' Eddie is upset. Not with him! With me! 'It's all right, man, I know him.' 'We don't,' says the spade. 'Just give me five minutes,' Eddie begs. And then he grabs me by the elbow and pulls me outside.

" 'Just give me five minutes!' I lay into him. 'Five minutes to get rid of me, right? Well, I got news, Eddie. It ain't gonna take that long.'

" 'Sally, I'm sorry,' Eddie says. 'I know it's been rough for you.'

" 'Rough? It ain't been rough! It's been easy, Eddie. All day long with nothin' to do. You wanna tour with Father Divine and the Chocolate Chicklets, find somebody else to play the tambourine.'

" 'Don't cut out on me, Sal,' Eddie says. 'This month was an experiment. Something I worked out with Wendell. Something I had to try. I don't know how it worked out. But we came up with something that's not like anything else . . .'

" 'Great! Where will I read about it? *Ebony*?'

" 'The people you saw inside were only part of it. There've been others. Names you'd recognize.'

" 'Too bad I never got to meet them.'

" 'The whole project was on the sly. It was the only way to go. I had to do this!'

" 'Yeah? Who forced you?'

" 'You don't understand!'

" 'Ain't that the truth. A big dumb guinea, what's he gonna understand? Give him an organ grinder and a monkey.'

" 'One month is all I asked,' Eddie said. 'Three weeks is gone. Sally, I need one more week and then we hit the road again, just like before. You can leave if you want to, but I hope to hell you don't.'

" 'Why?'

" 'Because wherever I go, I don't want to forget where I'm coming from.'

" 'Sure, Eddie.' I tried sounding tough, but Eddie's hands were on my shoulders and there were tears in his eyes. 'I'm your rear-view mirror, right?'

"He just shook his head like he was saying no, more than that, more than that.

" 'Well, what the hell,' I said. 'It's a living.' "

"So I left," Sal said. "And we hit the road again, just like Eddie promised. You know what happened next."

Sally stood up and took off his cummerbund. His gut sagged out.

"Beer and pizza," he said. "Before long I'll need to wear a corset for this show."

"So there *are* tapes," I said. "You figure Eddie actually came up with something?"

"Yeah, I guess so. Something. Christ knows what. You want that last slice? I'll throw it out if you don't."

"No thanks."

"Fuck it, I'll skip breakfast," Sally said, reaching for the last slice and a last beer to wash it down. "Like hell I will. Let me tell you something, Wordman. For all I care, they coulda buried those tapes with Eddie."

"You don't care?"

"I got a simple little act. Twelve songs. Run through 'em all in forty-five minutes, with time-outs for wet hankies and under-the-table feels. They find those tapes, what's in it for me? I can't play that stuff. Do I hire the Sweet Gospel Singers?"

"They're worth money," I reminded him. "Right now they'll pay anything."

"Sure. But I won't see a dime, Wordman, and neither will you. Entitled or not, they'll find a way to screw us out of it. They always do. Guys like you and me, they strike oil under your backyard garden, all you get is dead tomatoes. No thanks, I'll keep plodding."

"Aren't you curious about what Eddie was up to? Money aside?"

"I used to wonder. It ate me up. But now . . . it's been so long." Sally stopped and studied me, as if deciding whether or not I could be trusted with what he was going to say.

"Ever want to be famous?" he asked.

"I don't know."

"Not like a president or a movie star," he said. "What I mean is achieve distinction at something. And have people know it."

"Yes. I guess so."

"Me too. Yeah, me. Believe it or not. And Eddie was my shot at it. I thought we could go all the way together. After he died, I got crazy. Still do, sometimes, when I hear about the deals they make these days. Or hear some dipshit kid doing one of our songs on television. Or watch one of those big concerts outa doors, a helicopter delivering some British junkie to an audience of thousands just waitin' for the noisy squirt to rip 'em off. Yeah, it gripes me when I think how big we coulda been.

"But I can handle that, these days. Because I remember Lakehurst. And in my heart I know that I wouldn't have gone all the way. Because I was countin' on friendship to carry me along. That was my mistake. I know it wouldn't have happened. I'da got dropped off somewhere along the way.

"Yeah, some nights it's like he was still alive. I get mad at him all over again—want to slap him around and shake him up. I'm mad at him for livin', and I'm mad at him for dyin' the dumb way he did. But then I remember Lakehurst, and I say, 'So be it,' and I keep on living."

"Hey, Wordman!"

I was walking back to my room, past the swimming pool, and she was sitting on the edge, dangling her feet into the water.

"Pool's closed." I pointed to the sign. "No lifeguard. Swim at your own risk. Guests only."

"I'll tell them I'm your guest. All right?"

"I guess." I sat down next to her.

"No late show tonight," she said.

"I'm sure that's okay with Sally."

"Were you with him all this time?"

"Yes. Where were you?"

"Here. Waiting."

"Where's Mannheim?"

"He left."

"Did he get what he wanted?"

"I suppose. He always does. He works hard."

"It seems out of proportion. This Eddie Wilson revival

can't last forever. They'll have to find someone else to rediscover, I guess."

"What will you do then?"

"I don't know yet."

"I like what you're doing now." It came so out of the blue, I couldn't resist a double take, checking to see if she were talking to me or to someone standing in back of me.

"Doing what?" I asked.

"Going back into the past. I find that very interesting."

"I'm not so sure."

"It's worth trying. You're doing what everybody thinks of, one time or another. I mean, the future just comes to us. It arrives, no matter what. But turning back into the past takes work. And pain."

"Sure," I joked. "Like a fish swimming upstream to lay eggs and die."

"You shouldn't think of it that way," she scolded, and that surprised me. There was no reason for her to mind the jokes I cracked at my own expense. "Will you let me know how it turns out?"

"How do I reach you? Through Mannheim?"

"Not necessarily," she said.

She pulled her legs out of the water and reached for her shoes.

"Well, goodnight," I said.

"I'm wet up to my knees."

"They took in the towels."

"Do you have any?" she asked.

"In my room. Hang on, I'll go get—"

"Wait!" She put a hand on my shoulder and pulled me down, like there was something I'd missed, but she didn't tell me right away. Instead, she laughed at me some more, the way she'd laughed when I clumsily inquired if Elliot Mannheim were her "boyfriend."

"You really are a product of the fifties," she said. Her lips were at my ear, and I could feel her hair touch my face—that funny feeling halfway between a tickle and a caress. "What do I have to do to get in your room, Mr. Ridgeway? Jump all the way into the water and ask to borrow your bathrobe? My hair takes hours to dry. I'll jump in if you want me to, if it'll make you feel better. But then you'll be fucking a woman with lots of long wet hair."

She stood up. "Shall I jump?"

I held her.

"Don't jump." And then I laughed. She was right. A product of the fifties. I was the same kid who'd sat reading poetry in Vince's Boardwalk Bar because it seemed like a cool thing for a drifter to do.

"Good," she said. "What I want now is a towel. And a bed. And a long carnal evening. I want to sleep late. When I get up, I want a big breakfast. I'll be hungry as a lumberjack."

She stretched, tipping up on her toes and reaching out her arms, as if she were just awakening.

"How does that sound to you?"

"Fine," I said.

"You don't have to be someplace in the morning?"

"No." And then it occurred to me. "I'm taking some time off."

I awoke the next morning and studied the stranger in my bed. Susan Foley plunged into sleep as completely as she cast herself into sex, like she was riding a bobsled into sweet oblivion. Arms thrown wide, and light brown hair spilling over the pillow, and a smile on her face that I still couldn't quite believe had anything to do with me.

Being unfaithful after so long was like losing my virginity all over again. I didn't feel guilty, and I hadn't thought I was evening the score with Doris. But I was nervous. If I hadn't pleased my wife—and I evidently hadn't—how long had it been since I'd satisfied anyone at all?

"Remember last night when Sal needled you?" she asked.

"About what?"

"He said, 'Should I tell about the first time you got laid?'

You blushed and changed the subject."

"Because *you* were there," I admitted.

"You had your eye on me!"

"Yes. From when you met me at the bar. No, before. When Sally's act was dying, and I caught you looking at me. That's when."

"What would you have done about it?"

"Nothing."

"You miss a lot that way."

"I know. That's what Sally was kidding me about."

"What happened?"

"It's embarrassing. Why do you think I blushed?"

"Positions have changed since then. Wouldn't you agree?"

I supposed they had. She sat astride me after we finished, reluctant to dismount, and I enjoyed staying inside her, waiting to see if the tide was washing in or out. She leaned forward so her elbows were at my side and her breasts against my chest, and she gazed into my eyes like I was a book she was eager to read.

"Tell me," she said.

The longer Eddie and the Cruisers played at Vince's Boardwalk, the better they got. Night after night you could watch it happen, the group staking out a sound, a tone, a style that was distinctively its own. That summer was our time. And that tacky stretch of shoreline—humid, tar-blistery streets, rotted wood, salt air, deep-fried food—that was our unchallenged territory. We were lords of the plywood jungle, those miles of jerry-built beach homes with barely enough of a yard between them to hang out a wet bathing suit or toss an empty beer can. You can look up who was big that summer—Pat Boone's "Love Letters in the Sand," Debbie Reynolds' "Tammy," Elvis' "Teddy Bear," all Number One. But not in our neighborhood.

I'll never forget the round of cheers that sounded as soon as Vince unplugged the jukebox, no matter what was playing, and the Cruisers moved toward the stage. It was like the national biggies were okay, but what we were into was the real thing. Eddie would bounce up and down in front of the mike and shout his trademark, saying, "Let's get on with the music!"

Vince never had a better summer. From ten o'clock the bar was jammed, and the action flowed out onto the parking lot, the streets, the nearby beach. More than once they nearly drank Vince dry. I'm not kidding! The draft beer went first, then the cans and bottles, even warm ones, and by God, that wasn't the end of it. They started in on the hard stuff. Not just Scotch and rum and bourbon but those dusty, weird hair-tonic bottles you get one call for a year: anisette, rock-and-rye, Fernet-branca!

In mid-August, at the season's manic crest, there came the night I dreaded: my first appearance as a Parkway Cruiser. I was scared to death, and Sally didn't help much; he took out a newspaper ad, "See Frank Sing and Dance!!"

Eddie wanted to make it as easy as he could, so he decided that he'd bring me on for the last show on a Saturday night. "Smuggle him onstage," Sally said. "By then they'll be so polluted they won't care if he wets his pants. Some show business debut!"

The closer it came, the more jittery I got. I dropped things, I spilled drinks, the resin slid off my perspiring hands. I had no business being up there with Eddie and the Cruisers. What a colossal miscalculation, to presume that I had anything to offer that crowd of seasoned drunks and dancers. I could hardly sing, I didn't dance, I barely played. Did I have any business up there with savage Sally and heartbreaking Hopkins and black, mysterious Wendell and Eddie the boss magician? Frank B. Ridgeway in this group?

I rushed over to Eddie as soon as he came offstage, convinced I was at last telling him what he'd waited to hear.

"What's the matter, Wordman?" He was in the back room with Joann. They retreated there often between sets: they even called it "our house." Sometimes they closed the door, but I didn't mind. Eddie was my closest friend, I thought, and Joann—well, just knowing that she was in the room, on my couch, could set me up for the day. Remember Sophia Loren in *Boy on a Dolphin,* right when she came out of the water? Joann Carlino was like that all the time. She was the most potently sexual woman I'd ever seen. I craved her in a way I never craved my wife. But that wasn't all. Because she surely knew my feelings and she handled them well. She didn't laugh or tease or put me down. I thought—still think —that in an odd, funny way, she liked me. Don't ask why. But she was certainly the first to spot what was wrong with me that night.

"You're ready, aren't you, Frank?" She knew I wasn't. "Eddie, he's trembling!"

"What is it?" Eddie asked.

"Eddie—Christ, Eddie, it won't work! You know it and I know it, so please, please don't put me through it. Joann, tell him."

"What won't work?" she asked.

"You've done this stuff a dozen times in rehearsal, Word-man. You wrote half the stuff."

"But that's different. It's not like being up there in front of them!"

"I think you're ready," Eddie said, "and I'm the leader of the band. I want you on board after summer, just like we talked about. It's not that you need us. I think we need you."

"Eddie, I'll write, I'll read, all that. But I can't perform. Sally's right!"

"Sally's full of shit. Ask him in a nice way, he'll admit it himself."

"Eddie, I watched that last set. Not just you guys but the audience, too. I saw the look in their eyes. They ate you up, every one of you! And I just can't picture it. I just can't see them looking at *me* the same way."

"Calm down, Frank," Joann said. "*Think* about it. Who are those people? You're so much smarter."

"Yeah," said Eddie. "You know that crowd. What's so special about them?"

"It's not like they're your jury," Joann added. "They're not out to get you."

"I look at them, they're tougher, they're older. They've done so many things I haven't."

"Like what?" Eddie asked, before Joann could stop him.

"It's . . ." It was out now. Maybe she'd always known. I guessed she had. But now I couldn't even pretend. "They're experienced," I stammered, "and I'm not."

Usually, Joann was the sly, smiling kind who took everything in. But now she jumped up, led Eddie out to the door, and closed the door.

I sat down on my cot, a choked-up, perspiring wreck. If I could have locked the door from inside, I would have stayed there all night, let them pound away and plead till they had no choice but to go on without me. At dawn I'd be at the bus terminal. I'd be home for lunch, I swear it. It was that simple.

The door opened and I jumped up, ready to start protesting all over again.

Joann came in with another girl who'd been in and out of Vince's all summer long. If I saw her now, I wouldn't recognize her. But that night I saw tight short-shorts and a braless T-shirt and black hair and olive skin that looked still warm from the beach.

"Carol," Joann said. "You know Frank, don't you? The newest Cruiser?"

"Sure," she said. "I've seen him. The cute one."

"See, Frank," Joann said. "You're a hit already."

She hit the light switch and slipped outside the door. Through the crack, I saw where she was standing guard.

"Joann says you're nervous about joining the Cruisers," Carol said. "I don't blame you. But you must be good if they let you join."

She approached the couch, slipping off the T-shirt with her first step, her shorts and sandals at the second, and then she was sitting next to me.

"You play the guitar?" she asked. I'd never touched bare breasts before or felt them swell. Hers filled my hands.

"Well?" she asked.

"The guitar. Yes, I play it."

"Do you?" She'd undressed me now and lay down beside me.

"And I sing background behind Eddie," I told her while she pulled me on top.

"Terrific." I felt her legs winding around me, her heels moving up and down the small of my back.

"And lyrics too."

"You're ready, then."

"I've rehearsed . . ."

"You feel ready. Oh, for sure."

She guided me inside, and before long, the years, the walls, the nerves and life itself came tumbling down, then and again, till it was time for the Cruisers' third set.

The door cracked open and Eddie stuck his head inside.

"You in there, kid?"

"Yes."

"You all right now?"

"Yes."

"Okay. Now we got that out of the way, let's get on with the music."

I never saw Carol after that night. The next day, Sally mortified me with the report that a marine drill sergeant had been through looking for a wife named Carol. They all kidded me a while. Except Joann. She never mentioned it, which was just as well, because as painless and fine as the initiation had been, and as easy as women were in the months ahead, I already knew that in a perfect world, she would have been the one who shared the back room with me.

· · ·

Susan Foley did have a lumberjack's appetite. It was a good thing I'd done the talking during breakfast.

"This Joann Carlino," she said, "was Eddie's mistress?"

"I always thought of her as his girlfriend."

"But Eddie was married . . . and not to her."

"Yeah. But I didn't know it then. Not until the funeral. I went there expecting to see Joann. Instead there was this other woman, and old Mr. Wilson said she was his daughter-in-law. Could have knocked me over. It's the only time I ever saw Mrs. Eddie Wilson."

"What did she look like?"

"Blond, trim. Nice . . . Pretty. But not a rock-and-roll girl. Not the type for Vince's Boardwalk."

"No Joann."

"I looked around the edges, checked the cars. She wasn't there. I felt bad about that. I wondered how she was spending the day."

"Did you ever see her again?"

"No." It came out like a confession. I wondered why I hadn't even tried. Now it seemed like the most natural thing in the world. Yet it had been beyond me: character is fate. "Later that week I stopped off at Vince's for a beer. One of those sentimental things you do, even though you know they're corny. A beer for Eddie. A couple minutes in the back room. Their 'house.' And Vince told me she'd been in the day of the funeral. And she said to tell all of the Cruisers goodbye. End of story."

"I'm not sure how we should leave things," I told Susan Foley.

"There's no problem with me. You don't have to *do* anything."

"What if I want to? What if I want to see you again?"

"Sure." She scribbled her address and phone number on a napkin. "Where do you go from here?"

"I'll keep checking into things."

"The tapes?"

"Yeah . . ."

"I thought they didn't exist."

"Well . . ." I stopped. I didn't like how quickly she'd caught me up. And how readily I lied to her. "Whether or not they exist, it's fun looking for them."

"What if you found some tapes? What would you do with them?"

"I don't know. Listen to them first. . . ."

"I mean, would you sell them?"

"Hold on! Finding is one thing—owning is something else. I mean, if someone has them now, why should they give them to me? And whom do they belong to? Really. The current owner? The estate of Eddie Wilson? There's a lot of questions."

"Don't get too tangled up in questions," she said. "That's a piece of free advice. Want more?"

"Sure."

"Okay." She smiled and touched my hand. "You're a nice man. I'd hate to see you hurt."

"Who'd want to do that?"

"I don't know. I'm just suggesting that if you find the tapes, they might be . . . a little too hot to handle by yourself. I know Elliot looks like a kid to you. But he has connections. Lawyers, agents, industry people . . ."

"Did he ask you to tell me this?" I interrupted.

"Yes," was the disarming answer. "But I would have told you anyway."

"In that case . . . thanks." Remember, I thought: friends and how to use them. Mannheim had something to teach me in that line.

"Who's next?" she asked.

"Kenny Hopkins."

"Do you know where to find him?"

"It'll take some phone calls."

"And the other fellow?"

"Wendell? That'll be harder."

"And Joann Carlino?"

"She wasn't on my list."

"Oh really? Sounds like she ought to be."

"It might be a mistake. After all this time. She'd be nearly forty. Italian mamma. Moustache and kids."

"You don't believe that."

"No, I guess not. But it's a gamble."

9

Among the purple hearts, there was talk of a stranger in the camp. He came last night in an unmarked car, which he parked in the visitors' lot. He walked slowly from trailer to trailer, like a salesman or a meter-reader.

Nobody passes through here unnoticed. That's what appealed to me about the place. These senior citizens are like hamsters, shuffling and stirring at all hours, never very busy and never quite asleep.

Martha Darmstadter, the gray panther, came out to challenge him.

"Who you lookin' for, sonny?" Omar Bradley would be "sonny" to Martha. She'd been watering her sapling grapefruit. She pointed the hose straight at him, like the nozzle was a can of mace.

He turned and left without replying.

Not much of an incident in the workaday world, but around the camp the stranger's visit was the biggest news since Minnie Schumacher's stroke. Herman Biedermann guessed the stranger was a Jehovah's Witness. Ed Riley scoffed at that. No doubt about it, the intruder was a spy from the tax assessor's office, making sure that all the trailers had the wheels and licenses necessary to classify them as vehicles, not residences. Ex-electrician Al Ferraro countered that the stranger was almost certainly from the cable TV people, checking for bootleg wires from one trailer to another.

"Was he around my trailer too?" I asked.

"You bet," Martha answered. "He stood there for a while, like he was getting ready to knock on your door."

"That's funny," I said, thinking aloud, "because I'm the only one who doesn't have his name outside."

Or any sign of occupancy. No nameplate. No tiny garden, no barbecue or lawn chairs, no ceramic dwarves and deer, German elves and Negro stableboys. And then I realized that was how they found me, how they'd operated from the very beginning: by process of elimination.

Then and now, I wouldn't go out of my way to see Kenny Hopkins. There always seemed to be a distance between us. And Hopkins kept it that way, as if he were an upperclass fraternity member and I was a freshman pledge and those positions were timeless and unalterable.

He kidded me longest about my lost virginity. Sally fielded his marine corps scare story and let it go at that, but Hopkins derided me in subtler ways, boasting of his accomplishments—arcane positions, oral sex, two girls in one night—anything to minimize my little bout of "hide the wienie." I had a long way to go before I was a man, he said, and then he'd launch into a revolting-but-titillating tale about a certain mother-daughter combo over in Bridgeton.

I won't say we never had fun, because fun was all he lived for, and some of it lapped over. Hopkins could steer us around an argument, and at least once I saw him avert a major blowup between Doc and Eddie. That was the incident with Claude Richards, and I was surprised that Mannheim hadn't asked me about it, because it was the sort of story that becomes a legend.

I don't know if Claude Richards is still alive. The last time I saw him was on a television show several years after Eddie died. Richards was then the host of a teen-hop special at the New York World's Fair, and all I recall is that it was sponsored by the franchiser of Belgian waffles, which Richards cooked and ate on camera. But in the late fifties, Richards was an East Coast institution, the video-daddyo of Channel 10. Everybody watched his afternoon dance show. Including the Cruisers. Whenever we pulled off the road, we gathered in somebody's room to check out Claude Richards and the Milkshake Show, or whatever it was called. The game was to rate the girls, of course, and Hopkins ran the game. His tests and charts and points system turned the Milkshake Show into a papal conclave. He had more words for breasts than I'd ever heard—boobs, tits, chalambos, casabas, watatas, lungs, melons, knockers—and he used them all.

Then Doc booked us on the show.

"You've got to be kidding!" Eddie said. "That's not for us."

"It's for anybody wants to make it," Doc insisted. "You know what a plug on that show means? That Richards is a hit-maker, chart-breaker—"

"—music-faker. They lip-synch the words! You want us to stand up there like a row of dummies?"

"You're a dummy if you don't! You want to play shore bars the rest of your life? Shake the sand outa your shoes, man! What's with you, Eddie? You not happy performing in a place the plumbing works? That your idea of class? A sign on the door says restrooms-for-customers-only?"

"I'm not mouthin' words!"

"I said you'd show."

"Hey, Doc, listen close." Eddie moved right up to him and lip-synched "fuck you." And left the room.

"What's wrong with me?" Doc protested to the rest of us. "What'd I do to deserve this crap?"

"I don't mind going on," Sally volunteered, now that Eddie was gone. "It's nothin' to spit at. I know lotsa people watch it. And the bread ain't bad, right?"

"What about you, Wordman?"

"I'm all right . . ."

"Set him up with some broad in the dressing room, and he'll sing like Caruso," Kenny interrupted.

". . . but it's got to be okay with Eddie. If he's out, I'm out."

"And you, Wendell? You vote too."

Poor Wendell sat there looking like the sickle-cell poster child. So often he was out of it, and never more than those macho afternoons we spent appraising white teeny-boppers in saddle shoes, pleated skirts, and tight sweaters. He never voted in any of Kenny's games, unless we begged him to break a tie.

"Aah, he's been lip-synching all his life," Sally interjected, and for once I didn't mind the rudeness, because it let Wendell off the hook.

"What do you think, handsome?"

"I love it!" exclaimed Hopkins. "Are you kidding?!"

"Lot of good that does me," Doc said. "I got two yesses, two gutless maybes, and one strong no. The no has it. This could've been a step up for us, too. Record companies, TV spots, Vegas. You'd think Mr. Wilson never heard of 'em."

"Don't worry about Mr. Wilson," Hopkins answered. "I'll work it out with him."

"How?"

"Never mind how. We'll be there."

We arrived on time, well groomed and neatly dressed. Claude Richards wasn't around, but his assistant gave us our cues and marks, moving us around like we were manikins in a showroom window. Then we retreated to our dressing rooms. And changed.

I hope they saved the tape. Or maybe I don't. The gang that stormed the Milkshake Show stage had nothing in common with the eager-to-please, spic-and-span crew that had coasted through rehearsals. We dressed like thugs. We were thugs! Eddie turned his back on the audience—because he was afraid his parents would see him, Sally said—while Hopkins and I danced together, cheek to cheek. It was about the silliest thing I've ever done, but it got us through an impossible bind. And it was my best memory of Kenny Hopkins, who dreamed it up and convinced Eddie. When Claude Richards raged at us after the show, Kenny's excuse was that we were all just going through a phase.

That was his slogan. "This is just a phase I'm goin' through." He said it so often, and in so many different situations, that it was impossible for me to recall him without its coming to mind immediately. He'd be leading some drunken girl out to the parking lot, ushering her into the back seat of his, or anybody's car, and he'd peer back over his shoulder, smile, and say, "Just a phase, Wordman." I'd find him miserably drunk in the men's room at Vince's, with a bear hug on a toilet bowl, and he'd say it while he retched and heaved: "Just a phase I'm going through." Opening a paycheck, crashing a car, getting in a fight with some Polish kids from Metuchen, it was all just a phase. It got so that Eddie, introducing him onstage, said, "Watch it, ladies, we got Kenny Hopkins on drums, just going through a phase."

Still, Hopkins and his slogan made me uncomfortable. The rest of us liked to think we'd go on forever, but Hopkins and his saying suggested we were kidding ourselves: this was only an episode. That's not to say he didn't work, but his approach was that of a lifeguard on a nubile beach, a waiter in the Catskills. It was seasonal, summertime, soon to be over.

I was nervous about calling Kenny Hopkins, not sure of what to expect. I couldn't rely on my memories of him, and I didn't trust his memories of me.

"Kenny Hopkins? Is that you?"

I was in a restaurant phone booth in Phillipsburg, New Jersey, and I'd used only a fraction of the coins I'd piled on the counter in front of me. One call went to the alumni office of the college Hopkins attended for a year before flunking out and turning Cruiser. The second went to the business phone number they gave me, a bank called First Mountainside, in the New Jersey suburban town of that name. And now I had the phone number of Hopkins' home, readily provided when I insisted my business was urgent.

"Yes . . . who's this please?" There were family noises in the background, kids and TV. I wondered what Kenny's wife looked like. He was always spelling out requirements for his ideal woman: "hair down to her ass," "great rack of tits," "tight little ass," "legs like satin," on and on.

"It's Frank Ridgeway."

"Frank . . ."

"From the Cruisers. Remember me?"

"Of course I do."

"I'm driving through your area tomorrow night, and there's something I have to talk to you about. I know this is short notice but—"

"Is it a problem of some kind?"

"Uh . . . sure it's a problem."

"Then I'd be glad to help you. How's . . . let me check . . . eight o'clock tomorrow morning, down at First Mountainside."

"Great! I'll be there. See you then, Kenny."

"Yes. Good to hear from you . . . Frank." First names didn't come easily to him. Neither did nicknames. He was the only one who never called me "Wordman."

There was no reason for me to return home when I did, but Mountainside was only thirty minutes from where I lived, and it seemed perverse to sleep in a motel just miles from the house I nearly owned and the wife I used to love.

I hadn't been gone that long—three days, two nights—but driving through familiar streets, I had the odd feeling you get when you return to a place you've left years ago. It felt like I'd already moved away.

I drove down Butler Street, past our house, as if I were checking out an old girlfriend's home: a light in the window meant she was home, a dark window meant she was out with someone else. I'm not sure which I was hoping for, but Doris was out. The whole place was dark. I drove down two more blocks, to where Butler dead-ends against the highway right-of-way, pulled a U-turn, and headed back. Butler. I was the only one who still called it that. Three years ago, when they finished filling empty lots, there was a petition to change the name to something more prestigious. Butler, they said, sounded like a row of servants' quarters. Doris voted for the new name, while I held out for Butler: a house divided. The mail now comes to something called Old Sawmill Way.

I found a note in the kitchen.

Frank:

I want to talk soon. We've got to clear this up. I can't go on living in limbo. I need to know what you think.

Doris

I took a beer out to the back of our half-acre lot and sat down on the grass, listening to the trucks rush down the highway to New York. Some nights you could hear them, some nights you couldn't, depending on the weather. In our neighborhood, they were the weather. I wondered where Susan Foley was tonight, what she was doing. Susan was a Cruiser.

Her approach to sex had a lot going for it, I guessed. It was fun, it put you in touch with yourself, it trimmed away inhibitions and repressions like so many dead branches. And it was a nice way of getting to know interesting strangers: it beat sitting in a movie house or pickling your brains at a singles' bar. But I was a child of the fifties. I asked awkward questions awkwardly. I couldn't help wondering what things meant and where they led, and just asking those questions betrayed the forlorn hope that things ought to lead somewhere and ought to mean something.

Ah, but Susan Foley would surely have an answer for me, or at least another question. Come now, what's it mean to live with someone who doesn't love you, and whom you've stopped loving? Where does that lead, except to trading in betrayals? Either way—hers or mine—you wound up in a motel room with a stranger.

She was right, of course. I came from a middle generation. Our parents stayed put: one house, one spouse. Our kids lived and rutted in vans. And we were somewhere in between, restlessly encamped in neighborhoods that weren't neighborhoods anymore, where for-sale signs flourished like hardy perennials and a golden wedding anniversary was as old-fashioned as a quilting bee.

In the house, the phone was ringing. I got up dutifully, half hoping that I'd miss the call by the time I arrived inside. But my caller waited.

"Frank?"

"Yes."

"This is . . . you know . . ."

"Who?"

"Susan . . ."

"Where are you?"

"Still here."

"You sound closer. Like a local call."

"I wish. Did you find Hopkins?"

"Yeah."

"Where, New Jersey?"

"Yes. I'm seeing him tomorrow."

"There's a show on TV tonight. One of those celebrity news shows. I was just looking through the TV listings, I saw they're having a segment on Eddie Wilson."

"That's why you called? To tell me about the TV show?"

"I'd have found another excuse. I just wanted to tell you that . . . you're a likable guy."

"Did you say lovable?"

"That too."

"Same to you, lady. But I wasn't supposed to ask what happens next."

"It's complicated. At *both* ends. But I hope we meet again. I bet we do."

"How?"

"I'll take care of that," she said.

The program on Channel 4 was one of those brisk, frothy anthologies of celebrity profiles: a video magazine for people who found *People* tough going. Its hostess, Charlene Madison, was a promiscuously enthusiastic beauty who specialized in intimate conversation with the famous. She mangled the language a bit—"hopefully" and "enthused" were her forte—but she had wonderful legs, glossy black hair, a passable rack, and what's more, she seemed about to proposition everyone she interviewed, from Reggie Jackson to the Incredible Hulk.

The show was almost over before they got to Eddie.

I saw a woman walking through a cemetery: a fortyish blonde who nonetheless seemed somewhat matronly. She carried a bunch of flowers.

"Phyllis Wilson Hackett, a Lambertville, New Jersey, housewife, visits this Vineland cemetery at least once a month. Sometimes she brings her two children or her husband, a township engineer. Or, as today, she comes alone, to weed or decorate or merely visit the grave of her first husband."

A brief shot of the gravestone, with Eddie's name and dates. They hadn't changed.

"Yes, Mrs. Hackett's first husband was the man now recognized as one of the forebears of current music—the premier rock-and-roller Eddie Wilson . . ."

They found it! There was Eddie on Claude Richards' show, staring insolently at the camera, then abruptly turning his back, as if determined to remain a man of mystery. I caught a tiny glimpse of myself, unrecognizable, and heard a snatch

of "Far-Away Woman." Then it was back to the grave, with
Phyllis hunkered down next to the tombstone, like they were
on a date together.

"We married right after high school, in June 1955 . . ."

Black-and-white stills: yearbook profile, a wedding picture, a honeymoon beach shot, Eddie mowing a lawn someplace. And quickly back to Phyllis and the tombstone, in time
to see tears well.

"Eddie started in music right away. It's all he ever wanted
to do. People said he should be an engineer, what with Sput-
nik and catching up to Russia. But Eddie lived for music.
Lived and died . . ."

A change of scene. And costume. Dressed like Annie Hall,
Charlene stands in front of a Greenwich Village oldies record shop. Through the window we see hairy ferrets in army
clothes rummaging through record bins. The owner
emerges, a heavy balding subway type.

"Most popular records have the life span of a daily newspaper . . ."

Shots of *Billboard*'s Top 100 lists, several years of lists,
Scotch-taped to the store walls. Jump from one absurdity—
"When the Moon Hits Your Eye Like a Big Pizza Pie"—to
another—"Purple People Eater." Who remembers? Who
cares? Bits and pieces are played. Then the camera finds "On
the Dark Side," Number 27, March 1958. And we hear it,
coming right out at us, irresistible.

". . . but sometimes they come back to life, bigger than
ever. It starts in specialty collector stores like this . . ."

A locked glass case protects a treasury of 45's: "Love Me
Tender," $30; "Peggy Sue," $60; "Dock of the Bay," $15.
"Far-Away Woman," $50.

"Mr. Cohen, why have Eddie Wilson's records taken off
almost twenty years after they were released?"

"I didn't see it coming. Not this one. I'm no prophet. But
looking back, I'd say the guy had the same kind of appeal
you see in James Dean. You know? Innocence is what I call
it. He was loud and raunchy, all right, but the bottom line

is innocence. And that commodity, lady, is always in short supply."

Shots of reissued albums in a newer store, of a *Variety* ad announcing upcoming production of *The Eddie Wilson Story*, and finally, a British group, The Funky Company, performing "Down on My Knees" in a crowded amphitheater.

That's it, I guess. It's over.

It is not over.

Charlene drives up a pleasant residential street, parks in front of a well-maintained Victorian two-story, walks up the steps to the verandah, where Mr. and Mrs. Wilson are waiting.

"Hi there," she greets the two palpably nervous oldsters. Mrs. Wilson rises to shake her hand. Eddie's father, with a cane in his hands, doesn't budge. He motions Charlene to a nearby chair.

"Rock and roll was pretty controversial music back in the fifties. Did you approve of your son's decision to become a rock-and-roller?"

"Wasn't my decision to make," snaps the retired dentist. "Was *his* decision. My old man said I should be a farmer. I felt like drilling in people's mouths. That was *my* decision."

"How about you, Mrs. Wilson?"

"Whatever he decided." She has trembly hands. She folds and smooths an imaginary wrinkle in her dress.

"Stop that wobbling," scolds the old man.

"I'm not sure we wanted him to be playing a guitar forever . . . for the rest of his life, I mean. He had a wife to support, and we hoped that someday there might be grandchildren . . ."

"He never borrowed a cent!" the old man interrupts. "Not from us or anybody. Bought everything cash on the barrelhead. That's how I was raised. That's how he was raised. My wife didn't have anything to complain about. Neither did his. She still doesn't, I figure."

Charlene smiles. Old folks say the darndest things.

"Did you like his music, Mrs. Wilson?"

"No lies, Mother!"

"Well, it wasn't quite what . . ."

"Hated it! Couldn't stand the stuff!" He leans forward, leering. "I come from a time when we touched the girls we danced with, 'stead of throwing them off walls."

"How do you folks feel, hearing Eddie on the radio again after so many years?"

"We're glad that young people find something—"

"Not a bit surprised! All they've been doing is copying him for twenty years. I've got ears. Copycats is what they are. You call them rip-off artists. My day, we called 'em copycats!"

The two women retreat inside the house, up the stairs, down a hall.

"This was Eddie's room," his mother says. "We kept everything as it was . . . only neater, of course."

A bed with an Indian blanket. On the walls, pictures of fifties cars and baseball players, and Playboy-type bunnies, minus contemporary pubic hair. A closetful of clothes, shoes on the floor, a sleeping bag in back. In one corner, a broomstick with a rack of 45's and a pile of l.p.'s, with the Cruisers' album on top. And Eddie's radio, an old-fashioned Philco beehive.

"The fights we had about that radio!" his mother reminisces. "Eddie played it all hours of the night. 'Why can't you listen to music during the day and sleep at night, like other folks?' we'd ask him. And Eddie would say he had to listen then, because night was the only time he could pick up stations from New York and Philadelphia that played the kind of music he'd like to hear. So many nights, he'd sit up in the dark, listening to that radio. His father said he was like a spy, receiving secret messages."

Charlene touches the radio. She strokes it.

"It's an antique, now," Mrs. Wilson says. "But it still works."

"May I?" Charlene asks.

"Please."

She reaches for the knob, faces the camera.

"Eddie Wilson now has been dead for almost as many years as he lived. But in his short span of years, he had time enough to do more than listen to music in a dark room. He made some music of his own, put it on the network, sent his message."

She switches the radio on.

" 'Far-Away Woman.' "

She smiles.

"Message received."

Time for a commercial. I started to turn off the TV, but before I arrived, the show was on again, with Charlene Madison back in the studio, trading tune-off banter with her co-host, a former quarterback.

"Billy, I'm sorry to say there's a footnote to our last story. The Eddie Wilson revival hasn't been an unmixed blessing, especially for his parents. Last Sunday, while the Wilsons were at church, someone broke into the Wilson home. They searched and robbed the house."

"That's awful, Charlene. Did they know whose house they were in?"

"I'm afraid they did. That's the worst of it. The intruders moved from cellar to attic, but the only room that's missing anything is Eddie Wilson's. They cleaned it out, Billy. I spoke to Mr. Wilson today. He's hopping mad. Says if they come back, they'll get a souvenir they won't forget."

"That's one feisty gent, Charlene. Who would do such a thing? I mean, what kind of sick mind would . . . ?"

"Eddie Wilson material is very valuable. That's the theory the police are working on."

"Some world!" Billy reflects. "Next week, we'll visit with Cheryl Tiegs, John Belushi, and baseball's 'Mad Hungarian' relief pitcher, Al Hrabosky."

You know how it is, when you leaf through your college alumni magazine? You see that so-and-so is a senior counsel and someone else is taken seriously in the State Department and yet another ex-classmate is performing surgery? And you remember them, not as future lawyers, diplomats, or doctors, but as dormitory masturbators, dance-weekend drunks, exam-time plagiarists? You know that somebody has got to be kidding.

That's how I felt when I found that First Mountainside was a church not a bank, a red brick neo-Colonial complex across the street from a shopping center, with a school, a rectory, and an ample parking lot in which the Reverend Kenneth Hopkins waited to keep his appointment with me.

"So it really is you!" he exclaimed, as he walked over to the car.

He was a good-looking man, blond and trim. He wore brown corduroy trousers, a purple turtleneck sweater, and some brightly striped running shoes.

"How are you doing, Kenny?" I asked, as we shook hands. "Are you the Reverend Kenneth E.?"

"That's me. And my father before me. I kept it a secret when I was a Cruiser. Now I keep the Cruiser stuff a secret."

"Just going through a phase back then?"

He acknowledged his old slogan with a smile that was only slightly forced. "I've been expecting you."

"Expecting me?"

"Yes. Or someone like you. Come inside where we can talk."

He led me across the parking lot, through a side door, and down some steps to one of those bright, multipurpose basements where teenagers are supposed to play Ping-Pong and drink Coke instead of hanging out on street corners. In the rear was Hopkins' office, a book-lined Protestant confessional, with comfortable seats and a cup of coffee for all comers. There was no one in the basement. So far as I could see, we had the whole place to ourselves. Still, he looked out cautiously and made a point of closing the door.

For a moment we just stared at each other, measuring memories against changes, checking out the growing and the aging. We both did it, so neither one was embarrassed. Then Hopkins broke the silence.

"What's going on, Frank?" he asked quietly.

"What do you mean?"

"I saw that television show. People tearing apart the Wilson house. And now . . . here you are."

"Well, Eddie's back, they tell me."

"What does that mean?"

"I know it's crazy. I don't understand it myself. You're the preacher. Know much about miracles?"

"Miracles? Not much."

Just then the door pushed open, and a woman backed into the office carrying a good-sized coffee urn. Hopkins helped her set up the urn. Then he introduced his wife, Jeanette, an utterly plain, pleasant woman who stared at me as if she expected to give my description to the cops. She left only when her husband pointedly thanked her and held open the door. Even then, I guessed she was eavesdropping right outside.

"No tits, no ass, buck teeth, but I love her," Hopkins whispered. "Usually she doesn't bring the coffee machine till after lunch. She saw that show last night, and then I made the mistake of telling her that you'd be coming by. I think she put the two together. She tossed and turned all night."

"Me—and the break-in?"

"I told her it was a coincidence," Hopkins said. Then, after an appraising glance, he added, "I hope I was right."

"Relax, Kenny. It wasn't me."

"The others, maybe. Not you. Sally. Doc. What the hell is going on, Frank? It was twenty years ago! I don't understand."

"I was in touch with Doc," I began, as calmly as I could. "He contacted me right after the radio started playing 'Far-Away Woman.' He thought that Eddie made some tapes at Lakehurst which might be hot stuff now. He floated a rumor himself to that effect. He asked me to check around and see what I could find out. He knew there were other people out looking."

"Is that your job, Frank? Out treasure-hunting with Doc Robbins?" Kenny was angry. He regarded me with the kind of hostility you feel when you get up to answer the doorbell, expecting company, and it's a salesman. "Well, I'm going to tell you all I know, and then you can go. I don't know what was happening at Lakehurst. Not that I didn't wonder. Who wouldn't? . . . Well, one day I got tired just sitting around the house. It ticked me off, the way Eddie cut me out. So I called down to Lakehurst. He wasn't in, of course. The switchboard girl at the motel said he was almost never in. And she didn't mind adding that he was kind of a pain, with calls piling up from out of state, New York and Alabama and all. That puzzled me. I wondered what the hell Eddie was doing. So I called up Doc and got me a job on a cruise ship. And, believe me, it was a ball!"

"What do you think Eddie was up to?"

"I don't know. I assume it was something fairly grandiose. And that nothing came of it. That's all I know. Now if there's nothing more . . ."

"It wasn't just the tapes, Kenny. I mean, I'm curious but I don't care about the money. There were some other questions."

"Like what, Frank?"

"I thought that by going back I could . . . I don't know . . . establish contact with whatever we had going for us back then. There was a special feeling to that year. Maybe I didn't realize it at the time, but I do now. Whatever we had, I miss."

"What was it we had, you miss?" He spoke like a minister again, probing tactfully, listening. I had a feeling he was interested. "How would you describe it?"

"A feeling. That the future would be good, that we'd grow right into it, like driving down the road on a summer night, and that everything would kind of come together, work and love, into one continuous adventure, that we could look down the road and see the distance we'd traveled and the miles ahead of us, and it would all make some kind of emotional sense. . . ."

"We were young then," he volunteered when I paused, but my confession kept coming.

"After they started playing our music again, I went upstairs and found my record collection. Know what my record collection amounts to? About a dozen l.p.'s and maybe a hundred forty-fives, and not one of them is less than fifteen years old. They were sitting in a cardboard box I never quite threw out. Well, one night, I closed the door. I fished around for a plastic spindle to fill up the hole in the middle, and I played those records. All of them. You know what it was like?"

Kenny nodded, smiling though his face was sad.

"Those cheap little discs, scratched and dirty, with my initials on the label, sitting in the attic . . . they were alive!

The harmonies and falsettos and doo-wops. And the emotions. I listened to those songs, and I couldn't take it anymore. I couldn't face myself, and what had happened to me. The walls closed in. The house I lived in felt like a damn tomb! I had a tightness in my legs that made me want to run and a vague hurt feeling in my chest, and I had to get out of the house, into my car, out on the road, driving . . ."

I ran out of words. I found I was standing, pacing in the office. Describing the music reinfected me with caged restlessness. When I finished, I forced myself back into the chair and looked over at Reverend Hopkins, who had danced cheek-to-cheek with me on a television show a few lifetimes back.

"You must be good at what you do, Kenny, getting me to spill like this. We meet for the first time in years, and it all comes out. It's amazing, considering . . ."

"Considering what?"

"We were never really friends, were we?"

"It's okay, Frank," he said. "I have a confession of my own to make. Not much of a confession, but I think you'll get the drift. It's that . . . I know how you feel."

"You too?"

"Me too. I've got a broomstick of forty-fives myself."

He said it so shyly, with such a show of boyish shame, you'd have thought he'd confessed to owning a deck of dirty playing cards. I studied him and he glanced back at me and we smiled. Then we laughed, and before long neither of us could stop. We laughed and laughed till there were tears coming out of our eyes.

"Isn't it odd?" Kenny was asking. "We bought a summer home last year, up on Lake Hopatcong, and I hired a bunch of kids to add on a kind of porch-sundeck. A bunch of shaggy kids, each with his own van or pickup truck. They hammered away and I tuned out. I was working on a sermon. And then I heard them singing, shouting, harmonizing. 'On the Dark Side.' Loud and off-key and full of fun. I remember sitting there, asking myself, 'Why am I hearing that song? I'm nearly forty, I'm a clergyman, and that song still lives. Why is this happening to me? Me of all people?' "

"Why you of all people?"

"Don't you see? Because I was the one who was sure it wouldn't last."

We had walked across the street to the shopping mall, where there were benches and fountains and miles of shops.

"There's some ministers, and some doctors too, if you came to them the way you came to me, they'd suggest that maybe you just want to be a kid again. Or, put it another way, that you don't want to grow old. Have you considered that?"

"Sure. Kenny, I work with kids. I've seen them every day for a dozen years. Could be I'm jaundiced, but they don't have anything I want. And they don't have what we had. *That's* the disturbing thing. Whatever it was, it didn't last."

"And you'd like to plug back into . . . whatever it was. And see it continue."

"Yes," I answered.

"I see." His response sounded noncommittal. "I don't know what to tell you. You tell me about Doc and Sally, it's hard for me to imagine what there is to find. And Eddie's dead. And poor Wendell . . ."

"Hold it. What about Wendell?" I'd meant to ask about him, but I hadn't gotten around to it. I now realize that I had a bad feeling about Wendell Newton. I felt that Wendell was dead, simply because I couldn't picture him alive. The more I thought of that frail, talented black kid, the surer I was that he couldn't have survived from then till now. No way.

"Come on over here and have a seat," Kenny said. It felt like we were in a bad-news hospital ward. There was a fountain at the heart of the mall, crowded with footsore shoppers and pregnant mothers and dutiful husbands resting up for their next foray into Bamberger's or Korvette's or Two Guys from Harrison. Kids and ice cream all around, and the piped-in music was "Raindrops Keep Fallin' on My Head."

··· *Eddie and the Cruisers* ···

"It didn't work out for Wendell. See, Frank, at Christmas we go to hospitals and institutions. Singing carols and passing out little gifts and putting on parties. A couple of Christmases back, we went to Rahway."

"He's in prison?"

"Was. First I saw him, it looked like he was on the staff. He seemed to have the run of the place. But that's only because they're used to him. Like a mascot."

"Shit! Prison?! Wendell?!"

"Only sometimes. Next year, I met him down at Matawan. From prison to asylum. He commutes."

"Oh Christ!" I buried my head in my hands.

"I'm sorry, Frank," Kenny whispered, placing an arm around my shoulders while I sobbed. I remembered wondering whether Mannheim had found Wendell in whatever Bedlam they confined him, and if he'd delivered my message about life turning out to be longer than expected.

Kenny accompanied me to my car and we both stood there for a while. The parting was awkward because I think we knew it wasn't likely we'd meet again. I saw Kenny straining to find the right note for us to end on.

"I'm worried about you, Frank."

"I worry myself."

"Old songs, old memories . . . I don't know whether to clap you on the back or warn you off."

"Just a phase?"

"I'm not so sure. There's something haunting about those times. I understand why those songs make you restless. But if you go back into the past, at least be sure you see it whole. There were bad times too. Hassles. Arguments. Things I'll bet you've forgotten."

"What do you mean?"

"I remember one night in Ohio, Eddie played hell with you."

"I haven't forgotten. Things weren't the same after that night. You're right, Kenny."

"Think about it, Frank."

· · ·

After seeing Kenny Hopkins, born again, I decided it was time to check in with Doc Robbins. He'd asked me to call in now and then, and though I didn't kid myself about his motives, it felt good to know that there was someone else on my team, even if it was Doc.

I dialed the direct line Doc had given me.

"KCGM. Ed Hickey here."

"I beg your pardon?"

"Edsel Hickey." The voice sounded like the name, rural and out-of-fashion. "No jokes, mister. It's been a bad couple days."

"I was calling for Doc Robbins. I thought this was his personal line."

"What's your name?"

"Ridgeway."

"Well, Doc ain't here anymore, Mr. Ridgeway, I'm sorry to have to tell you."

"When's he due?"

"He ain't. He's dead."

"Dead?"

"Yes sir. Dead. And that's puttin' it mildly."

"What happened?"

"Somebody killed him. He was on the air two nights ago. Somebody musta come in and got him. All anybody knows is that the same record starts playing again and again, with no interruptions. Five times, Paul Anka singing 'Having My Baby.' You know what Paul Anka quintuplets can do to a listening audience? They called the station. No answer. They called the cops. The cops picked me up, since I had the keys. I'm the one who opens up mornings, with the weather and stock prices."

"You're sure he's dead?"

"Son, I cleaned up the place. He's dead. I got the mops and pails to prove it."

· · ·

Doc's death hit me hard. Maybe it was because I'd seen how he was living in that forlorn tourist cabin, or because my own house was empty now. Anyway, it hurt. I thought about his loud suits and jive talk, his schemes and deals, and I realized how I was taken with the man. He was out-of-date now. He smacked of carnivals and confidence schemes, one-night stands and offices rented by the week. The music business of the fifties suited him. He blew into radio stations with a briefcase of 45's and a bottle of Jim Beam. "Have I got a record for you!"

And now he was dead. Not dead: murdered.

"There's no shortage of crooks in the world." I could hear him laughing at me as I puzzled over things. I doubted it was Mannheim. Sure, he might be a hustler. But I couldn't see him as a wrecker, or a killer. Still, for Doc's sake, I decided to check him out.

Mannheim had said he worked for *Rolling Stone*. That's what he'd told Sally. *Rolling* fucking *Stone*. I bought a copy and called the office number on the masthead. I asked for someone who knew about assignments, explaining that I wanted to verify that a certain free-lancer was working for them on a certain story.

"What's his name?"

"Elliot Mannheim."

"What's the story?"

"Eddie Wilson. I used to play with him."

There was a long pause at the other end. I thought we'd been disconnected.

"Hello . . . are you still there?"

"Yes."

"What about Mannheim?"

"He's not on assignment for us."

"You never heard of him?"

Another gap.

"I didn't say that. I said he wasn't working for us."

"But you do know of him?"

"Listen Mr. . . . uh . . . Ridgeway. You called the switchboard and asked to talk to one of the editors, right?"

"Yes."

"They put you through to me. Did I . . . when I picked up . . . did I give you my name? Or just say hello?"

"Just hello. I still don't know your name."

"That's good."

"Why?"

"Because now I can tell you. Have nothing to do with Elliot Mannheim. You hear me? Nothing."

"Yes, but . . ."

"Nothing."

He hung up.

Eddie Wilson is dead and Wayne Newton plays Vegas forever, and if that doesn't shake your trust in the Almighty, nothing will. But for me, Eddie's death was a disaster of a more personal kind. Two months before the accident, and one month before he holed up in Lakehurst, Eddie and I fell out.

It was all my fault. In April 1958, Doc Robbins told us we'd been offered a booking he was inclined to turn down. It was out of our territory, in Ohio, and the money wasn't that great. We hadn't played that many colleges, since we knew the equipment was often terrible and the hours long. So Doc was running the offer past us, for form's sake, knowing we'd much prefer to spend that weekend in an out-of-season bar in Asbury Park. Then he mentioned the name of the college.

"That's where I went!" I exclaimed. "That's my college!"

"No wonder they're so cheap," Sally muttered. "What'd they throw in to sweeten the offer, Doc? Library privileges?"

"Dance weekends are incredible out there. You should see what happens. The whole place goes crazy!"

"How's the trim?" Hopkins asked.

"It's an all-male school, actually."

"Oh, terrific," Hopkins said. "We play 'Far-Away Woman,' what do they do? Face Mecca?"

"Pull out their high school yearbooks and beat off," Sally jeered.

"You don't understand," I persisted. "That's what makes it so wild. Six hundred guys haven't seen a girl since New Year's. They bring them in by train, by car, by the busload —cattle-cars, they're called. It's like they were dropped into a prison."

"Place sounds like it belongs on *Zoo Parade*," Hopkins said.

"Cut it out," Eddie said. "They must be doing something right." He'd been watching Claude Richards, but now he was smiling at me. He'd delivered a compliment, certified my membership. "You want to go back there, Wordman?"

"Yes," I said. "Please, I really do."

"Why?"

"I just . . . I don't know . . . you'll understand, when you see the place."

"The hell with it," he said. "We'll go."

Why? Why did it matter so much to return as a Parkway Cruiser to that horny, cloistered hillside I'd abandoned just a year before? At first, I assigned myself high motives, literary-sounding: "Tintern Abbey," *Look Homeward, Angel.* But that was nonsense. I didn't want to see the place so much as I wanted the place to see me. I wanted to snow them, titillate them, blow them away—the professors, the guys down the hall in the dorm, the faculty wives I'd coveted —I wanted them all to eat their hearts out! While they'd been filling up blue books and lobbying for tenure, I'd been out in the world. I'd played bars, written songs, gotten laid. I was a Cruiser! Catch my act, see me tonight, talk about me when I'm gone. "Oh yeah, Ridgeway. Crazy son of a bitch. Lit out of here and joined a rock and roll band!"

I remember that westward drive in springtime. I remember it so clearly that if I drove the same route today, I'd associate certain conversations with landmarks, a whole soundtrack of memories all along the road. I remember how dawn found us crossing the Pulaski Skyway, with Jersey's polluted marshes turning gold below, and warehouses, factories, and railroad yards stretched out forever, and a convoy of early garbage trucks stirring up hundreds of birds that had been nesting on a mountain range of landfill refuse. "Good-bye, Garden State," Eddie said, waving at the three-ring sign over the Ballantine brewery in Newark.

"This is where we're from, Wordman," Eddie said. I'd never seen him higher. "People drive through here, they roll up their windows so they don't have to breathe none of the air. Not me!"

He rolled down the windows and took a deep gulp of New Jersey.

"Ain't that ripe! Man, I thrive on it. I make music outa it. It knocks me out! You got miles of swamp and mountains of dumps and all different-colored rivers. You got automobile graveyards and radio transmitters and ball parks and breweries all mixed up, birds and rats and people making garbage and using garbage and pilin' it up to the damn sky. Holee shit, man! I love it! No wonder the Statue of Liberty faces the other way."

Then the mood changed. We left the factories behind us, and the bedroom suburbs, the people and the territory that belonged to us. Sally, Wendell, and Kenny were in the station wagon, Eddie, Joann, and I in the new Ford. As soon as we climbed Jugtown Mountain in western New Jersey, there was an odd feeling in our car: in front of us lay undiscovered country. The radio thinned out and nearly died, with inches of silence between country-western stations. There were

hex signs on the barns before long, and Amish wagons along
the shoulder of the road. Eddie grew more somber by the
mile. It touched me to know that this was something he was
doing out of friendship for me.

"They mostly from the East, these college friends of
yours?" he asked.

"All over," I replied. "Don't worry about it, Eddie. They'll
eat us up."

"You sure? Who else they have on these dance weekends?
Who'd they have last year?"

"They brought in Woody Herman for the dance."

"Oh, no! A big band?"

"That's for Saturday night. Saturday night is like a prom.
Dressy. We're doing the Friday-night dance. That's the wild
one."

"Yeah? Who'd they have for that?"

"Bo Diddley. He tore it up. You should've been there. The
dean of the college, when he was introduced, he said, 'It's
nice to meet you, Mr. Diddley.' Mr. Diddley! That cracked us
up."

Eddie gave Joann an oh-what-have-I-gotten-into look. To
me, he remarked about how hard it was to compete with a
black act.

Through the old railroad tunnels along the turnpike, past
Pittsburgh, through the grim mill town of Weirton and on
into Ohio, where we overnighted just across the state line,
I kept chattering about the college, working hard to make
it interesting. I was all full of it: eccentric professors, brilliant put-downs, famous pranks, notorious alumni. Now I
realize that, almost as much as I wanted to cut an interesting
figure back at college, I wanted to impress Eddie and the
Cruisers. And—to tell the belated truth—I wanted to fascinate Joann Carlino, the same way I'd wanted to fascinate
her when I sat holding a poetry anthology at Vince's Boardwalk Bar.

Considering how it turned out, it's easy for me to reproach myself. I was using people to make myself look

good. I was using a decent-enough college as a backdrop for a homecoming fantasy: the prodigal dropout returns. Worse yet, I was using the Cruisers to authenticate my adventures in the outside world. Most of all, I was using Joann Carlino.

That's what it came down to when I pictured it. I didn't visualize myself performing onstage to wild applause. I knew better than that. No, all I wanted was to walk into the dining hall on a Friday night with the unprecedented Joann Carlino on my arm. Was that so much to ask? There'd be six hundred men in there, sitting at tables covered with fried fish and french fries, bug juice and Jell-O molds, and we'd stroll through, Frank Ridgeway and Sophia Loren, and that one moment, that charged, gaping, incredible tableau, would mean that the dropout who became a drifter who became a Cruiser was a winner! It was impossible, I knew, and it was false: she was Eddie's girl. Still, I pictured it.

Now you know what was in it for me. It's a fantasy that reflects no credit on me, nor does the nightmare it turned out to be. The memories of that weekend still make me sweat and tremble, and it doesn't do any good, knowing how long ago it was, or that Eddie's dead, or that everybody else who was there has probably forgotten. I remember—and that's enough. And yet, one final point before getting on with it. As bad as it was, I sometimes think that in bringing the Cruisers to that college, in putting Eddie up onstage beneath the dark oil paintings of dead Episcopalians, in picturing Joann Carlino in Pierce Hall, I was struggling to bring two worlds together. I was trying to complete myself, to become full and whole. It didn't work, but that's what I was trying. And it was something I never tried again.

We came up the Hill in midafternoon, Friday, eight hours before we had to play. Usually, we showed up with twenty minutes to spare, and if we'd pushed it, we could have made the whole trip in one long day. But I'd told them not to try it. The extra time was my doing.

Dance weekend was well under way. The first women—
"eager beavers"—arrived on Thursday, sitting in the back
of lecture halls while their dates prayed they wouldn't be
called on. They kept dribbling in, in time to witness last-
minute preparations. There was a "pig pool" for the guy
who landed the ugliest blind date, and voting for the "asshole of the year" cup at a clandestine ceremony in the cornfields at dawn, and there were the usual training meals:
eating a stick of butter which would line your stomach and
protect you from getting drunk.

Still, on first sight it was beautiful. Guys promenaded
their dates around campus, politely pointing out the chapel,
the president's residence, and the new library, so tentative
and polite they might have been leading a walking tour
through some historic neighborhood. They introduced dates
to each other, like gentry on a promenade, and they carried
their ladies' suitcases—one round blue suitcase, one square
blue suitcase—into spare faculty bedrooms and vacated dor-
mitories.

Yet the spring madness was already stirring. Music
blasted out of open windows, and beer kegs were rolled out
onto the grass. Beer, music, and—now I sensed it—privilege. I pointed out the beer and music. The Cruisers sensed
the privilege. Gothic architecture and sloping lawns intimidated them, like they were high school seniors with bad
grades.

"Hey, Wordman." Sally approached me as we checked
into the college guest house, which I'd never noticed was
such a genteel, Molly Pitcher–Whitman-sampler place. "This
shindig tonight, how we supposed to dress? I mean, what
should we look like for these people?"

I'd never seen Sally so shaky. Wendell was Wendell, black
for every occasion, and Hopkins had his eye out for "fraternity girls." Sex was his equalizer. But Sally was lost, Joann
was rattled, and Eddie wasn't helping.

"Eddie decides what we wear," I said. "You know that.
Why should this be any different?"

"I can't suit up like no Bo Diddley," Sally groused. "I can't juggle the mike or boogie round the stage, I guarantee you that. Eddie, how we dress tonight?"

"Put a sock in your crotch," Eddie answered, gloomier than ever. "It's your college, Wordman. What's the dress code?"

"Wait a minute!" I protested. "Why is this suddenly such a big issue? We've played colleges before."

"Sure we have," Eddie retorted. "We played Saint Something down in Delaware, where the dropouts from barber school get scholarships, and Fairly Ridiculous up in Madison, where you go if the army won't take you, but we never played this kind of finishing school!"

He looked at Joann, regretting the outburst, as if he'd broken a promise not to say something. Then he faced me.

"This was a mistake. They're different here. These aren't our people."

I couldn't miss the implication. I wasn't their people, either, if I were part of this. From where I stood, quitting college and joining the Cruisers was a rebellion, a nifty adventure. From where Eddie stood, it looked like I was slumming.

"They're kids, college kids, is all," I said. "They're no better than you, they just—"

"I didn't say they were better!" Eddie shouted. He surprised himself, shouting. Next he spoke quietly. "I said *different*. You want to remember that."

We all went to our rooms then. Sally never did find out what he was supposed to wear.

That afternoon, alone, I walked around the campus. Already, the return was a failure. I'd wanted to stroll with Eddie and the rest of them through libraries and classrooms, turning heads. But now I meandered by myself, at loose ends, like some pathetic alumnus who returns with a straw hat and a hip flask, searching for F. Scott Fitzgerald's party. I greeted people here and there, professors and students, but none of them knew I was a Cruiser. They all guessed I'd come back for the weekend, as usual without a date.

The campus had a special loveliness in springtime, when violets dappled the grass and bright forsythia exploded onto sunlit walks, and balmy afternoons stretched into mellow evenings. That's what I'd wanted them to see, but the Cruisers weren't budging from the guest house. Sally was wretched because where there was usually a television in his room, there was a Colonial spinning wheel!

What was familiar to me was alien to them. And, I had to admit, I liked this green, peaceful, secure world. I was glad I'd escaped, but at the same time I realized that someday, inevitably, I'd return. I knew I wouldn't be a Cruiser forever.

They embarrassed me, just now. It was that bad. I was like some smooth student whose callus-handed father and ungrammatical mom had dropped by for an unexpected visit. I wanted the Cruisers to be gone at the same time that I hated myself for bringing them. How could I have gotten them into this? Had I forgotten what it was like? Tonight, the college wanted raunchy music, a gross group, the blacker the better. They wanted double entendres, tits and ass; they wanted to get drunk and vomit and brag about it.

"What's a Beta?" Joann asked. "A fraternity house?"
"Yes. Jocks."

I found her on the porch of the college guest house, pretending to read a magazine. Actually, she was checking out the dance-weekend traffic. Late-arriving college girls crowded the lobby, running upstairs and down. They had the routine down cold, these migrant croppers on the hand-job circuit. They traveled from college to college like journeyman boxers who fought in one tank town after another, never expecting a fair decision or an honest count: Wabash to Muskingum to Oberlin to Kenyon, a campaign of losing battles.

"And a smoker?"

"That's a party they have before the dance—a cocktail party in a fraternity lounge."

"I've been asked to a couple of smokers."

"I'm not surprised," I said. "Where's Eddie?"

"He's upstairs." She stopped and thought. "He feels this was a mistake, Wordman."

"What do you think?"

"What do *I* think?" She folded her arms in front of her, laughed nervously, and glanced around as if someone might be listening in. "I'm scared to death!"

"Oh hell, Joann!" They'd never seen the likes of Joann Carlino on this campus, yet she was intimidated by the coed bustle all around her. To her a college dance weekend was high culture, halls of ivy, reception lines, and punch bowls. Those little blowaway blondes in madras skirts and Oxford shirts were an elite race—clever, sophisticated, well-read. They humbled her.

"They told me I wasn't college material," Joann said quietly, like I was her confessor. "You know? The guidance counselor? Sophomore year, he'd already decided about me. Not college material."

"Joann, those guidance counselors are creeps, snobs, they—"

"I asked my guidance counselor what he figured I should do. He talked about being a beautician or a typist—did that appeal to me? Or maybe a secretary, working in some big office, with lots of men around. Or a nurse, but that was already reaching for the moon. That's what he said. But all the time he was checking me out, and he wasn't looking at my eyes. There's a ripe one. Tight sweater, crucifix, the works. Doesn't matter what kind of job you get, because in a year you'll be married and pregnant with the first of six, and they won't be college material any more than you are, cookie. Case closed."

"Joann, next to you, these college chicks are . . . remember that night at Vince's? That first night onstage? How I was?

That's the way you look now. Listen, these people are way behind us . . . "

"I don't think they think so. It doesn't bother them, it bothers you . . . "

She never finished. Suddenly, my freshman roommate, Keith Livingston, stood before us. He wore a blue blazer, chino pants, white bucks. He was from Short Hills, New Jersey, he owned an M.G., and he claimed that his girlfriend, standing next to him, would take it in her hands and play with it. On off-weekends, he drove into town and picked up locals, whom he called his "fucking machines."

"Ridgeway! When did you get back?"

"Just this afternoon." I introduced Joann to him, and he presented Lois, a "nice girl" whose picture had greeted me every morning for a year, wedged into a corner of our common mirror.

"You back for the weekend? The rites of spring?"

"Yes."

"That's perfect! Know who's playing tonight? They got the Parkway Cruisers! Mean-assed black group out of Newark."

"Actually, there's only one black in the group," I corrected, avoiding Joann. "I hear."

"That so? Hard to tell what's what anymore. Say, why not come by the dorm? There's a keg party. Everybody'll be there."

"When is it?" I asked, hoping that he'd leave so I could talk more with Joann.

"We're on our way."

"Well, I don't . . . "

"Come on, Ridgeway. What, you're not traveling incognito, are you? Have you eaten?"

"Not yet."

"We'll get you into the dining hall. They never check on weekends anyway. What's an elephant scab more or less?"

I looked at Joann. "Breaded veal cutlet."

"You've never had an elephant scab? Come on!" Livingston urged her. He wasn't subtle about his staring: I'm sure he was playing imaginary "motorboat" between her breasts. "They had a food riot this year. Did you hear about it? I guess not. Guys slinging handfuls of mashed potatoes at each other. You should have seen it. Well, come on, let's eat."

He bowed gallantly to Joann, who gave me a look that asked what she should do and received back a look that said . . . please, come. I knew she never would.

Joann Carlino got out of the chair, took my arm, and walked with me out of the guest house.

"Thanks," I whispered, "for not . . . you know . . . "

"I know," she answered.

"You're always helping me out of jams. It'll only be a little while. You want to leave a note for Eddie?"

"Eddie's talking to Wendell," she said. "Don't worry about Eddie. Sally went for a six-pack. Hopkins is out being himself. We'll hear about it in the morning."

We walked The Path, a broad gravel corridor through the heart of the campus, with the dorms at one end and an abandoned seminary at the other. The Path was the backbone of the College, the first walk you took whenever you arrived, and the last before leaving. In September, freshmen ran the gamut on The Path. In June, colorful processions pomped and circumstanced their way to graduation. In between, you never knew what you'd find. I'd seen Robert Frost quite early one morning. And, another morning, a quite naked faculty wife.

Joann Carlino stopped traffic on The Path. We were barely a hundred yards along when Lois started chatting with Joann, as if to draw some of the attention to herself, and Livingston pulled back beside me.

"Ridgeway, where did you find that . . . piece!" A high compliment, coming from Livingston. "She's incredible! I never knew you had it in you. Where were you hiding your talent last year?"

"I've been working on it," I said. Walking behind the girls,

I heard Lois jabbering about dance weekends hither and yon, how Oberlin differed from Ohio Wesleyan, and Joann faking polite interest, as if she'd been wondering the very same thing that morning. Meanwhile, Livingston was dying.

"I'd eat her on credit," he whispered. "How is she?"

I mumbled a nonanswer. It was strange. Livingston was knocked out the way I wanted them all to be knocked out, but now that it was finally happening, it felt all wrong. Joann Carlino was an overwhelming beauty, tall, dark, buxom. Lois was a nondescript teenager well on her way to becoming a matron. But more than looks separated them. There was a nasty edge in Livingston's admiration. Joann Carlino was the sort you lusted for, beat off over, banged your head against the wall about. Lois was the girl you married. That's the distinction he was making. I hated it then, and I hate it now, because it turned out to be true, for him and for me. But being true doesn't make it right.

"You know Mike Henderson? Sigma Pi? He was saying he thought he saw you on some television show, singing or something."

"Me sing?"

"I know. I told him he was out to lunch. Where have you been, though? Is she . . . what . . . Puerto Rican?"

"Italian, I think."

"A-fucking-mazing. We don't get many like her around here."

We stepped into the lobby of the dining commons. Inside the hall, I heard the slam of trays, waiters asking how many bug juices, how many milks. I smelled grease and disinfectant. I watched Livingston drop an arm around his girlfriend's shoulder and lead her down the long long aisle. You know the walkway that leads out into the audience at the Miss America Pageant? And you've heard about the main street of Pamplona, when they run the bulls? Put them together and you're entering Pierce Hall on the Friday night of a dance weekend, circa 1958.

Joann watched Livingston and Lois stroll down the aisle.

She hesitated, held back, surprised, amused, a little scared. There were hoots and whistles for Lois: not more than two or three hundred in the audience knew she was beating Livingston off pretty regularly.

"We can skip it," I told Joann. "It's no big thing. There's a hamburger place . . . "

Inside the hall, the audience grew restless, mooing like penned cattle, stamping their feet, banging utensils against plates and pitchers. Sugar bags flew through the air, like rice at a wedding.

"It's like the Jersey shore," I said. "That's what I was trying to tell Eddie."

But Eddie was right, and I was wrong, and I knew it even then. These raucous weekends were the flip side of a smugly patrician mentality. Call it wild oats, blowing off steam, letting your hair down—the wildness was all intramural, sanctioned by the college. It came with the tuition.

Livingston was looking back at us, like we were lost. He waved to us to come in. At the same time he leaned forward, as if to tell his buddies, "You're not going to believe this!"

"We better not," I said. I must have reminded Joann of the antsy kid who didn't want to join the Cruisers onstage because he was afraid the jaded summertime crowd would sniff out and destroy a virgin rock-and-roller. She put her hand on the inside of my arm and drew herself so close to me that I could feel her breathing.

Silence greeted us. A vast cavern of silence, like there'd be silence if Angela Davis showed up at a rodeo. An amazed, breath-holding, eye-popping silence till we were halfway down the hall, Frank Ridgeway, Class of '61, and Joann Carlino, black sweater, silver crucifix, blue jeans, her hand tightening around my arm, who had matriculated in a class they'd never join. Then one of the waiters dropped a tray of elephant scabs and the place turned into a zoo: howls, whistles, groans, screams, and cheers, all of it for Joann Carlino, my best friend's girlfriend, my homecoming queen.

· · ·

"Did I do all right at dinner?" she asked, when we walked back across campus.

"All right? Are you kidding?!" She held my arm, not as tightly as before but like we were a relaxed couple, strolling home at the end of a nice evening. I remember how the grass smelled then, and that owls were hooting down by the river, and that we met an elderly German professor who greeted us courteously and, when we left, gave Joann an Old World bow.

"When that Lois girl asked where did I go to college, I didn't know what to say."

"You told her you worked in the city. Fine!"

"And whether we were pinned or lavaliered . . . "

"Forget it. Did you enjoy yourself at all?"

"The man we met. Your professor. Him I liked."

"You never see him, dance weekends. He doesn't chaperone parties or go to dances. He just stays indoors and waits for the storm to blow over."

"If I could just sit in the back of his class, invisible, a fly on the wall, I'd like that."

"You don't have to be invisible," I said, stepping in front of her. The dreaded, hoped-for moment had finally arrived. "You're good enough to be here. You could make it in a place like this."

"You mean I'm good enough for you," she countered quickly. "That's it, isn't it?"

"Sometimes I think you're too good."

"How do you know I'm not?"

"I didn't mean . . ."

"Eddie said *different.*" She laughed, not that it was funny, but she wanted to stop the conversation from turning personal. Her laughing did the job. And Eddie's name. She pulled me forward.

"Thanks, Joann. For the lovely date."

"Are you being sarcastic?"

"No."

"You're welcome, then," she said.

We were close enough to the guest house to see the cattle-car from Denison, a busload of blind dates for desperate underclassmen, kids without cars or fraternity connections, losers and loners and closet cases. I explained how it worked: how upperclass proctors matched the dregs of both schools in advance. Now, when the bus pulled in, the poor girl's name was called and her date met her at the door. "Want a beer?" "Not yet, thank you." "There's a party up in my room." "Uh-uh."

"A year ago, I was in that crowd," I told Joann.

"How'd you make out?"

"I didn't win the pig pool."

"That's something."

"I came in second. The guy who won, I think his date was missing a nose."

She laughed at that and held my arm tighter. I think she liked me when I was at my most awkward. My helplessness brought her closer. Whenever I asserted myself, she pulled away. But not that night. No, that night I was a regular smoothie. I turned and opened my arms, and my mouth was on her mouth, nothing she could do about it. I remember she opened her mouth, just a little, just a moment, just touched my tongue ·with hers, and then it ended. The kiss stopped there. Her hands reached my shoulders and gently pushed me away.

"Let's go back," she said.

They were waiting on the porch, watching us come down the walk and through the door, where Joann split off and went upstairs, and I stepped out alone.

"Show time yet?" I asked.

No one answered. They slouched in their chairs, feet up on the furniture, smoking cigarettes and drinking beer, like they were posing for a tough-ass album cover. I saw they decided to dress tough, too—worn jeans, T-shirts, leather jackets—like we'd dressed on the Claude Richards show. I was in ordinary khaki slacks, Hush Puppies, and a blue short-sleeved shirt.

"I'll get my other stuff on," I said. I'd packed my Claude Richards outfit: black slacks and a used shirt that said "Ricky's Sunoco" on the back.

"No," Eddie said.

"Only take a minute . . ."

"I said no," he insisted. "You stay like that." I looked into his eyes and saw there was nothing I could do. They told me, too, those hunter-hunted eyes, that Eddie knew.

If you could go back and choose one night to see Eddie Wilson and the Parkway Cruisers, to catch us when we really cooked, it would have to be that spring night in Ohio, that one incredible show which summarized everything we were about and foreshadowed our doom.

I don't know why it happened just then, what there was in that audience of college snobs and drunks and makeouts that brought out Eddie Wilson's fine and angry genius. There were lots better audiences closer to home. But maybe that's what did it: the unfamiliarity, the tension, the manifest hostility with which Eddie faced the audience. Or it could have been personal. It could have been just me.

They hadn't waited for us to start the party. A local group, not a bad one, had been playing a solid hour of white rock and roll—Everly Brothers, early Presley, Gene Vincent, Eddie Cochran. We set up behind them while they were still working, gazing out on a crowded hall. You'd look back at it now and maybe you'd laugh: short hair, old clothes, dance steps that are out-of-date. But laughing is the easy way out. You'd miss something if you only laughed.

The locals were no slouches. They finished with a rousing five-minute version of Bobby Freeman's "Do You Want to Dance?" They nodded as if to say "top that" when they moved off . . . and they stuck around to see if we could.

Somebody from the college social committee popped up at

the microphone and began a long, flat speech. It sounded like we were there to accept an honorary degree, not play a dance, and that's when I knew that Eddie would be wild that night.

" . . . and to Dean Thomas . . . "

"Get on with the music!" Eddie shouted.

". . . and the campus senate, who provided . . ."

"Get on with the music!"

"Okay, everybody. Here they are, Eddie Wilson and the Parkway Cruisers!"

The crowd cheered, pushing toward the stage to get a good look at us. Here and there various ex-classmates had spotted me, and the word was passing through the audience, but it didn't feel right. Eddie and the others—except for Wendell, who always wore a suit and tie—were dressed like gas-station attendants. I looked like a stranded motorist. I was sure people were wondering what I was doing up there with the Cruisers: Had I won a bet? Or lost one?

"You got some fine college here," Eddie began as soon as the applause died down. "All the advantages. Ivy walls."

Hopkins hit the drums.

"Lecture halls."

Another hit.

"Full-dress balls."

Drums and guitars. I faked and fumbled, wishing they'd told me they were doing a special intro, because I was sure everybody was watching to see whether I really belonged.

> "And you got the Cruisers
> For the nasty stuff . . .
> For the get-down music
> And the hangin' tough
> Better grab a woman
> Don't mention your name
> 'Cause after tonight
> She won't be the same . . ."

Then it exploded, from gospel chant to impromptu song to a rocking, nasty version of "Down on My Knees." Out of touch as I am with music since Eddie died, I still refuse to see how anyone could surpass what he did that night. We played for nearly two hours, no breaks, no patter, no tuning or stalling, Eddie rushing from one song to another, and the way he pounced on the songs, the way he explored, prolonged, teased, reprised, exhausted them, you had to think —and I later confirmed this with some other people—that he was fucking the songs. We all thought it. At the time, though, we were struggling to keep up.

He destroyed the audience. The difference between what they expected and what they received was the difference between a swimming pool and a tidal wave. Oh yes, it was just like that. They'd come to dip and stroke and splash, but Eddie swept them away, spun them around, pulled them under, carried them off, deposited them gasping and disoriented on strange shores. I refuse to believe that anyone who was in the room that night could not have been changed by the experience.

How can I recapture that night? I can't sing it, play it, or relive it. All I can do is recall bits and pieces. One thing I recall is, how as soon as Eddie had established a certain musical feeling, so that everyone thought they knew where they stood, he'd abruptly jump to its exact opposite, force-marching us from one extreme to another.

One of our prettiest songs, for instance, was called "The Tides." It was a slow, harmonic *a capella* doo-wop that Doc Robbins had written. Written? Well, stolen. It was a prosaic meld of two other songs, Roy Hamilton's "Ebb Tide" and Nolan Strong's "The Wind." But the sensuality of our singing overcame the banality of the lyrics.

"The tides roll in"

Eddie sang, low and brooding, and behind him we harmonized

> "do-wee-ooh—do—wee
> And touch the sand
> doo-ooh-wee
> Roll out again
> ooh-waah
> Out of sight, of land
> ooh-waah
> So my love for you
> so my love for you
> May ebb and flow
> flow . . . love
> Depart the beach
> Return and grow
> grow love . . ."

And they'd all be slow-dancing, hanging on tight, while we harmonized a bridge, and I might as well tell you that nothing moves me quite as much as a slow, well-sung 1950s *a capella* doo-wop: it's youth, springtime, and first love, a whole state of feeling which Eddie promptly destroyed before our last harmony had faded. Before we knew it, he was jumping up and down, Mick Jagger's sardonic embryo:

> "Hand-holdin' women are not my style . . .
> Hand-holdin's fine, but just for a while . . ."

I glanced over at Sally. He shrugged his shoulders. We were hearing all this for the first time, this doggerel verse that spilled out between songs, the raw material of a dozen unwritten, never-written tunes.

> "When the lights go out, when the clock winds
> down . . .
> Got to find me a woman who'll go down town
> No hand-holdin' baby
> Who'll nip and tuck
> Want a girl off the streets
> Who knows how to . . ."

Kenny hit the drums as soon as he heard what was coming, and Sally hit the guitar. They were no prudes, but they liked steady work. Sally looked at me again. What goes on here? What the hell goes on? Out of control, Eddie rushed into the next song, a little number we'd cooked up for the Claude Richards show and decided against doing at the last moment.

> "Maybe she will, maybe she won't
> The girl say take it easy
> And I see her point
> But I want some more than kiss and tell
> Want to ball that baby
> Want to ring her bell
> Want to *know* that woman
> Stop her talk
> Want to groove my baby
> Till baby can't walk . . ."

The whole evening was like that—tender songs like "Call on Me" and "Blue Lady" juxtaposed with carnal raunch. And again and again, those scary, damn-near-demented introductions. The strangest of all he saved for last, right before "Far-Away Woman."

> "Want to thank you people
> For making the scene
> Now the show's about over
> And I'm gonna come clean
> Gonna present the Cruisers
> One by one . . .
> On drums . . . Kenny Hopkins.
> First guitar and sax, Mr. Wendell Newton.
> Second guitar, Sal Amato."

My turn came. And went. He didn't mention me. He turned away till someone—I'll always blame Keith Livingston—shouted, "You forgot somebody."

"Who'd I forget?" Eddie asked, like he'd made a bona fide slip.

"Over there. In the corner."

"Oh ... oh yeah." He spoke in a rueful, how-could-I-have-done-that voice. "In the corner we got Toby Tyler."

Laughs. I stood there, praying that would be the end of Eddie's joke.

"Not his real name. Stage name. Show business *nom de plume.* Toby Tyler. He's the little boy who ran away from home and joined the circus, isn't he? Snuck into the tent without a ticket, so he could see the wild animals inside. The savage beasts, the clowns and freaks. Let's hear it, everybody, for Toby Tyler."

Applause and laughter, mingled with a few shouts of "asshole!" and he launched into "Far-Away Woman," a fierce, stretched-out version. As soon as we ended, Eddie leaped off the stage, ignoring calls for an encore, pushed his way through the crowd, and vanished out the door.

The Ohio band took the stage to mop up. But they might as well have started setting the tables for tomorrow's breakfast, because there was no act on earth that could follow us that night. I left as quickly and inconspicuously as possible. I crossed the campus, walked into a fraternity party, snatched a six-pack of beer, and walked out again toward the college graveyard, opposite the guest house. I sat down on the grass next to a favorite spot of mine, a Civil War tomb, and started in on the beer. The grave belonged to a Union officer who'd been killed—beheaded, according to college legend—in the spring of 1865, practically on the last day of the Civil War. I liked his timing.

Well, it could have been worse, I told myself. Eddie could have told the story of my lost virginity. I could have died on stage, like opera singer Leonard Warren, or collapsed like Judy Garland, or had an egg smashed into my hair, like Emil Jannings at the end of *The Blue Angel.* Sure, it wasn't all that bad, little enough price to pay for a good year on the road. I'd made friends, played songs, gotten laid, and now it was over. Eddie had revoked my membership in the Cruisers. So it was back to college. A year from now, if I were lucky, I'd be staggering around in the cornfields, copping feels and blowing lunch on my way to the asshole-of-the-year party. This year, though, I'd better stay away. I might win *in absentia*, but if I showed my face I'd be in by acclamation.

"Wordman?"

She found me out there, when it was nearly dawn. I knew she would. I'd pretended I didn't see her coming, but I'd watched every step. I'd seen her search the porch and cross the road and look down The Path. "What have you been doing out here? Have you been here all night?"

"I like cemeteries," I said. "Old ones like this, anyway. You come back anytime and nothing's changed. There's no catching up to do."

"Are you drunk?"

"I wish. Did you see the show?"

"Yes."

"I thought it was terrific. If you like public executions."

"I'm sorry."

"Don't bother. You've got your own problems. The way he acted onstage, I figured you were in for it tonight."

"What's that mean?" she asked.

"I mean, the business. How'd it go? 'Fuck that woman till she can't walk'?"

Two fast slaps, one on the left, one on the right, and she was ready to deliver more.

"I'll take a bus back East," I said.

She knelt down then and touched me where the slaps had landed. "Eddie's up there crying. He's been crying all night."

"Why?"

"I don't know. Whenever I try to talk to him, he turns away."

"Is it because of us?"

"There's nothing between us for Eddie to cry about," she answered. I was hoping she'd at least think it over a little.

"Well, I guess you cleared that right up."

"Don't be like that. He needs you."

"Did he say he needed me?"

"I know he does. He's under pressure now, acting crazy. I can't reach him like I used to. Maybe you can help."

"Toby Tyler?"

"He's your friend."

That morning we headed home. It was a grinding, interminable journey compared to the buoyant outward drive. Everybody was fagged out, so we took turns at the wheel, with hillbilly radio stations to keep us company. The only time we talked was when we pulled off the road for gas and food. We were at a Howard Johnson's near New Stanton, Pennsylvania, eating fried clams, when Hopkins started boasting about some girl who "tuned his skin flute" the night before, and somehow he found a chance to call me Toby Tyler.

Eddie's hands were faster than Joann's. He grabbed Hopkins by the collar and pulled him across the table.

"That's it!" he said, shoving him back across. He looked at me, and I thought he might say something—smile, nod, shake hands. He just looked at me though, as if he were checking for the first time to see if I were there.

Eddie and I never talked about that night. Maybe he felt it was best not to, or maybe he was waiting till it was further behind us. So it happened that our friendship turned low-key and cautious. I still don't know whether my staying with the group made any difference to him. He seemed so far away, those Lakehurst weeks, but maybe Joann was right. Maybe he looked back from wherever he was headed and felt better, knowing I was still around.

12

There's one thing you have to know if you're around old-timers like my neighbors. Every event, from getting up to going to bed, is scheduled; everything fits into a fixed daily routine. Never change your routine, never upset your neighbor's: that's the social compact here. And that's what my hunters attacked.

The camp has been in an uproar for two days. Every trailer that has a phone—every trailer but mine—has been receiving odd phone calls, day and night. Naps have been ruined, meals interrupted, peace and quiet shattered. Sometimes it's a man who says he's from Tony's Pizza or the Nielsen Survey. Or a woman: Avon calling. Often it's rock music blasting over the wire. Sometimes silence.

The old-timers are helpless before this kind of attack. They can't disconnect. They never know when they might need an ambulance or a tank of oxygen. The phone's their only connection to the outside world, doctors and relatives. So there's nothing they can do but jump up and answer every call, no matter what.

It's like the place was under siege. The dawn patrol never assembles. Bleary-eyed and faltering, they slouch in lawn chairs outside their trailers, waiting for the next phone call. Yesterday, at my suggestion, Herman Biedermann called the phone company to see if the calls could be traced, and all they could tell him, when the answer came this morning, was that they were placed from various pay phones all within a twenty-mile radius of the camp.

This morning, the attack entered a new phase. Now they ask for Frank. And hang up. "Frank there?" "Say hello to Frank." "Tell Frank Eddie called."

I'm Frank. I felt guilty as soon as the phone calls started, knowing they were aimed at me. I went out of my way to be helpful. I was the one who urged Herman to contact the phone company. But now that they're asking for Frank, private guilt has been turned into public exposure.

"Get a phone of your own, why don't you?" Martha Darmstadter suggested.

"Frank, we need our peace and quiet," Ed Riley confided. "That's why we came here in the first place."

"If it's the money, we can all chip in," Herman hinted.

A phone of my own won't solve a thing, but I couldn't tell them that. So I lied. I told them I'd requested a phone but that the installation would take a week to ten days. By then, I thought, it would be all over. But Martha Darmstadter, who reams out public utilities for sport, double-checked me. The result is that I've been caught in a lie. They're meeting this morning, in her trailer. The caucus has lasted three hours already—pie and coffee included—but how can there be any doubt about the outcome? They'll ask me to move out.

"Normally I'd ask you to leave; I'd bounce you right out of here, understand?"

The deputy warden at Rahway State Prison, Herbert

Sanders, was like a lot of civil service blacks: the innate caution that brought them so far mingles with the angry premonition that they'll get no further. They pride themselves on going by the book, but they know they didn't write it.

"Yes, sir," I responded.

"You put your request in writing. We check you out. We check it with the prisoner. There's a pamphlet of do's and don'ts for visitors. You want to come back again, make sure you read it."

"I'll do that."

"You plan on coming back?"

"Maybe so."

"Good."

"Why . . . good?"

"He gets so few visitors—so goddamned few!"

The visitors' area was a fenced-off lawn, outside the cell block. Someone had tried to make it into a picnic area. Sapling shade trees stirred in muggy summertime air that smelled of Perth Amboy refineries and the polluted Raritan. There were swings and slides for kids and a fireplace for cookouts. Ignore the high-wire fence, the patrolling guard, the brick walls, and you might be in a park someplace, a park where all the men wore faded denim and all their wives were welfare-fat, and everyone spoke in whispers.

You could hear the gates opening and closing whenever prisoners came out. Reunions were constrained and awkward: an initial greeting, a touch of hands, a quick retreat to the farthest corner of the yard. I waited for Wendell at a picnic table near the door, gazing over the fence at a highway where early weekend traffic beat the rush to the Jersey shore.

"What's he in for?" I'd asked the deputy warden. I didn't want to ask Wendell. The way he shrugged, he made me feel I'd asked a stupid question.

"B and E, I guess."

"That's . . ."

" . . . not a railroad. Breaking and entering. I'll check his file. Stop by my office on the way out."

"Was he guilty?"

He laughed at me. "You don't get far talking guilt and innocence around here."

"How's he doing?"

"Just don't mention the Dewey Decimal System. Take a tip from me. Stay 'way from Mr. Dewey."

Sanders walked away, chuckling. I was the only white visitor, the only adult male visitor, in the area. While I waited, I wondered why it was that I'd lost touch with Wendell Newton, and with all the rest of them. We didn't have to play together after Eddie died, but we could have stayed friends. I exchanged visits, traded Christmas cards with dozens of people who meant less to me. So why not the Cruisers?

Looking back, I realized that I'd never even tried, not so much as a phone call or a postcard. That was my fault, no doubt, but not mine alone. The others weren't any different. They'd scattered just as I had, no turning or returning till now, and I was the first one back. So it wasn't just me. It was melancholy tribute to Eddie, who brought us together and whose death killed all thoughts of our staying whole. When he died, it turned us into fragments. Wreckage. And we knew it.

A shadow crossed the green-painted picnic table, fell over my shoulder and onto my hands, and then a man filled the space where the shadow had fallen and I was looking at Wendell Newton for the first time in twenty years.

"I remember you," he said, his eyes welling with tears, like remembering me was the proudest, finest thing he'd ever done. "You're the Wordman."

"Hello, Wendell." I shook his hand. I held it. "I remember you, too. I really do."

But I wouldn't have recognized him. He'd always been thin and frail, but back then he had a feverish energy that

159

made you forget how puny he was. I remember how he
sweated when he played, how the veins in his neck bulged
when he blew the sax. That was gone now. He was a skinny
fidget who wore Coke-bottle glasses, and his hair was mostly
white. It hurt me, seeing him like this. I couldn't help it; I
asked the question I'd decided to save for last, or not to ask
at all.

"Wendell . . . what happened?"

He smiled and shrugged, as if he hadn't quite decided.

"The sixties." He laughed a little at that, just in case he'd
said something funny. "It'll take some time before I get
nostalgic for the sixties. Now the fifties, that was tops.
Prime time. But after that . . . you don't want to hear about
it."

"Yes, I do," I insisted. "Where'd you go?"

He nodded, but I felt that he was forcing himself, playing
a tune his heart wasn't in.

"I didn't get far," he said.

"Newark?"

"Oh, I don't mean that. Oh no. I been all over. All those
places Eddie wanted to play. I toured with Ike Turner for a
while. Rufus Thomas. Eddie would have loved it."

"Then what . . . "

"It was never the same. Never the same excitement, the
same chances being took. It was just a job. A Sally-type job,
punchin' a clock, playin' notes, hoppin' back on the bus. I
missed you guys. Eddie. All of you."

"Wendell, if you'd contacted me . . . "

"Don't bother," Wendell said. "I don't want to hear you
talking like that. You guys were part of the best time I had.
There's nothing to apologize for. It ended, was all, and other
things came along. It's the way things go."

"But prison!"

"You want to know my record, Wordman, ask the warden.
He keeps score. Tell him I said he could tell you, dates and
details and all. I don't mind. I just don't want to talk about
it."

"You still play?"

"Sure," Wendell said. "Records and the radio. And in my head—there's music in my head. That's the music nobody else hears. The incredible solo instrument of all time. How about you?"

"What about me?"

It shouldn't have surprised me, but it did. I'd thought of the visit as a one-way investigation. It hadn't occurred to me that Wendell would be looking back at me, that they all would, and that they'd be pleased or disappointed by what they saw.

"Whatever happened to you, Wordman? I've wondered, I sure have. Trying to guess what you were up to. Time to time, down in the library, I try looking up your name, just trying to keep up with you. We got *Twentieth-Century Authors, Books in Print.* We got the *Readers' Guide to Periodical Literature . . .* "

I had to turn away then. I couldn't face him. I couldn't tell him that what he was looking for couldn't be found.

"Being a writer is something," Wendell mused. "And hard. It's got to be hard. I recall, you used to talk about it all the time. How many books you write so far?"

"Wendell . . . " That was the pivotal moment: I couldn't disappoint him. Not when losing touch already seemed like the most enormous cruelty I'd ever committed. "I'm working on one now. And you're in it!"

"Me?"

"And Eddie and the whole bunch. It's about the old days, when we were Cruisers together."

"Eddie's on the radio again!" he remarked excitedly. "You hear him? Old Eddie's fixing to be a star. You hear? Eddie's coming back!"

I wasn't sure what Wendell meant. It seemed like he believed that Eddie might really be coming back to life, or that he'd never died. What's more, I had trouble following Wendell—not just his logic but his speech itself. When he was young, what little he said came out so intelligently, so carefully pronounced, that Sally accused him of being a foreign student. Now, Wendell sounded old.

"You gonna see it happen, Wordman. Eddie in the big time! I hope his old friends won't be forgot."

"You listen to music, Wendell?" I was stalling. I was trying to make up my mind. Was Wendell crazy?

"I sure do. And you know, sometimes out in the yard, these kids we get in here stand around and sing. Believe it, Wordman, they do some of Eddie's and your songs. Jiving and doo-wopping and harmonizing. Street-corner stuff. And I hang back, it almost makes me cry. It gets me sad and happy all at one time to think, 'Hey, that's me singing! That's *me*. I was part of that!'"

"You were, Wendell," I said. I almost cried myself. "You were one of us."

"Hey, don't get down about me, Wordman. They treat me pretty good here. Oh damn! What's today?"

"Saturday."

"Oh damn!" He sat back down disconsolately. "Library's locked on Saturday. I wanted you to see the library. I figured you'd be interested. You got to come back and see what I done there."

"I'll come back."

"You promisin'?"

"Sure. What do you do?"

"I run the library, Wordman! You should've seen the mess when I took over. But now it's all organized, top to bottom, a place for everything and everything in its place. I guess you know about the Dewey Decimal System ... "

He was off and running before I could intervene, a tape unreeling inside the wreckage of his mind, dots and numbers playing where the music used to be. Not a subject you couldn't cover, not an area you couldn't find, Wendell said, once you learned the system. Mr. Dewey was some smart man: he got it all together.

"What kind of book you writing about Eddie?" he finally asked.

"I don't know yet."

"Well, there's fiction and there's nonfiction. It could be biography, I guess, or autobiography, or history or music. You send one over, Wordman, I'll tell you right where it fits. Any book at all, you just try me. You can't stump me and Mr. Dewey."

"I'm still working on the book, Wendell. That's why I need your help."

"You know as much as I do about those times, Wordman. You know what fits and what don't fit in a book. We were all in it together. That's what I was telling Mr. Hopkins."

"Mr. Hopkins?"

"Sure. You remember Kenny. He's a preacher now. Come's visiting sometimes. Got us a new *World Book Encyclopedia* for the library . . . "

"You talk to Hopkins, Wendell?"

"I sure do. We talk about the old days, him and me. I find myself remembering things I thought had slipped away for good. Old Kenny, he likes to reminisce."

"Lakehurst?"

"What's that, Wordman?"

"You talk to Kenny about Lakehurst?"

"Talk about 'most everything. It sure does please me, to see him come. He grew up fine, Wordman. Believe me, he's not like he used to be. He's changed. Used to always want me to date him up a colored girl. Always wanted to be doing it, he did, but you ought to see him now, you ought to look him up. You'd be surprised."

"Wendell . . . for this book I'm working on . . . there's a weak spot. I think you can help me out."

"You just ask. You just ask me anything."

"Lakehurst. That month in Lakehurst. None of the rest of us were in on it."

"No," Wendell conceded, almost as if he owed me an apology. "I guess you weren't."

"I need to know what was happening out there. What were you and Eddie working on? Ever since his records became popular again, there's been rumors going around."

"What those rumors say, Wordman?" For the first time, I sensed that Wendell was reluctant.

"All kinds of things. This one reporter came to me, he said maybe there were famous names out there, working on the sly. Elvis Presley. Buddy Holly. People like that. And Sally remembers crashing a party out there one night, and the place was filled with a bunch of blacks he didn't recognize."

"Sally wasn't never too good at recognizing blacks," Wendell said. "The Ink Spots, the Mills Brothers, maybe Billy Eckstine. That's about as soulful as old Sally got."

He laughed at that, not bitterly; he was never bitter. But he was uncomfortable about something.

"We got a few records in the library," he meandered. "It don't amount to much. Folks donate their seventy-eight's. Big bands. Kay Kyser. We got just about every Kay Kyser side there is."

"Wendell . . . "

"I promised I wouldn't say nothing about Lakehurst, Wordman."

"Who'd you promise?"

"The man himself."

"Eddie's gone, Wendell. Been gone. Nearly twenty years. You think he'd mind at this late date?"

"That's what Mr. Hopkins said. I try telling him, a promise is a promise. I just don't know what Eddie'd want, Wordman. Specially since you're workin' on a book."

"Twenty more years, we might all be gone, Wendell. What's the meaning of your promise then?"

"I know, but . . . "

"The music and the book . . . that's all that's left of Eddie now. The part that doesn't die. I want to make it a good book."

"Yeah, I hear you." He clasped his hands and looked down at the ground. "That Eddie. That crazy Eddie. Never left nothin' alone for long, that white boy. Always something else he wanted to do. Always wanting to bring

things together. Which is when they fall apart. You follow me?"

"I'm trying."

"You know how it started, the whole Lakehurst thing?
You were there. You ought to remember."

"When?"

"That night at the Regency."

I guess they're gone now, demolished, urban-renewed, or
grinding out kung-fu features: the Apollo in Harlem, the
Regal in Chicago, Uptown in Philadelphia, and the Newark
Regency. Vast, tumbledown, inner-city movie houses that
smelled of sweat and popcorn, where melty ice cream ran
down the aisles, springs popped out of chairs, and the black
legends of Motown were born.

It started as a joke. All of us were sitting around at
Vince's one afternoon, gabbing away, and Eddie asked each
of us what we figured might be the toughest possible place
for the Cruisers to play. Where could we go that would
really scare us?

"Don't take me no place where there's old folks," Sally
said. "St. Petersburg, Florida. They'd die on us."

"Or Roseland," Hopkins ventured. "Some big old ball-
room where the Arthur Murray graduates hang out. No
way."

"Country-western," Wendell said. "Those other folks just
walk away. Them rednecks come after you!"

"Your turn, Wordman," Eddie prompted. "Where's the
toughest place for us to hack it?"

"This is hypothetical, right?" I asked him. "I mean, we're
just bullshitting?"

"Yes."

"You sure?"

"Go ahead and say it, Wordman." I'm sure he already
knew what was coming.

"Negroes," I said. "Sorry, Wendell."

"Don't apologize to me, man," Wendell answered. "I

don't want to play in front of bloods. Not with you fellows."

"Hell yes!" Sally said. "He's right. 'Sheeeit, Rastus, whuts all that light up onstage!' Jesus, I'd enter a pissing contest with a skunk before I stepped on a stage in South Philly."

"Relax, Sally," Eddie said. "It's not South Philly. It's Newark."

These days, with Motown transplanted from Detroit to L.A. and Diana Ross a movie star and blacks copying white music almost as much as whites copy black, you forget the fear and awe with which we used to regard black music. Everything crosses over now—I won't say it combines—but it crosses over. Not then. They were worlds apart back then, with no connections, except maybe a late-night radio show that barely reached Vineland, New Jersey. That, I guess, was enough.

Sure, we knew about black music. We heard Little Richard, Ray Charles, Chuck Berry. Fats Domino seemed like a jolly old soul, and Frankie Lymon's "Why Do Fools Fall in Love?" was something we sang in the car, traveling from club to club, everybody taking parts, everybody but Wendell who was laughing too hard, just as he laughed at Sally's Amos and Andy bits and Hopkins' Johnny Mathis imitation. Yeah, black music was fine. But it was music from another world, a place we'd never travel.

Then one Saturday afternoon, we turned off the parkway near the airport and headed into Newark and, damn right, it was another country. We'd all squeezed into the station wagon. "If we get jumped, we *all* get jumped," Sally insisted. He left the hubcaps at his aunt's place in Asbury Park.

"Jesus, Wendell," Sally said, "you got any family in this town? Any relatives you know about? Some little pickaninny cousin can watch the car while we inside? Otherwise, we can kiss this car good-bye. Might as well not even lock up."

Boarded-up apartment buildings, bombed-out lots, drinkers and garbage on every corner. Sally jabbered nervously, "Hey, Wendell . . . get this

> 'What's the word?
> Thunderbird . . .
> What's the price?
> Fifty, twice . . .
> What's the action?
> Satisfaction . . .
> Who drinks it most?
> Us Colored Folks.'

Ever hear that one?"

"No sir," Wendell answered.

"Oh hell, Eddie, what're we gonna lead off with tonight? 'Stranded in the Jungle'? Our Al Jolson medley? And, say, when Doc booked us here, he didn't happen to mention what color we were. I mean, did he say black or white?"

"Neither one," Eddie said. "Italian."

"Very funny," Sally answered. "I tell you what. You put Wendell up front tonight. 'Wendell and His Trained White Slaves.' They'll love it."

"Calm down, Sally. It's near here."

Sally drove extra slow, rolling up the windows at every stop light. When cars full of blacks pulled alongside, he'd grab for a road map and run his fingers up and down, like he was looking for the road to Irvington.

"Hey, Eddie, who's starring tonight? Teresa Brewer? Gogi Grant?"

"Coasters and Drifters, Doc said."

"None of them spade bird groups. No Flamingoes or Orioles or Robins or Crows?"

"No, I don't think so."

"Penguins? Meadowlarks? Sparrows?"

"You want to be a bird group, Sally? The Five Chickens?"

"They whip out their knives, we'll be the Funky Capons.

Then we can all grow tits and sing falsetto. How much we makin' for this suicide mission?"

"Doc set it up," Eddie said, "like always. Why? You want to change your next of kin?"

"Oh? Doc took care of it? The good doctor? We're lucky we get a pail of chitlins . . . "

"Holee shit!" Eddie shouted. "Look at that line of people! What's going on here?"

"Must be they're waitin' for the library bookmobile," Sally said. "It breaks down, they get worried."

We'd arrived. They were lined up around the block, in front of liquor stores and barbershops and rib joints, and it felt like every one of them was watching us pass. We stopped, turned a corner, and the line continued, all the way to the marquee. As soon as Sally read the marquee, he was laughing hysterically.

"So Doc set it up, you say? Our faithful coach? Sure he did!"

I was sitting in the back seat with Wendell and Kenny, so I couldn't see the marquee. All I heard was Sally howling.

"That does it, Eddie. That's fucking *it*! Let's split!"

"We're here," Eddie said, but even he seemed down. Whatever was on the marquee was an unpleasant surprise. I leaned forward, over the front seat, but I still couldn't see.

"Don't break your neck, Wordman," Sally said. "I'll read it to you. Marquee says tonight we got the Coasters, the Drifters, LaVern Baker, Lee Andrews and the Hearts. You know what else we got tonight? Amateur night!"

"We'll do it," Eddie said. "I swear to God, we'll do it."

"Amateur night is what we're booked for! Can you dig it?! The Parkway Cruisers are giving it away for nothing! A benefit performance for a worthy cause. Spades!"

"Parking lot's around the back," Eddie said quietly.

"You kiddin' me?"

"Pull in."

"My grandparents never owned no slaves. Came over in

the twenties in a ship they hammered together out of old Mazola oil cans. I don't owe these colored folks nothin'."

"Pull in, Sally."

"Uncle's bakery got knocked over once already this year. I figure we already donated for civil rights, you know?"

"Pull in."

You can guess what happened that night at the Regency. White group faces audience of hostile blacks. Only other white face in the place is the Jewish theater owner, so he doesn't count. Otherwise, its solid rows of stingy brim hats, do-rags, imitation leather jackets. Tired domestics fresh from dusting Goldberg's apartment. Men passing the bottle after a hard day at the car wash. Surprise, laughter, scattered boos when whitey appears onstage, all turning to astonished appreciation when the honky boogies like Blind Lemon himself. Before long the house is rocking. They're dancing in the aisles, jumping onstage, begging whitey to do another one just like the other one. "Sheeit, where them ofays learn to play like that?"

Guess again. For one thing, it was amateur night at the Regency, and amateur night was an evening of almost medieval cruelty: Mardi Gras, inquisition, and pillory all in one. Never was an audience more skeptical, more jaded, more ready to destroy careers before they began. We all have an enormous appetite for other people's failures—no victory occurs in a vacuum—and amateur night served up a smorgasbord of losers to an audience of have-nots. It was an orgy of humiliation, a night for fools, and a fool presided, a faggoty black comedian with a spotted clown suit and a dunce hat and a long cane. That was the hook, and few escaped it. He was always in the wings, staring at groups waiting to go onstage, confident that his moment would come. At the first sign of audience restlessness, he'd peek around the edge of the curtain; a few more derisive laughs, and he'd tiptoe out onstage.

Sometimes the performers saw him coming. I remember a gang of school kids, heartbreakingly hopeful, singing their hearts out on "A Sunday Kind of Love." They'd rehearsed steps, spent money they couldn't afford on shiny shoes and nearly phosphorescent suits, and the moment they stepped onstage, they fell apart. They tripped over wires, missed harmonies, and the lead singer's falsetto broke like chalk against a classroom blackboard. This time the clown came out fast—sometimes he gave an act time to pull itself together, but not this one—and the audience shouted unanimous approval. But the lead singer saw him coming and darted away from the advancing cane, like a hookey player skipping away from a truant officer, only he was still trying to sing. So the clown stepped on the microphone cord, picked it up, and advanced toward him, hand over hand, till he reached where the lead singer was kneeling at the edge of the stage, reaching for notes that were off the scale, praying for a reprieve, and the clown popped down beside him, mimicking his gestures, and finally the kid collapsed, handed over the mike and ran offstage.

"Nice crowd, nice place," Sally muttered in the wings. "Classy. Very classy."

"Kid sounded okay to me," Hopkins said. "Coulda let him finish."

"Hey, Eddie," Sally whispered, "you know anybody could use five identical suits with matching shoes. An undertaker, maybe? Quintuplets die in a car crash, he'll be sitting pretty."

Eddie ignored Sally, but I remember he looked worried. He talked to me.

"I'd love to knock them on their asses tonight, Wordman. I'd trade a dozen Claude Richards for an encore here."

"Are we ready?"

"Are they?"

A blues-singing bus driver. A Johnny Mathis drag queen. And a beautiful black woman who wanted to be Dinah Washington was jeered at, hooked, and led offstage in tears. The clown looked at us as he passed. "Be seein' you."

"Wendell," I asked, "has there ever been a white group here before? Is this a first?"

"Been plenty white groups here," Wendell answered.

"Yeah?" challenged Sally. "Who?"

"This here used to be an opera house. That was a long time ago."

"Thanks, Wendell. I feel better already."

The clown picked up an offstage mike.

"Okay, ladies and gentlemen. Are you ready for somethin' different? I mean something un-pre-ce-dent-ed, you catch my meaning? Mr. Eddie Wilson and the Parkway Cruisers. Make 'em feel at home. They ain't. Eddie Wilson!"

The curtain took forever to rise. "Coulda been worse!" Sally whispered. "He coulda said we were South African sailors in the market for poontang."

Now if Elliot Mannheim ever hears about the Regency, he'll turn it into a triumphant evening. Or maybe I've underestimated him. Maybe he'd go the other way, recount a tragic failure, a noble ahead-of-time effort to span what was still an unbridgeable gap between white and black America. No matter, the truth is that we played three songs pretty well, received a polite hearing, closed to moderate applause, avoided the hook, got offstage and out of town in one piece. Now, to Sally that was a triumph to rank with Livingstone and Stanley. Catching up with the Russians was small change compared to our daring escape from Congolese New Jersey.

Not for Eddie. I now realize that, just as dance weekend was my effort to bring worlds together, this was Eddie's. Wendell said it best, that morning down at Rahway: "Always trying to bring things together . . . which is when they fall apart."

That Newark night Eddie learned there were people his music couldn't reach, a world he couldn't enter. Eddie wanted it all, wanted it now, and that was the night he learned he couldn't have it. That night, it was his turn to play Toby Tyler.

"He wasn't the same after that," Wendell said. "Maybe you others didn't see the difference, but I sure did. You remember what happened after we finished playing?"

"No . . . not exactly. Didn't we just pack up and leave?"

"You guys did. You waited in the station wagon."

"That's right. You and Eddie were missing. You disappeared someplace."

"We caught the show. The pro-show. Some hell of a show it was too, even from way up in the balcony. Me and Eddie in the last row of nigger heaven. Condrums and bottles on the floor, broken seats, the two of us. Know what we saw that night?"

"No."

"We saw . . . he saw . . . folks doing what he couldn't do. The Coasters working on 'Searchin' ' and 'Young Blood' for half an hour. The Drifters singing 'Ruby Baby.' Lee Andrews and the Hearts doing 'Teardrops.' Those last years, before the Beatles and psychedelic shit and all, those last years were good. People forget how good those black groups were, how strong they came on, singing, dancing, carrying on. Eddie ate his heart out, because they were where he wanted to be. He wanted to bring it all together. That's what killed him."

Eddie hadn't given up. After the so-so reception at the Regency, he was determined to bring off the impossible, some fantastic union of black and white music. Now, more than ever, he was drawn to the dark side. During the months before Lakehurst, when I assumed he had simply withdrawn from the rest of us, he was out with Wendell, embarked on the last struggle of his life.

"Wherever we were," Wendell said, "we went into colored neighborhoods. Clubs, bars, whatever we could find, driving for hours to hear Jimmy Reed or Muddy Waters or Howlin'

Wolf. That was some Cruise! You never knew, did you? And it was all leading up to Lakehurst. That was our top-secret project!"

He laughed at that, laughed nervously, and then—I swear it—he nodded, as if he were saying good-bye now, the time had come for parting. He looked at me, looked away, fidgeted and trembled.

"That crazy Eddie," he sighed, and started humming something. He put his head in his hands, nodding back and forth, forgetting I was there. I was losing him.

"Wendell?"

He kept humming. Nothing I recognized, words and notes mixed up, like one of those endless improvised songs that kids sing in the back of cars.

"Wendell?"

He glanced up at me, squinting, as if there were already a distance between us. And yet, I remember wondering why this was happening, why now. Had I done something to Wendell? Or was Wendell doing something to me? Did the very mention of Lakehurst force him into incoherence? Was he avoiding the truth? Or ducking out on a lie?

"What were you doing there?" I shouted, as if the problem was his hearing. He heard me fine.

"We pulled it off . . . me and crazy Eddie . . . Mr. White and Mr. Black . . . kings were there . . . and nobody knew!"

"What did you pull off?"

"Leaves of grass, Wordman. Leaves of grass."

He reached out and grabbed my hand, holding tight while the rest of him dropped away, humming and singing. He swayed and nodded and held my hand, or I held his, till I was quite sure he was gone. Then I called over a guard, who removed my hand and helped Wendell back inside.

"They tell me he's kicked off again," Deputy Warden Sanders said. "Singing and all."

"It's happened before?"

"Hell, yes. We'll keep him for a day or two. If it doesn't

stop, we'll ship him down to Matawan."

"I thought it was my fault."

"No. Don't blame yourself. It's just Wendell. Three months, six months at a stretch, and he's perfectly okay, fiddling in the library with his goddamned Dewey Decimal System. Did he . . ."

"I heard all about it."

"Then, someday, he blows a fuse. Just sits in his cell, rocking back and forth, drooling music. We ship him down South Jersey. Few weeks, they ship him back."

"How long will it go on like this?"

"I'm a warden, Mr. Ridgeway, not a fortune-teller."

"What's he in for? And how long?"

"That's right, you asked about his record. I was wrong. He's in for B and E this time, but the first occasion he stayed with us, it was manslaughter. That was 1963."

"Wendell killed someone!?"

"His old lady. Female, white, and dead. Served five out of fifteen, spent a year on the streets, came back in 1970. Been in and out ever since."

"And nobody visits?"

"It's all here on the outside of the folder. Let's see . . ." Sanders ran a finger over the manila folder, then threw it down. "Not my day. I was wrong. Just lately, Wendell's gotten popular. You're the fifth this month. Not bad, considering . . ."

"Considering what?"

"Well, Wendell's been hard to catch. He's been in and out."

"What does that mean?"

"We don't advertise it, because the newspapers would climb all over us. But we have a small furlough program whereby some of our better risks can be signed out for two to five days in the custody of a responsible sponsor. Wendell's been out twice lately."

"Who's the sponsor?"

"That's confidential. So's the list of visitors."

174

"I'd like to see that list."

"Can't show it to you. Cost me my job, someone found out."

"You'd be doing me a favor."

"What about him?"

"There's not much I can do for him, is there?"

"You could come back. Take an interest. You could care. He won't be in here forever. He could've had parole last time he was up, if there'd been anyone on the outside. Place to stay, promise of employment, financial support, that kind of thing. You his friend?"

"I used to be."

"You *still* his friend?"

"Yes."

"You'll be back?"

"I'll be back."

He tossed the folder on the edge of the desk, swiveled around in his chair, and looked out his window at the exercise yard.

I picked up the folder and scanned the list of authorized visitors for Wendell Newton—names, addresses, dates of visits.

It was a revelation. A regular oldies-but-goodies reunion for the Parkway Cruisers.

The Reverend Kenneth Hopkins had brought the word of God over from Mountainside, New Jersey, on more than one occasion. And it was he who'd furloughed Wendell out of prison. I guessed it made sense, entrusting Wendell to a clergyman like Kenny. But I wondered why he hadn't mentioned it, why neither one had said a word to me. It was out of character for both of them. Why so quiet about the good deed?

There were other surprises.

A potential employer, Mr. Salvatore Amato, had stopped by for an interview, right after he'd wowed the young-at-heart in Ohio.

Mr. Elliot Mannheim, writer, of New York City, had

stopped by. Purpose: research. I wondered if he'd delivered my message to Wendell: life turning out to be longer than expected.

And one visit a year, ever since Wendell came inside, from Joann Carlino of Toms River, New Jersey, right down the road from Lakehurst.

13

Half a mile from the prison, I found a phone booth, dialed Joann Carlino's number, and after half a lifetime, heard her voice.

The tape said, "I'm not at home now. If you like, leave a message when you hear the beep. I'll be back soon." She didn't give her name.

"Joann," I said, "this is Frank Ridgeway, from the Parkway Cruisers. Remember? I've been looking into some things that might involve you. I can't be more specific over the phone. I think we ought to talk, the sooner the better. I'm driving down today, and I'll call you when I'm in the neighborhood."

The parkway was hopeless by the time I headed south. I used to be part of the bumper-to-bumper crowd. I loved it all —the traffic, the pitch-and-putt golf courses, the surf-and-turf restaurants, the bars and beaches, the very idea that this was the lowest, commonest vacation on earth. If you could find enjoyment this way, you could be happy anywhere, I used to think. Have fun in New Jersey—that's an accomplishment. Make music out of New Jersey—that's a miracle, straight out of Whitman.

Leaves of grass.

I crossed the Raritan Bridge. How proud we used to be that this was the world's most polluted river, where nothing lived, and hell, you even got your feet wet, you could die!

After Perth Amboy, I pulled off the parkway and decided to try the old shore road, Route 9. We used to like the old highway. Cluttered and littered, it ran from Newark to Atlantic City, connecting the toughest city in America to its tiredest resort. It was New Jersey all the way: nothing planned, nothing pretty, one business after another lining the road, crowding traffic like pigs at a feeding trough. Spend a buck, make a buck. But beyond the suburbs there were some surprises. There were Colonial-looking farming towns, rundown fishing villages, swamps and fields, and pine barrens. And strange people. Black crop-workers, Jewish poultry farmers, Methodist teetotalers. Once a wrong turn brought Eddie Wilson and the Parkway Cruisers into a Tolstoyan Russian community, with Cyrillic signs and an onion-steeple church. You never knew. In the summer, we used to feast along the road, at stands that sold blueberries and peaches, clams and crabs, and beefsteak tomatoes you couldn't match anywhere outside of New Jersey.

There's something glorious in piling into a car when you're young and driving twenty, fifty, a hundred miles for a hoagie sandwich, or hot pretzels, or strawberry-rhubarb pie. It's the one thing the Cruisers had in common: a lust for the grub we found along the road. We were always making discoveries and returning, to make sure our discoveries hadn't changed. We called it "foraging," and the foraging title changed hands weekly. I remember the sausage-and-peppers place in Plainfield that Eddie claimed, and Kenny staking out a beer-and-bratwurst spot in Union, and Joann finding a chowder stand just in from the Long Branch pier. My contribution was a hamburger place with great onion

rings and a sign I couldn't resist: "We grind our own meat."
And Wendell! That was something. When it came Wendell's
turn, we all expected soul food. Sally was elated: at last, a
connection for barbecued ribs and smoked pork, greens and
beans and sweet-potato pie. "Hey, Wendell, just make sure
it's a carry-out place, okay? You get the food, the rest of us'll
watch the car." So where did Wendell take us? An ice cream
parlor, an 1890's ice cream parlor, in Red Bank. "Would you
believe it?" Sally whispered later. "An ice cream joint. Good
ice cream, cute, and I didn't have to break out semaphore
flags to snag a second cup of coffee. But Jesus! And did you
see what he ordered?" I hadn't noticed. Ice cream? "Yeah,
but what flavor?" What? "Vanilla." No doubt about it, Sally
thought, Wendell was strange.

There were good times, all along the road. As soon as I
thought of one, I remembered another. They just kept coming. I remembered the talks we used to have and how we
enjoyed each other's company, the funny arguments we got
into. It was my job to start the argument. I still remember
some of our debates: Would rock and roll ever be concert
music? If the Russians occupied America, coast-to-coast,
what were the chances for a long-term guerrilla movement?
If the nation elected a bachelor president, what, if any, sex
life would he manage while in the White House? Then there
was the time I opened a discussion on sexual positions. That
was a setup. Kenny Hopkins had continued to roast me
about my inexperience, so we all dumbfounded him by claim-
ing that there was nothing quite like making love on the
hood of a car. Ah, the feeling of engine-warm metal beneath
your bodies, the slight buckling of the hood as you pumped
away, holding onto windshield wipers with your hands and
bracing your feet against the hood ornament. So much better than wrangling around inside, cramped by steering
wheel and gearshift. That weekend, we—the Cruisers and
half the clientele of Vince's Boardwalk Bar—caught Hopkins on top of a Nash.

Of all our foraging expeditions, the one I most remembered was to a place that Sally discovered, an Italian restaurant in Pennsville, just across the bridge from Delaware. The meal was a blowout. To the rest of us, pasta was spaghetti, and it usually came out of a can, cold and orange, with meatballs attached. What you couldn't finish, you gave your dog. Sally straightened us out about pasta. Tortellini, fettucini, linguini, spiedini—it sounded like an aria. And Sally was in his glory. For once he was the leader, host, boss, the center of attention. It made me feel good, seeing him so happy.

"Hey, Sally," I said, "I was just wondering . . ."

"Oh no, give me a break!" Sally groaned. The others joined him. "I was just wondering" was the ritual opening. "Not another one of them knuckle-headed questions!"

"Can't we ever have a peaceful meal," Kenny protested. But he was smiling.

"Hey, what's the matter?" Doc Robbins asked. He wasn't usually with us, so he could pretend he didn't know what was coming. "The bookworm's got a question. Something's bothering him."

"Oh Lord," Wendell sighed.

"Hey," Doc said, defending me. "This is one sweet kid. How many times has he come to our rescue with a timely piece of information, an obscure fact, a fragment of little-known lore? If it weren't for him, would we know that the Mason-Dixon line cuts through South Jersey? No. We'da missed out on that. Or that Leon Trotsky, leader of the Red Army, once worked backstage at Minsky's Newark? Remember?"

"It's a wonder we made it so far without him," Sally said.

"These are things that keep me up nights," Hopkins added, "tossing and . . ."

"Just stay off the hood of . . ."

Doc cut Sally short. "Ladies present," he said, gesturing at Joann. It was curious, how her being there never stopped any of us from saying what was on our minds, but if I told you it was as if she wasn't there at all, I'd be lying. Because when she was absent, we missed her, our conversations went flat. We needed to know that she was there, next to Eddie, drinking her club soda and watching over all of us.

"Okay, Wordman," Doc said. "What's on your mind? What's troubling you, my boy?"

"Well, I was wondering, Sally . . ."

"Why me!" Sally pleaded. "How come I have to bear the brunt?"

"Because this was some great meal you put together. Half these things aren't on the menu. You have to know what you're doing to put a feed like this together, and since you obviously do know, I was just wondering . . ."

"Here we go . . ." Hopkins said.

"I was wondering what has given you the most pleasure in life. If you had to choose, I mean, between food and . . . sex?"

Sally's answer was what we called a "King Farouk." He put his head into the plate, face down, as if he suffered a postprandial coronary.

"Sally passed," I said. "Okay, Doc, which way would you go?"

"If it came to giving up ginch or starving to death? I don't know, nobody ever died doin' without . . ."

"But it's not a question of need," I clarified. "It's a question of pleasure."

"Yeah, I see." Doc seemed genuinely perplexed. And even a little embarrassed. "I never had to give up either one. I've taken what's around, meals and tail. Never been a picky eater. Never gone out of my way neither . . ."

"So?"

"I couldn't say and—you know what? I wish I could." He stared down at the table, as if considering one alternative. Next he looked at Joann. "Hi babe," he said, pretending to leer. But he was still stumped.

"Food and sex. Food or sex." He mulled it over. "That's what it's all about, I guess. Supposed to be. But . . . I don't know, kid . . . I must be playing another kind of game."

"What game might that be?" Sally asked. He couldn't pass up taking a shot at Doc.

"Beats me," Doc confessed.

That was one odd moment! It was like we'd all glimpsed a part of Doc we weren't supposed to see. An empty part, perhaps, but that didn't make it any less revealing.

After that the conversation settled into normal patterns, Kenny carrying on about carnal delights while Sally—emphatically no fag, he made clear—pointed out the regular merits of three squares a day. He even worked it out. Assuming twenty-one meals a week ("we ain't even talkin' about snacks"), and three fornications, a sexual coupling had to be more pleasant than seven meals combined!

"You eat like I eat," Sally said, gesturing at the pantheon of pasta, "it's a hard question." He allowed that other people, blacks and other non-Italians, might have an easy time choosing sex. But, as for him, his pleasantest memories of his mother were in the kitchen. "And my old man would probably say the same thing."

"Eddie?" I usually didn't call on Eddie. I used Wendell as a tie-breaker. But there was something about Eddie that day, a rare, outgoing mood, as if he were delighted that we were all living up to his best expectations of us.

"Some dumb-ass question you fed us for dessert," he began. "Might as well ask what tastes better in the air, hydrogen or oxygen. Take away either one, it ain't air. Or which eyeball you see more out of. Answer's obvious if you ain't half blind. Anyway, Doc had it pegged from the beginning."

"I did?"

"Sure. The question wasn't food or sex, pick one. Not originally. It was what gives you the most pleasure. Am I right?"

"Yes," I acknowledged. "But if it's not . . ."

"Doc said there must be some other game? Right?"

"I certainly did."

"Well, speaking for myself now, and no criticism intended, I'd pick music."

Sally's mouth dropped open. Crazy Eddie had done it again! He shook his head at him, as if he were sad to see how they were growing apart. "Hell of a thing for a guy to say in front of his girlfriend."

We all turned to Joann. Even Eddie seemed concerned—he hadn't intended to say the wrong thing—but now it bothered him.

"I vote for music too," she said. "I also vote for the musicians. How about you, Wendell?"

"Music."

"I guess that settles it," I said.

A moment later, we were on the road again, the same highway I was traveling this afternoon headed for my meeting with Joann. I hadn't been back along this road in years —no reason to go—but now it came back to me: how we loved New Jersey the way you love an old shirt or a baseball mitt that's broken in. And none of us, now that I thought of it, had gotten very far away: a journeyman musician, a high school teacher, a convict, and a parson. Nor had Joann Carlino of Toms River. She'd traveled least of all . . .

Leaves of grass, Wendell said.

Right. Mostly right.

Make it *Leaves of Grass.*

A couple weeks after the Regency, Eddie, Joann, and I were driving around through South Jersey. It was a proper cruise—no timetable, no purpose, no fixed destination. It could last for twenty minutes or three hundred miles. Often, we'd make lots of stops: an Italian sausage place, a fruit stand, a junkyard. We even read historical markers. Other times, we stayed in the car from Cape May to the Delaware Water Gap and back again.

These days it takes an effort to remember how emotionally important driving was to us. People recall the fifties and they picture drag-races, playing "chicken," hot rods, and submarine races. That's easy. But there was more to it than that. A lot of my best memories of Eddie concern our "cruises," the things we found and the things that found us. Some mornings we'd wake up and take off, hurling ourselves across the landscape like young horses galloping across a green meadow. And there were nighttime drives down piney roads, through darkness that our headlights barely pene-trated, and we were like kids around a campfire, scaring each other with ghost stories. I remember stopping on coun-try lanes where we'd get caught by a storm, the rain drum-ming on the car roof, and it felt like we were sitting out a typhoon in a tin-roofed hut. Or some nights we'd drive up to the Watchung Hills and scan the miles of lights below: the decorous gridlike suburbs, the shopping centers where klieg lights poked up into the sky, the streaming highways and bridges, and on the very edge, the vast glow of New York City. On rare nights, you could just spot the tops of Manhat-tan's tallest buildings. That excited us.

That morning in South Jersey was a special kind of cruise. Eddie had been down since Newark, and I guess Joann wanted my help in cheering him up. Autumn was coming, and we were going to look at the leaves, she said.

Near Manahawkin, we saw that the landscape had changed drastically since our last surveillance. "ADULT LIVING," the billboards advertised. A whole new commu-nity had been cut into the pines, built and paved and peopled. It was one of the first of the New Jersey retirement com-munities, and we drove through it at ten miles an hour, on streets that were named for birds, like Robin, Heron, Mea-dowlark. We gazed at the residents, who were raking leaves, and setting traps for moles, and admiring the year's last flowers, chrysanthemums. Autumn of the year and autumn of life came together for us that day.

"Any morning there'll be a killing frost," I said. "We're due."

"Who gets frosted," Eddie asked. "The people or the flowers?"

"I wouldn't like the winter here," Joann said. "I wouldn't want to be old here in the winter."

"There's Indian summer to hope for," I said.

"Hey, what is Indian summer?" Eddie asked. "Years and years, I've heard that expression."

"After the first frost," I said, "it sometimes turns warm again. You get these mellow days, sunny and brisk. A time for hayrides and—"

"But, oh Christ!" Eddie burst out. "What do they do when winter comes? I mean, what happens all day long? The mail arrives. That's the big event, I'll bet. They call each other on the phone. They eat. What else? Sleep? Tell me this, Wordman. You get to be a certain age, what do you figure it feels like just going to bed at night and not knowing for sure you were gonna see the morning?"

"I guess . . ." I opened my mouth but it was one of those times you start a sentence without knowing how you'll finish it. Luckily Eddie interrupted me again.

"Hey, let's go!"

He pulled to the side and was out of the car in no time. He nodded to a pair of old people who were raking leaves, or trying to. That was why he'd stopped. There were lots of leaves, and a gusting wind kept the leaves well ahead of the old-timers' rakes.

"Come on!" He shouted, yanking a rake out of the old man's hands, gesturing for me to take the woman's. They backed off, astonished, while Eddie swept across the lawn. He made a contest out of it: Which of us could build the largest pile? I worked hard, but Eddie went at it like a madman, giggling wildly, raking up huge piles of oak and maple leaves.

"Free Italian-sausage-and-peppers sandwich to the one who picks up the last leaf!" he shouted.

We raced along, stuffing the leaves into plastic bags. The piles dwindled down to handfuls, and before long we were on our knees, chasing the last few stragglers across the lawn.

"You pick the winner, Pop," he called to the old man. His wife looked shocked, but the old-timer got into the spirit.

"There's one over there near the mailbox!" he called out. "A maple over by the garden hose! Oooh, a big red one just came down! Get it!"

I'm sure he rigged the contest. Eddie and I were down on our knees, scanning a lawn that was as immaculate as a vacuum cleaner could have made it. We were sweating, and our hands smelled of dirt and leaves. Stems and twigs were in our hair, and our jeans had round wet patches at the knees. We were crouched on the grass when Joann came up behind us, holding a red-and-gold maple she'd been saving for the endgame.

"The lady wins!" the old man shouted. "Hot diggity!"

An hour later, still munching cookies they'd forced on us, we found ourselves near Camden, just across the bridge from Philadelphia. Camden's not such a good town for leaves. Or trees. Flat, fucked over, mostly black, Camden is to Philadelphia what Newark is to New York: a place you drive through.

"Time we turned around," Eddie said.

Nobody argued, but there are a lot of old-fashioned traffic circles in that part of Jersey, exits feeding off them like spokes off a wheel. I screwed up the turn, and somehow we found ourselves in downtown Camden, where even the dirty bookstores closed at sundown.

"What a place," Eddie mused. "Who the hell ever lived here, anybody ever heard of?"

"I know one!" Joann popped up. "A famous person, too."

"Who?" Eddie asked.

"Guess."

Eddie didn't respond. Maybe he was blue. Then again, maybe he was stumped.

"Give up?" she asked.

Eddie shrugged. "Sure."

"Jersey Joe Walcott," she said. "I read it somewhere."

"There's another famous man came out of Camden," I said.

"Who's that?" Joann asked.

"You guess." But there weren't any takers. "We'll drop in at his house."

I was in luck that day. My memories of a class trip I'd taken ten years before didn't betray me. And Walt Whitman's home hadn't been urban-renewed, although everything around it had. It stood there, an island of wood and stone in a sea of empty lots, smashed brick, shattered glass.

"Oh yeah," Eddie said as we pulled up in front. "Walt Whitman. Guy who built the bridge."

"Come on, Eddie," Joann chided. "The guy they named the bridge after!"

"No shit!" Eddie said.

"Like Pulaski and Goethals," she said.

"Yeah. And Triboro."

"Let's go in," I said.

"They let you in?" Eddie asked.

"Sure."

"What for?"

"Just to look around. See where he worked, lived, died. So you get inspired, maybe."

"Okay," Eddie agreed. "I could use a little of that."

I won't make too much of Eddie's visit to the place where the senile, half-paralyzed poet spent his last two decades. I'll leave that to Mannheim and his kind. Yet he won't be wrong if he argues that something of Walt Whitman stayed with Eddie for the rest of his life.

Like all such shrines, the Whitman house was presided over by one of those dear officious volunteer ladies who are the last-ditch custodians of culture in America. She was surprised to see us, so close to closing time, and a little alarmed. We didn't look like your average literary pilgrims. But once we paid admission and convinced her we weren't casing the place, she escorted us from room to room, happy to show us everything: the front parlor, with the poet's rocking chair and fireplace, the back room, with the bed from which he completed the ninth, or "deathbed," edition of *Leaves of Grass*.

Joann loved the place. She was everywhere, poking into corners, peering at pictures, peppering the hostess with questions. What was it? A nesting instinct? An antiquarian streak? A tiny respite from the impasse her affair with Eddie must have reached? I don't know, but she stayed indoors forever. Eddie, meanwhile, strayed outside, and I followed, into the backyard. I remember there were some fruit trees and a vegetable garden that was about shut down for the season, and a rickety wooden bench you weren't supposed to sit on. We squatted on the grass and rested our backs against the seat.

"We can go anytime," I said, afraid that he was bored. "We've seen all there is to see. It's just an old house."

"Leave her stay a while yet," Eddie said. "She likes it here. I like it too."

"I was hoping you would."

"Maybe someday, they'll make a museum out of the back room at Vince's. Hey, wouldn't that be something? This here bed is where Frank Ridgeway worked on 'Far-Away Woman,' and Eddie Wilson sat right over here on a case of empty Schaefer bottles."

"That would be strange."

"So's this. Think about it. If Whitman came back today, he'd find the house the same as ever. He could climb right back into the bed he died in. Or step out into the yard. Same pear trees. Same bench. Same old vegetable patch. Nothin' ain't changed. But the minute he stepped out onto the streets of Camden . . . holee shit!"

I laughed at that. Eddie had this way of saying "holee shit!" that always broke me up. He had a big grin on his face as he headed back to the car.

I went inside and found Joann. We started browsing

through pictures of turn-of-the century Camden and stayed till closing time. When we found Eddie, he was waiting for us outside, sitting on the hood of the car. He was staring across the street, so wrapped up in what he saw over there, he didn't notice our approach.

I can tell you what he was looking at. I can't tell you what it meant to him, though, but I can guess. The Whitman house, I've said, was surrounded by empty lots strewn with junked cars, ripped mattresses, cans and bottles, all the detritus of urban decay. Here and there, on the horizon, there were a few other surviving houses: a flash of laundry, a scrap of garden, an unbroken window. Out of these houses, at dusk, kids came to play. That's what Eddie was watching: black kids throwing rocks at birds, foraging over bins of garbage, scraping together a baseball game on a lot where a slide into home plate would mean death from a dozen kinds of tetanus. They played though, till it was too dark to see grounders or line drives, only the fly balls against the sky. Then, when it was too dark even for that, they walked home, kicking, jiving, poking past the poet's house, trailing clouds of "mothah-fuckahs."

Eddie pulled a pack of cigarettes out of his shirt pocket and offered them around. I didn't smoke much back then, but I took one anyway, sensing that Eddie didn't want to leave. Joann lit up too.

"It doesn't connect, does it?" Eddie said, blowing a cloud of blue smoke into the autumn air. "From there"—he pointed to the Whitman house, then to the war zone where the kids had played—"to there."

"No."

"It came apart somewheres," he said. "They don't know nothing about each other, him and them. He's just a name on the bridge to Philly."

"He's been dead a long time," I said.

"I know that, but . . ." he gestured at the ruins " . . . what about this?"

He pointed down the street at the black kids. You could still hear them announcing what they would do to each other's ass, come morning.

". . . and them?"

"I got this for you," I said. It was the only answer I could give. A paperback edition of *Leaves of Grass.*

He seemed genuinely surprised. And moved. He thumbed through it, though it was too dark to read.

"I like the title, anyway," he said.

"It's from the both of us," I said, a total lie. Joann had been in the backyard, examining the poet's pear tree, when I purchased the book.

"Thanks, you two," Eddie said. He grabbed us each by the arm and walked around to the side of the car, and for once the ride home was the way it used to be, relaxed and full of wonder, windows open to the night.

No, Eddie and I never rapped about Walt Whitman. We didn't recite poems or mark them up or try putting them to music. Fact is, I never saw that paperback again. If you told me Eddie chucked it in the garbage at the next gas station, I couldn't prove you wrong. To this day, I don't know if Eddie more than flipped through *Leaves of Grass.* I know that I made a point of buying a copy for myself, though, and carrying it around. I wanted to read what I hoped Eddie was reading. I wanted to invite him to talk. But all he ever did was kind of wink at me.

"*Leaves of Grass?*" he'd ask.

"*Leaves of Grass,*" I'd respond, till it became a joke, a password, a kind of riddle. Sally thought we'd scored some hash. "What the hell goes on here? You guys smokin' cattails?"

"*Leaves of Grass?*" I'd ask when Eddie was sitting alone on the edge of a bad mood, or when he'd come out of a motel room after a night with Joann. "*Leaves of Grass?*"

"Oh yeah, you bet. *Leaves of Grass.*"

"*Leaves of Grass?*"

"Bet your ass, *Leaves of Grass.*"

Now I'd heard it again, twenty years later, from a troubled felon at Rahway State Prison, and I was pretty sure that Eddie'd been trying for something grand and broad—something Whitmanesque—down in Lakehurst. He'd been trying somehow to pull it all together, to cover the landscape, the poet's empty house and the ghetto's scavenger kids. Who were Wendell's "kings"? That I didn't know, and I didn't know whether Eddie had even touched what he'd been reaching for. But I bet Joann Carlino did.

Leaves of Grass.

14

Around Lakehurst I got lost. For twenty minutes, I wandered through the pine barrens, till I suddenly came upon a vast, ghostly landmark that told me exactly where I was. Worn and rusting, the Hindenburg's ten-story-high hangar loomed out of the scrub pine, a dark colossus against a dead gray sky, and I knew I was five minutes from the turnoff to the quonset. I never debated returning to the quonset. I didn't even bother flashing the turn signal. I just turned.

The sandy road wound through the pines and maples and oak, all of them dwarfed and scrubby. It crossed over a slow dark river whose waters were stained brown by cedar roots and fallen needles, and then emptied out onto a clearing, with just enough room to pull a U-turn. Across the clearing stood the quonset, depressing and uncared-for, as I remembered it. I'd thought the termites would have gotten it by now, or rust, or the fires that swept through the barrens, but there it was, refusing to fall down and die, Doc Robbins' acoustical wonder.

Why bother getting out of the car? I didn't have fond
memories of the place. There'd been little enough to see back
then. What now? Still, I stepped out, slammed the door, and
walked toward the quonset. No point in going in, I said. Just
—you know—walk around it once and leave. That's what I
did, circling at a distance of, say, twenty feet. The windows,
one on each side, were painted black. But the paint was
scratched so you could see inside. You couldn't see much.
But you could see—I saw—that there were lights inside.
And the lights were on.

I came around the front, stepped onto the rotting wooden
porch, reached for the handle, turned the knob.

And stopped.

There was someone in there. I swear it. I heard someone
cough—a warning cough, like a snake's rattle. Don't mess
with me, man, stay outside.

I pushed the door open.

The lights were off now.

I stayed outside, looking in. I couldn't see much. The back
of the room was dark. And the sides, and the space right
behind the door. I saw an empty floor and puddles of water,
that was all.

I stood there, like a kid on the steps of a haunted
house, afraid to enter but lacking a strong enough excuse
to run. Someone was in there. It was the surest thing I
knew. A derelict, I told myself. A bum. But what bum
would take refuge in such a damp and moldy shell on a
warm summer afternoon? No reason to take shelter, not
here, not now.

I backed away, a step at a time. Why go in? Because I was
one-fifth of a group whose leader rented the place for one
month twenty years ago? What kind of reason was that? No
telling what the quonset had been used for since then, what
deals went down there, what might be stashed against the
walls, or buried in the floor.

I opened the car, slid behind the driver's wheel, turned the
key. The engine jumped to life.

And the quonset door slammed shut. Loudly, triumphantly, shut.

I sat in the car. There'd been no reason to come to this dead place, and there was no reason to stay. That was then and this was now.

You visit graves, right? But you don't go digging them up. You drive past the house you used to live in when you revisit the old neighborhood. But you don't go banging on the door.

I stared at that door slammed shut in front of me, as if whoever were inside knew I wasn't the type to force my way in.

I decided to surprise him. Surprise myself. Just this once.

I reached over to the glove compartment, pulled out a flashlight, and got out of the car. I snapped the flashlight on when I was still a dozen feet in front of the quonset door. I kept coming.

I knocked on the door three times, and waited. Play fair. Open and aboveboard. Another knock.

No answer.

The knob turned—no lock—and the door pushed open in front of me. I brought up the flashlight and pointed it inside, onto the same patch of floor I'd seen before.

I stepped into the doorway and raised the light.

"Anybody here?"

No answer.

"Is there someone in here?"

Nothing.

I stepped inside. One step is all I got.

"Someone's here."

A voice, faint and hoarse, from far back in the quonset. My light didn't reach that far. A voice, faint and hoarse and terrifyingly familiar.

"NO!" I screamed. "NO!!"

"Get out, Wordman."

I threw the flashlight into the quonset, where it shattered on the floor. Screaming, I ran for the car. Crying, trembling,

I raced through the pines, careened out onto the highway, like a mortally wounded animal running—too late, in vain— from the scene of his own death.

What had I expected? A bum, a drunk? An escaped con from a nearby work farm? Maybe a mental patient—South Jersey was full of institutions. Or maybe—granting the impossible premise that the intruder in the quonset had something to do with the Parkway Cruisers—maybe I'd expected to shine my flashlight on Elliot Mannheim's predatory face, or Kenny Hopkins', or even Sally's. Even Wendell Newton's. You can escape from a prison, can't you? But there are some prisons you can't escape.

Eddie.

The Airship Tavern was a roadhouse Eddie used to like. Twenty years later, it hadn't changed: tar-paper shingle siding, a neon sign shaped like the Hindenburg, and a bartender who looked me over twice before drawing a draft beer.

I sat there for half an hour, sobbing, shaking, struggling to get a handle on a situation that didn't have any handles. "Eddie's back . . . larger than life," Doc Robbins had said. Doc was dead. And Eddie? "Eddie's on the radio again, Eddie's coming back!" Wendell had exulted. But Wendell was half crazy, wasn't he? What did he know? What did I know? Was I half crazy too?

Somewhere—then, or now, or sometime in between— there was something I'd missed, and that missing something had plunged me into the middle of a nightmare. A lurid tabloid horror story: James Dean biding his time in a sanitarium, Elvis alive in Brazil, Buddy Holly up in the mountains. Forget the shattered car, the smashed plane, the broken bodies; forget the televised funerals and the thousand mourners, the so-final-seeming tombs. There was something I'd missed, and now I was paying for it.

I ordered more beer and tried hard to reenter the normal world. I studied little things. The foam in my beer. The labels

on the bottles along the bar. I stared at a jar of Polish
sausage, pickled in brine—formaldehyde—and I gagged. I
watched a TV quiz show. I started feeling better, thought
that I was coming around. Someone played the jukebox, and
that was all right with me, till "Far-Away Woman" sounded.
I spun off the stool, looking for someone to accuse, and
lurched toward the men's room, vomiting. Nausea, cramps,
sweats, tears: all hit at once. I felt that I had eaten something spoiled, something that had been dead too long. I stag-
gered from sink to toilet, and finally passed out on the bathroom floor. When I awoke, the linoleum felt cool beneath my
cheek; the sweat was drying on my clothing.

"Coffee's all you get, friend," the bartender said when I'd
washed up and come back out.
"Okay with me." He poured it black and strong and nod-
ded approvingly when I asked for change to make a phone
call.
"Hello?"
"Joann?"
"Yes."
"Frank."
Like a million other phone calls. It surprised me to be so
suddenly and easily in touch with the largest fraction of the
life I'd never lived. It cost a dime, was all.
"I've been expecting you," she said. "Where are you?"
"Airship Tavern. Eddie's old place."
"You got lost?"
"Yes . . ."
She lived fifteen minutes away, she said. She proceeded to
give me some fairly complicated directions, listening to me
repeat them back to her, correcting me when I slipped.
"Be nice to see you again, Frank," she said as she hung
up. That was it. Nice. Competent and friendly and in control,
like she was a real estate agent arranging to show me some
likely houses.

· · ·

This time I drove slowly, straight past the turnoff to the quonset. You could hardly see it in the dark: a slightly wider opening between the trees. I shuddered as I passed. Pull yourself together, Wordman. There's got to be an explanation.

Sure there is. You're crazy. That explains it. You saw the wreck, didn't you? You watched them pull his body out of the car. You attended the funeral, right? And twenty years later, stopping by the quonset on a summer afternoon, he's in there, standing in darkness, like he'd been waiting all along for you to show.

Only he hadn't. That was the most frightening thing of all. I'd intruded. I was unwelcome. An enemy. He knew it and I knew it.

How are you supposed to react when the dead come back? Who wrote the book on that one? Is surprise appropriate? Joy? Well that wasn't what I felt when I recognized his voice. I'd been terrified. I ran away. I knew that the return of Eddie Wilson was something to be feared.

He'd been one of my nicest memories, till this afternoon. Remembering him made me feel good. But he'd been a memory, like a picture you treasure, or a souvenir. That's the way I'd handled him. That way he was manageable. But now I'd kept pressing and rummaging in the past, and somehow, without knowing it, I'd crossed a border that divided then and now. The past had come to life, and I feared it.

We've all seen those articles about how people react to the coming of death: how denial turns to rage turns to acceptance. I think that the people who survive a death go through a similar process. I remembered feeling all those emotions about Eddie's early, pointless passing. And when I was done mourning, I learned to live with the fact that he was gone. A life became a memory which I pictured in the sepia tones of an old film. But now the process had reversed itself. The old picture flushed with new color. Eddie was back. The past no longer contained him.

So how about it, Wordman? Are you crazy? You think that Eddie's back? Or that he never left?

No. I couldn't buy it. I wasn't crazy. But there was craziness around. That was for sure. And somebody was taking advantage of it. Someone was using the past, using memories like weapons. And that, I thought, was the most brutal kind of ambush.

A dozen mailboxes and a sign that invited people to come pick blueberries: those were the last landmarks in Joann's instructions. I turned down the road she'd told me to follow to the end. I passed some small lakes and an abandoned poultry farm, with roofs caved in and weeds growing through the bottom of wire runs. After the blueberry farm, the macadam turned to sand, the pines closed in, more like weeds than trees, and the road curved farther into the barrens.

I'd been all full of Eddie Wilson, ever since that Sunday morning at the Safeway. If the dead live on in the memories of the people they leave behind, then Eddie Wilson had lived in me. I'd replayed all of it—words and music, ups and downs. I couldn't believe that anyone could have thought more of him, more about him, than I had. For sure, no one would remember me that way. And my reward for remembering was a voice that set me screaming. Now I couldn't bear to think of him at all. Picturing his face set me trembling. A bar of his music made me gag.

That outraged me. What was happening to my memories of that Cruiser year hurt me more than my wife's infidelities, my students' indifference, my own failures and defaults. It hurt me where I lived, in the only place and time I'd really been alive. That was unforgivable. That made me an enemy of whoever was out there. I thought of him as a traitor, whoever he was. Not a murderer or a thief, but a betrayer of memory, of the bond of private feeling that links the dead with the living, that holds a generation together, that enlarges the fallen and guides survivors.

The road crossed a wooden bridge and ended in what

looked like a picnic site. There were campfire ashes and soda cans, and a path leading down to the river, to a place where it looked deep enough to swim.

But there wasn't any house.

Half an hour, I said. By then it would be dark, and I didn't want to stay there in the dark. I turned the car around, pointed it back the way I'd come, switched on the parking lights, and waited.

No mistake, I was sure of that. She gave me the directions carefully, I repeated them, she corrected me. I followed them, and everything was just where she'd said it would be. Except her house.

I was exactly where Joann Carlino wanted me to be. At the end of a dirt road, in an empty clearing, near dark.

Fifteen minutes down, fifteen to go. That morning I'd talked with what was left of Wendell Newton. That afternoon, a brush with Eddie's ghost. Now I'd spoken with Joann. A full day, all things considered, and I wanted it to be over. I didn't want to sort things out or weigh possibilities. I didn't care anymore whether I'd guessed right or wrong. All I wanted was for it to end.

Ten minutes left. It wasn't the hardest problem in the world, I told myself. Not when there were just two basic possibilities. Two possibilities for Eddie, two possibilities for all of us. Either we were alive or we were dead. Dead or alive —that's all it boiled down to. Nothing in between. Dead or alive. Not even a multiple choice.

Five minutes. Close enough. Leave now. Nobody's timing you. Oh hell, give it the full five. Dot the *i* and cross the *t*. And blow. Make like a Cruiser. But one last call before leaving.

I opened the door, stepped out, looked around: a stood-up date. When I'd arrived half an hour before, I'd been scared. Now I felt plain foolish. I double-checked to make sure there were no houses within earshot. Then I shouted, loud as I could.

"Joann!"

So much for the foolishness. Now came the fear, for real. A flashlight snapped on inside a nearby grove of pine. Its beam was powerful. I covered my eyes.

"Joann, is it . . ." I held my hand over my eyes, opened my fingers, squinted out, but all I could see was that glaring light.

"Whoever you are . . . I can't see . . . put it down, please . . ."

The flashlight didn't budge. It pinned me against the car, like an escaping prisoner caught against the wall, a deer blinded by a poacher.

"I came here because I was told to!" I pleaded. Maybe it was a farmer outraged by trespassers.

"Joann Carlino asked me."

No move.

"You want me to leave? Is that it? Okay . . ." I reached for the handle to the car door.

That decided it.

The flashlight closed in on me. Whoever held that light was running straight at me, and I knew that if one hand held a flashlight, the other could hold a gun or a knife. But still I couldn't move. I tried, I swear I tried, but nothing budged, not even a scream, because my lungs couldn't pump the air to carry it out of my throat, and now my executioner was five feet away and I guessed I'd die without knowing what it was all about. But the flashlight dropped to the ground. I blinked in the sudden darkness, peered out, and saw her standing in front of me.

"Hello, Wordman."

"Joann . . . why . . . this . . ."

"I had to check you out, but you wouldn't get out of your car . . ."

"What's going on?"

"These past few days . . . phone calls . . . and the house, there's someone watching it, and then you called and . . . I thought it was you . . . There's someone around . . ."

"I know there is," I said.

"I live just down the road, but I had to see if you—"
"Get in the car. I'll drive you home."

She owned the blueberry farm. A hundred and fifty acres to which she admitted pickers in the summer and hunters in the fall and Christmas-tree choppers in December. A barn where she lodged horses for suburban equestrians. An old brick farmhouse where she said she lived alone. First I saw the property. Then, when we were inside, in the kitchen, I saw Joann.

Never go back. Isn't that the conventional wisdom about old flames? Remember them as they were, and let them get better as the years go by, till your memory becomes a work of art, your grain of sand a pearl. But never go back or everything falls to pieces. Now, here I was, risking everything. I admit it: it was the longest possible shot. I admit more: I didn't just want to find that she was alive and well, that she'd earned money or aged nicely, that she'd gone on to college or into business. I wanted more. I wanted to feel exactly as I used to, the same surge, the same rush. I wanted to want her, right then, that first minute.

And I did.

She was still Joann. That was the important thing. There were gray streaks in her hair, and maybe she was ten pounds heavier, but it hadn't collected in any one place that I could see, and even in muddy boots, slacks, T-shirt, and windbreaker, she was still Joann.

I know what you're thinking, because it's what I would think myself: that I made too much of a woman, that I placed an impossible burden on her, mistakenly regarding her as the key to the life I hadn't lived. Okay, but every life has a pivot. And she was mine. She had been, she still was, my turning point. And, what's more, I bet she knew it. While I studied her, she looked at me. Her fear faded. The old sly smile crept out again when she saw how I was looking her over.

"You haven't changed much, Wordman."

"Maybe I should have."

"So where do we start?" she asked. "Now? Twenty years ago? In the middle someplace?"

"Better start now. Anyone else here?"

"No."

"Anybody live here, except you?"

"No."

"Who's got keys?"

"My sister on Long Island."

"Lock the doors."

She peered out front, where we'd come in, then turned to check the back.

"Done."

"Windows."

"Closed. Latched."

"Do you have a gun?"

She reached into the pocket of her windbreaker, pulled out a pistol, and set it on the kitchen table.

"I wasn't sure about you," she said.

"What convinced you?"

"When you came out of the car and called my name. Hearing your voice again. And when I blinded you with the flashlight, you just stood there, like you couldn't help yourself. And I remembered."

"What?"

"The way you used to be."

"How was that?" I asked.

She laughed mischievously, as if at the memory of an old joke she wasn't sure she should share with me.

"Helpless," she said. That was the joke.

My dismay must have registered. It wasn't the way I wanted her to remember me.

"Oh, you know what I mean," she added. "Nice and smart and all, but always kind of lost. Needing someone to give you a push or a shove. Otherwise, just waiting for things to happen to you."

"Oh."

"Don't take it so hard, Frank. It's just your nature. And when I saw you at the dead end of the road, standing help-less, blinded by the light, I knew that there was no way you could be behind what's been going on lately. No way. Not you . . ."

"Thanks . . . I guess."

She still treated me like I was a kid. The other Cruisers were men, but not me, and twenty years didn't change that. Job, seniority, home ownership—they might fool other peo-ple, but not Joann. A long time ago she decided that I hadn't quite grown up. Maybe you could take it as a compliment, since it suggested my best work was still in front of me. Sure, on paper you could call it a compliment. But not sitting at her kitchen table.

She brought out a pot of coffee, a bottle of brandy, and a plate of gingersnaps. She sat in one chair, put her feet up on another.

"Why'd you come, Wordman."

"Things have been happening lately. I think that I'm in danger. And that you're in danger too."

"Wordman to the rescue?" She tried, but she couldn't quite take me seriously.

"Yes," I said. "Rescue you, and me . . . and . . . Eddie."

I told her everything except for that encounter in the quonset. There was no fitting that in anywhere. The rest of the story fell into place. The Safeway. Mannheim. Sally in Ohio, Kenny in church, Wendell in prison. Doc Robbins dead in Pennsylvania.

Yet even as I told her the story, I sensed that I wasn't really answering questions. I was asking them. I was estab-lishing my need to know about Wendell's "kings" and the *Leaves of Grass.* It felt like she was Eddie's surrogate, his earthly representative: all requests to him would be handled by her.

"You haven't changed," she said, when I finished. "You always had so much on your mind."

She sat there, mulling things over, and I thought that of all my questions, she was the largest mystery. I didn't know her, for all my years of wondering. It brought me up short, how easy it had been for me to idolize Joann Carlino and yet remain ignorant of the most basic facts about her. I sensed that it would be a challenge loving her; not a romantic challenge so much as a daily test. Even now, I could tell she was judging me, measuring whether I was worth her time. Did I deserve to share her confidences about the past? What business did I have, sitting in her kitchen, asking questions about Lakehurst?

"You used to have the answers," I said. "Got any answers for me now?"

"Some," she nodded. "And some questions."

She poured a shot of brandy into her coffee. "It's a funny thing about secrets. About keeping secrets, I mean. First you keep secrets because that's what you'd promised you'd do, right? You said you wouldn't tell anybody, and you don't. Time passes and still you keep your mouth shut. More time. Years. People die. People disappear. And you keep the secret for a different reason. First, because everybody was alive. Then, because they're not ... they're gone. Then you're gone too. Bingo. End of secret."

"Wendell said the same thing, more or less. I don't know, I think most secrets are meant to be told eventually. It's not like a vow of eternal silence. It's more like a trust. You put yourself in someone else's hands. You count on them . . ."

"That's just what that kid Mannheim said," she countered. "Only he's a little smoother than you are."

"When was he here?"

"Yesterday. He had money."

"For the tapes?"

"What tapes? He wanted an interview."

"No deal?"

"No deal."

"How about me?"

"What's it mean to you, Wordman? After all this time, what could it possibly mean?"

"Eddie was your guy," I said. "Okay? But he was my friend too. So maybe I'm entitled."

"Entitled to what?"

"To know. That's all."

"Know? All you want is to know."

"That's all," I answered quickly, hoping to impress her with the simplicity of my mission. Money wasn't the point, or fame, or music. The truth was all.

"Why do you want to know?" she asked, unimpressed. "What good is just knowing."

"Can't you just tell me?"

"Why should I? Eddie was my guy. You said it. What's left of him? Some records I can play when I feel blue. A couple of snapshots. And memories. That's all I have. And you're asking me to share it."

She wasn't quite as tough as she sounded. I sensed in her the kind of tension that precedes confession. But she was still plenty tough.

"I keep hearing about Lakehurst," I started quietly. "I heard about it from Doc. You know what he was after. I heard about it from Sally, who's still hurt he wasn't included, and Kenny, who wondered about Eddie calling long-distance, night and day. But Wendell was the one who did me in. He said that Eddie was trying for something big. I want to know what it was. What kind of gamble he was taking."

"But *why?*"

"Because I've never gambled myself. I maybe should have, but I haven't. I pulled up short where Eddie went flying over the edge. Well, he used to say he could learn stuff from me, but it's too late for that. Maybe I can learn from him, though. Even now."

She pondered that a while. It wasn't going to be easy.

"Joann!" I pleaded. "What else can I say?!"

"Okay, Wordman." She got up and walked over to the

sink, staring out at the dark like she wanted to pretend she was talking to herself. "You guessed right about Lakehurst. Eddie had this idea of . . . I don't know what you'd call it . . . bringing people together. That trip to Newark? And that time in Camden? It was all pointing toward Lakehurst."

Her voice trailed off; her back was still turned. Her fingertips drummed on the counter.

"I've had it to myself so long," she said.

"I . . ."

"Skip it. I'll get it out. Eddie used his contacts. So did Wendell. They arranged for some people to come out and jam. Big people. You say Wendell called them kings? I guess they were. It was all secret. I mean *secret*. They never even acknowledged each other. You understand? No names. No introductions, no acknowledgments. They called each other Mr. Black and Mr. White, depending. No names, no pictures, nothing down on paper. They came to play, is all."

"Did they know they'd be taped?"

"Yeah. But everybody had veto power. They never had to use it though."

"Because Eddie died?"

"Not just Eddie. About everyone who was there has died. The ones I recognized, at least. They weren't such a lucky bunch."

"Joann . . . who was out there?"

"Eddie, Wendell . . . and . . ." She took a deep breath. "And Sam Cooke, for a night or two. Otis Redding. He stayed longer."

"Who were the Mr. Whites?"

"Buddy Holly. Square-looking glasses and spit-curl. Some others I didn't know. It was some strange party."

We sat silent for a while. Her secret was mine now too, and it took time to grow accustomed to joint tenancy. Yet I could tell that despite her reluctance, she was glad she'd told me. From now on, the responsibility for telling or not telling was something we'd be sharing. But I wasn't worried about that right now. The audacity of Eddie's concept bowled me over. This time, he'd swung for the fences. *Leaves of Grass.*

The ground rules for the Lakehurst sessions were strict. In addition to what she'd already told me—no names, no acknowledgments, no publicity, no release of material—they provided that no nonmusicians were permitted inside the quonset while the Mr. Blacks and Mr. Whites were playing. So there was an odd collection of go-fers, girlfriends, bodyguards, and sidekicks in the parking lot. Sometimes the real action seemed to be outside, where there was food and booze, hillbillies and bluesmen rubbing up against each other all night long.

"We were like a collection of left-out kids," Joann remembered, "pretending we were having the best time. You know? 'They can keep their silly old music! We're having more fun anyway!' But then, by God, when they started playing, we shut up fast. Nonchalant-like, we'd edge over as close as we could without actually putting our ears to the door."

"What about the music?" I asked.

"Sometimes you'd hear bits and pieces of something kind of familiar. Usually they played old stuff first. But there was lots I didn't recognize. It was hard to tell though."

The Mr. Blacks and Mr. Whites took breaks of course, and Joann decided that was the best way of telling how things were going. Sometimes they came out laughing and joking, even imitating each other. One of the Mr. Whites pretended he was Blind Lemon Snodgrass, a Delta blues singer of unmatched obscenity. To which a Mr. Black responded with a devastating impression of the early Presley. Once, they all burst out the door laughing, threw off their clothes as they sprinted across the parking lot, and dove into the river.

But there were other times when they came out separate and sullen, withdrawing to their cars. "One of the white singers came up to Eddie and asked him if he ever heard the joke about the man who mated a jellyfish and a lobster. Know that one? He wanted to breed a lobster without a shell. But he got a jellyfish with a shell. Then the guy who told the joke nodded and left. 'Nice try, kid.' He never came back."

"How did it end? Did he finish what he set out to do?"

"I don't know. It just kind of stopped. The month was over, everybody was gone, and it was time for the Cruisers to hit the road again."

"But was he up or down about it? You must have been able to tell."

"I don't . . ." She faltered. "He was hard to read, Word-man. He was up and down, crazy. Sometimes you'd think he'd hit gold. Other times, he said it was all a . . . you know . . . a crock. I don't think he'd decided. Sometimes . . ."

"Yeah?"

"Well, there was this one day . . ." She looked up in alarm, like she'd just crashed into a scene that it hurt to remember. I knew the feeling.

"What happened?" I put the question as low-key as I could, but it was still a solid minute before she met my eyes. I'd thought that once she told the Lakehurst story, there wouldn't be any more obstacles. Everything would be easy and open. But I was wrong. The past was a labyrinth, with no long vistas, no easy turns. You never knew what you'd come up against.

"Did you ever hear," she finally asked, "of a place called Palace Depression?"

Palace Depression? At first I drew a blank but then, with Joann prodding me, it came back. Not that there was much to recall: a feature story or two and an item in *Ripley's Believe It or Not*. I'd never even been there, but I knew that Palace Depression had been an offbeat tourist attraction, like the Margate elephant or the diving horse at the Steel Pier. During the thirties an eccentric hermit in Vineland,

New Jersey, had scavenged junkyards and trash heaps for the makings of a home. Not a home, a castle, a hobo's San Simeon. Part Hooverville, part Disneyland, Palace Depression was an amalgam of discarded appliances, hammered-out cans, empty bottles, junked automobiles. It was an odd place at any time, and an odd place for Joann to mention now, or for Eddie to want to visit, the day they finished at Lakehurst.

"I met him in front of the quonset," Joann said. "The place was locked up already. He'd called to ask me to pick him up first thing in the morning, before breakfast, and I arrived on time. He was sitting in front, his back against the door, his guitar and suitcase at his side, and I had this uneasy feeling that he'd been sitting there awhile, you know? Like all through the night, maybe."

Eddie had nodded at her, thrown his things in the back, but he hadn't said a word. He made her feel like a chauffeur, Joann said, but she sensed that something was wrong, something deep, and she kept quiet. And then, closing the car door, Eddie stepped around to where she was waiting and threw his arms around her. "He didn't kiss me, I don't think he wanted me to see his face," she said, "and he still didn't talk to me and that was because—I'm pretty sure—he didn't trust his voice. So we just stood there holding on to each other. It was the kind of hug—you might think I'm saying this now, but it's what I thought at the time—it was the kind of hug that people give each other at a funeral."

When they were in the car, driving away from the quonset for the last time, Joann had asked Eddie where to. He told her to head for Vineland, and that unnerved her.

"Eddie's parents lived in Vineland, and he had a wife in Hammonton, which you have to go through on the way," Joann said. "I guess you never knew about all that."

"Not until the funeral," I said. "That's the first and last I ever saw of Eddie's wife. Not counting that television show the other night."

"What did you think of me, when you found out?"

"It didn't change anything," I said, but I'm sure she missed my deeper meaning: that I had always wanted her, couldn't have wanted her any more than I did. And—I knew too well—could not have done any less about it. "I just hoped you were happy. I mean, that you had been happy."

"It didn't make me seem . . . dumb? Tramping around with a rock-and-roll singer who was married? Whose chances of getting a divorce were zero? I know *I* felt pretty dumb sometimes. The dead-end, no-win, untogether proposition of all time. God!" She laughed. "Talk about hopeless!"

"Then why did you . . . ?"

This time she laughed at me. "Eddie."

I nodded. The only answer I'd ever get.

"We're all allowed one or two."

"Mistakes?" I asked.

"Maybe you could call it that," she said. She didn't say what she'd call it, but I knew she had a better word in mind.

"Where were we?" she asked. "I got off the track."

"Palace Depression . . ."

"We drove through Vineland like we were in a rush to get to Philadelphia. Eddie didn't look left or right. You'd've never known that this was where he was from. The place was outside town. There were signs pointing to it, but they were old, knocked down. And even when we got there, if Eddie hadn't been with me, I wouldn't have known I'd arrived. There was a fence all around, and a 'Keep Out' sign that the municipality had posted. But Eddie knew another way to get in, around back."

It was the back door to a junkyard. Neglected since the death of the owner-builder, raided and vandalized by neighborhood kids, Palace Depression was dying.

"The whole place gave me the creeps," Joann said. "You could still see that it had been nice once. A kid could find it fascinating and ingenious. A terrific place to play. I mean, there were bathtubs set into the ground for fishponds, and birdbaths made from toilets, and sidewalks lined with upside-down bottles, beer and soda, so when the sun hit them you thought you were walking on stained glass. And the house—the castle, I should call it—was three stories of hub-caps and car hoods and refrigerator doors and I don't know what all. You could see the old man who built the place had something. I don't know what you'd call it, a joke, or a goof, or a piece of art . . .

"But now it was over. The place was falling down. Every-thing you touched gave way; every step you took, something moved. And whenever the wind came up, even a light wind, something shook or rattled. There were flies and rats, too. You'd better believe, I wondered why Eddie picked this of all days to show me where he used to play.

"There were a couple old barber chairs sitting in front of what was left of the castle. Chipped porcelain, green bronze, cracked leather seats that some kids had stuck their knives in. But Eddie sat me down in one and climbed up in the other, facing me. Then he spoke.

" 'They never decided what to do about this crazy place,' Eddie said. 'Even when the old guy was building it, and later, when people came to see it, they didn't like it so near town. A fire trap. A health hazard. A zoning violation. It was a hot topic around here. I heard my parents talking. But they couldn't keep me out of here. I hung around so much, the old guy let me be the ticket taker when he stayed inside with a bottle. Other times, I helped with repairs. That tickled my old man. Young Eddie training to be a repairman at a junk-yard.'

"He leaned back in the barber chair for a moment.

" 'Now it's all going back to being what it was. Junk to junk. A year or two from now, you won't be able to find this place. For sure, this is the last time that I come back.' "

That was when Joann took her chance. Usually she let Eddie tell her things in his own time. But lately he'd had this way of just digging himself deeper and deeper into a hole.

"Why are we here, Eddie? And how are you? And all that?"

"That about covers it," Eddie said. The way he sat in that

barber chair, with wreckage all around him, he reminded Joann of a king at the end of his dynasty. Any minute, they'd come for him. "What I liked about this place was the idea of it. Of taking all this . . . stuff . . . and bringing it together. I even thought that would be the title of the album that came out of Lakehurst. Palace Depression. Till I found another title."

"What was that?"

"Leaves of Grass."

"And . . . what about it?"

"What?"

"Did you get it?"

"I got what I had coming to me," Eddie said.

"Would you do it again?"

"No." That much Joann could see. There was only one Lakehurst in him. And one had been too many.

Eddie got up out of the barber chair and helped Joann out of hers.

"I don't know why I came back here," he remarked.

"That's when I knew," Joann said. "See, Eddie and I never made any deals. I want you to know that. We never talked about the future. And I thought the reason we never talked about it was that the present was so fine, why ruin it by planning ahead? Just let each day roll. But that afternoon at Palace Depression I knew there was another reason. I knew it in my bones. There wasn't going to be any future."

The phone was ringing. Joann got up, walked to the doorway between the kitchen and living room, lifted the receiver. She listened a second, waved me over, and handed me the phone.

Someone was playing "Far-Away Woman" at the other end. When the song finished, the line went dead.

"Half a dozen times a day, the last few days," she said. "Last night I thought I heard something. There was a car sitting in the driveway, with the parking lights on. First off, I think it's some kids, making out. Then I look closer. Know what kind of car it is? A 1951 Ford, like Eddie used to drive! You know what happened then? I'd turned on the lights when I got out of bed, so I was silhouetted against the window. Whoever was out there could see me. And did. And blinked the lights, high and low and high again, just like Eddie used to do. What's going on, Wordman?"

"They want the tapes."

"You sure?"

"Yes."

"You have something to do with that car, Wordman? Did I guess wrong about you?"

"No."

She wasn't convinced, I could see.

"Then what *do* you want?"

"I don't want the tapes," I said. "You keep them to yourself, that's all right. You sell them, that's fine too. I just want to get the story straight."

"What makes you think I have the tapes?"

"I'm guessing. Tell me I'm wrong, Joann. Tell me there weren't any tapes. Tell me you lost them. Tell me they were in the car with Eddie. Whatever's true . . . you tell me anything, I'll believe you. You always had my number."

"Yeah," she smiled, "I guess I did. But now?"

"Yes."

"Still?"

"Still."

"Then how come I never heard from you, Wordman? I always thought that you'd be coming around. 'Come see about me.' Know what else? I would have given it a try with you. You beat hell out of the guy I married. After Eddie, I wasn't particular. So what ever happened to you?"

"I guess . . ." She waited, but there was no way I could finish.

"No apologies necessary, at this late date," she said. "I used to figure it was Eddie got in your way. Even after he was dead, I was still Eddie's girl to you. But that wasn't it, was it? It was just . . . just . . ."

"Just me." She had me, from day one, through forever. Maybe that's why I'd never showed. She had me without half trying. She had me now.

"Even when I knew it wasn't in the cards, I used to . . . I don't know . . . root for you. Wherever you were. Hoping that you were up to something good. Something big. Something I might even hear about, if I kept my ears open. Funny, huh? Joann Carlino sitting on a farm, waiting to hear about you on the Academy Awards or something. It didn't turn out that way, did it?"

"No, it didn't," I confessed.

"No more music."

"No. The music stopped. And the words."

"Something you needed, you didn't have."

"I guess. Sometimes I think it was . . . you."

"No, Wordman. 'Cause you could have had me. What you needed was whatever it took to come after me. And now this . . . this reunion. Kind of a disappointment. Eddie and the tapes. Eddie and the tapes. That's what you're into. Oldies but goodies. That's all you want to talk about."

"It wasn't just the tapes," I protested. "It was you too."

"Me too?" She got up, collecting the cups and saucers. They clattered in the sink. One of them broke, I think.

"Me too?" She laughed at me. Not the head-tossing jeering she was entitled to, but the quiet chuckle you save for an incorrigible loser, a likable flop.

"I didn't mean . . . "

"Save your breath, Wordman. It doesn't matter. It's past one. You can stay if you want."

"Okay."

"On the couch."

She switched off the lights and went up the stairs while I stretched out and pulled a blanket over my body. I could hear her walking, opening her dresser, climbing into bed. It was just the sort of corny teenage situation they used to write songs about. I lay awake, trying to put some lines together. What a clever endearing way to redeem an awkward situation, to make up some lyric and serenade her from her front lawn!

> You walk up the steps
> To sleep alone
> I lay awake below
> All on my own.

"All on my own" was awkward. I never got past it. If Eddie were around, I'd have had the heart to complete the lyric and serenade Joann, I thought. But then, if Eddie were here, he'd be upstairs, loving Joann.

She came to me when it was still dark and placed her hands on my chest, wakening me with her whispering.

"Didn't you hear it?"

"What?"

"The phone's going crazy. You didn't hear it?" Her hands were shaking. I held them. They were cold. "Every five minutes for the past hour."

"Did you answer?"

"Yes," she said. She raised her hands to her face, carrying my hands along, and I felt tears. "It was . . . he said he was . . . Eddie."

We were both shaking now, two scared people in a dark farmhouse, and the phone upstairs kept ringing. I told her about the quonset. That didn't help a bit.

"Did you ever see his body, Joann?"

"No. He let me out down the road. We'd had an argument. He was so low, and I tried to cheer him up. Dumb me. Kissing him and ruffling up his hair, like that would make it better. He let me out. That was the last I saw of him. Ever. . . . You?"

"I was in the following car. I thought I saw him. I mean, there was a body, halfway through the windshield. Head, arms. I thought it was Eddie. I don't know. I ran toward the car, but the gas tank went, and after that . . . "

The phone was still ringing.

"Don't answer it," I said.

We listened to it ring. That wasn't much good either. Each ring sounded different. Some rings were sad and some were mad, and when the phone finally quit ringing, it left a certain anger in the air.

"Do you think . . . there's some way . . . that Eddie could be out there?" she asked, and I was dismayed to notice that her voice was hopeful.

"No way," I insisted, sounding surer than I was. "Why would he stay away so long? Why would he come back now?"

"You stayed away yourself," she countered, "just the same as Eddie."

Every time she said his name, it came a little easier. Eddie, Eddie, Eddie, like a refrain in a song. My boyfriend's back and there's gonna be trouble. Hey, bird dog, get away from my quail. You really got a hold on me. Some hold it was.

The phone rang again. Once. And stopped.

"That's it!" she burst out. "Swear to God, that's Eddie. One ring, that's our signal. It means get ready, he's coming over. He'll be here any minute."

She rushed upstairs, almost forgetting me. "You better go, Wordman. He finds you here in the middle of the night . . . I wouldn't want Eddie to get the wrong idea."

Now—not five minutes from now—but now was the time to choose. Did I believe in miracles? Did I want to believe?

Joann Carlino had cast her vote. That one ring of the phone had turned the trick. Eddie-my-love was on the way over.

I couldn't buy it. I didn't believe. I didn't want to. I admit it, shamefully, with a sense of betrayal: I wanted Eddie to be dead, to have been dead. God forgive me.

I went out the back door, closed it quietly, and stepped around to the driveway. Damn it! Whoever was coming had picked a perfect night for it. It was a balmy summer night, a light salt breeze punching through the humidity, and a full moon lifting over the pines. The top of the summer. They'd be open all night along the boardwalk. A wonderful night for midnight swims and late-night makeouts. Drink beer on porches, go for a spin, let the kids stay up. It was the kind of night that stretched the limits of the possible, that loosened lips and loins, that made believers out of doubters. Oh yeah, what a little moonlight can do.

I didn't want him to know I was there. I parked my car inside the barn, next to Joann's, and closed the door. Back in the kitchen, I picked up the pistol and slipped it in my pocket. The moonlight flooded into the house. It was bright enough to read a newspaper out on the front porch. But in one far corner, there was a pocket of darkness, just large enough to contain me. There I sat, waiting.

"Wordman? You still here? Wordman?" Twenty minutes later she came downstairs. I didn't answer. She stepped out onto the porch and glanced out to where my car had been. She stood there looking at the empty space. Perhaps she was whispering good-bye, but I didn't hear it.

She thought she was alone now, and I guess that made her nervous. I'd be nervous too. She was waiting for Eddie. It hurt me, sitting there, watching her wait, seeing her pace up and down, look down the road, loving Eddie.

There was no way of arguing with her. I could try to tell her that nobody came back from the dead, but after what had happened in the quonset, I wasn't sure. Or I could say that no lovers reunite after twenty years, but there I stood, proof that I was wrong. The then and the now, my careful compartments, were breaking down. Eddie, Joann, and I were all in a strange, illogical territory, where dates, tenses, time itself played tricks, and decades were brushed aside by a single phone call.

She jumped up and ran for the receiver.

"Eddie!" she cried. "Yes . . . yes . . . sure I do . . . I'll be here . . ."

This time he didn't keep her waiting long. Anyway, what

was ten minutes after twenty years? He gave her just enough time to go upstairs, dig out the tapes, and come back down. And then, like that, he arrived. He came jolting down the road in a boxlike '51 Ford, radio blaring, pulled into the driveway, and honked the horn—beep-beep-beep beep-beep —just like old times.

The horn-blowing was a nice touch. It sent chills down my spine. So did that old Ford sitting in the moonlight, beckoning her to start in right where she left off, like twenty years was just a detour, and death itself nothing more than a wrong turn. I guess I might have stopped Joann. I could have tackled her or tied her up or knocked her out. But it wasn't in me. She was on the edge of the sort of miracle we all dream about. If I stopped her now, she'd never forgive me.

Joann held back at the door, crying, afraid. She stood in the doorway looking out, waiting for Eddie to step out into the moonlight so she could rush toward him. But Eddie was too cool for that.

The headlights flashed to high, dimmed, flashed high again. The door on the rider's side swung open for her. The radio went down low, and that familiar voice called out to her.

"Hey, baby? What's the holdup? You know what I like!"

"Eddie," she whispered, but so low I could barely hear her. "Eddie!"

"Come on, honey!" Eddie shouted. "Let's get on with the music!"

That brought her out, running, crying, racing down the corridor of light that led from her front doorstep to the headlights of the Ford. She took her best shot at happiness, Joann did.

And so did Eddie.

I saw it, right where I expected to see it, a silver barrel pointing out from the driver's side, resting against the rolled-down window.

"There's a gun!" I shouted. Joann saw it, just as it fired.

She dropped and rolled across the grass.

Crouching in darkness, I pointed through the screen and fired three or four quick shots in the direction of the Ford. One of them somehow found a headlight.

The door slammed shut, the engine raced, and the old Ford cut across the lawn, spun onto the driveway, and raced down the road.

She lay on the grass unharmed, watching the car disappear down the road. You could hear him lay rubber when he turned onto the highway. Then the crickets and tree frogs reclaimed the night, and a dog that was barking somewhere down the road.

I knelt beside her. One look told me what she needed. No consolation. No I-told-you-so. Just my company, if only I could keep my mouth shut. I managed. She motioned for me to hold her. I managed that, till the night started turning gray.

"Thanks," she said. She put coffee on the table, toast and eggs, and pork chops she'd cooked for me. She only wanted coffee for herself.

"Are you okay?" I asked.

"I'm angry."

"At?"

"Myself, of course! I wasn't so smart last night. And you know what? I knew better. I knew it wasn't Eddie. The odds were—what?—a thousand to one against. You know what I was going to say, first thing? 'Where the hell have you been for twenty years?!' "

"You still went for it."

"I know. The phone call did it. And the car, blinking the headlights, beeping the horn. And that voice! Whoever it is ... they're good. It's frightening how good." She shuddered, but it passed. It felt comfortable sitting there with Joann, her watching me eat the meal she'd prepared on a sunny summer morning.

"After Eddie died, I made a promise to myself. A resolution, you could call it. Not to act on impulse anymore, not to let my feelings sweep me off. You can't live that way. Think. Plan. That's what I decided the day of the funeral. I kept that resolution, too. I did okay. Not great, but okay. Till last night."

"Funny," I said. "I made a resolution that was just the opposite of yours. Cut down on thinking. To go with my feelings more. Trust them. That's what got me in my car this summer. And brought me here."

"And now?"

"I want to find out who's out there."

"It's that important to you?"

"Yes. Enormously."

"Why?"

"I want to be able to feel right about it all. About Eddie and the rest of them."

"Who do you think it is?"

"First I thought it was somebody who was left over from the Lakehurst sessions. Not one of the big names. Some bodyguard or sideman. A small-timer with a long memory. Maybe that's it."

"What else?"

"Mannheim. Or somebody like Mannheim. A researcher digging into Eddie's career, or Buddy Holly's, anybody who came across that missing month. Those guys are crazy. They sift garbage, they reconstruct schedules from twenty years ago, laundry lists, tax returns, dentist's bills, they want it all. Anybody doing a job like that would come across that month in Lakehurst."

"You buy that?"

"No," I said. "Not after last night. Not after the way the phone rang, and the way he hit the horn. I'm afraid it's someone closer to home. Someone we know. Someone who knows us. It's gotten personal."

"All right," she said. "A Cruiser. Let's go through the list."

"There's Wendell," I began.

"But he's in prison."

"Not always," I replied, explaining Wendell's furloughs in the custody of Reverend Hopkins. Then there was Hopkins himself, the turtlenecked cleric who always kept his options open. If you believed in miracles, you could trust Kenny Hopkins. But Kenny had told me he didn't believe in miracles. And neither did I. People don't change that much.

There was Sally. That hurt, but it was hard to ignore him. All those years of playing oldies but goodies in motel lounges. His proprietary relationship with Eddie, his sense of having been ignored and wronged. Maybe Sally had convinced himself he had a valid claim. If so, he had the manpower to back it up. And a lead singer who sounded just like Eddie.

"So all we know is somebody killed Doc Robbins," Joann summarized. "Somebody robbed Eddie's parents. Somebody spooked you at the quonset. And came after me. It could be one of the old Cruisers. Or the new ones. Or somebody else altogether. Or some combination of the above."

"Yes," I conceded. Joann had this way of making me feel very unimpressed with myself.

"We know what they're after, though. The tapes they think I have. But you know what bothers me?"

"What?"

"*You* bother me. I don't know what you're after. I can't seem to get a handle on that."

"I was alive back then," I said. "It's odd how you keep waiting for your life to happen, to lift off the ground. You wait for that one period of time when you can say to yourself, *this is it!* Well . . . that was it."

"But it's over now. It's in the past."

"No it isn't. Why do you think you went running across the lawn last night?"

"Okay," Joann said. "Okay." She asked me to wait a minute while she went upstairs. I poured myself another cup of coffee and wondered what came next. Joann returned with an overnight bag in one hand and a small cake-size cardboard box in the other. She handed it to me.

"The tapes?" I asked.

"Yes."

I glanced inside the box, counting five boxes of recording tape. I wondered if I'd have the heart to play them. How could the results of that month in the quonset ever match the nobility of the conception? I'd almost prefer to keep hoping that Eddie, that all the Mr. Blacks and Mr. Whites, had pulled off a miracle. Isn't that what we always want to believe, when someone dies and we go rummaging through their trunks and attics, searching for the last masterpiece, the farewell message, the final expression? And wind up with bits and pieces, interesting failures, and ambitious plans, and we have to admit that's all there is, there is no more? We hope, by finding something more, to cheat death. But what we find, if we find anything, only confirms it.

"You're giving them to me?"

"I guess. If you want them."

"What's on them?"

"Would you believe it . . . I don't know."

"What? You never played them?"

"It was Eddie's secret."

"His death didn't change that?"

She shook her head and handed me her suitcase. I opened the barn door, put her suitcase in her Volkswagen. She started the car, backed, and turned. I followed, pulling alongside.

"Where are you headed, Wordman?"

"South."

"Chuck the tapes. That's my advice. They're trouble. What we had going for us back then . . . it's got nothing to do with what's happening now. No connection at all."

"I guess."

"You don't agree?"

"No."

"You'll play them, huh?"

"Yes. Once, anyway."

"Anybody asks me where the tapes are, what do I say?"

"You tell them. Don't worry about it."

"Okay." She started rolling up her window. Then she rolled it down again. "Sometimes I almost played them. When my marriage went bad, and I got thinking about the past. I thought there might be a message in there for me. Or at least a better good-bye than what we had."

"What stopped you?"

"I didn't want to say good-bye . . . "

"I get you."

"Not till last night. That was good-bye."

"I understand."

"And call me when it's over. If you . . . want to."

"Okay if I come back?"

"Oh, sure. Come on down. There's blueberries in the summer. Cut yourself a Christmas tree in December. In between . . . I don't suppose you hunt?"

"You know what I mean."

"Yeah. I do."

"So?"

"Sure," she said, rolling up the window. "Better late than never. 'Come see about me.' "

Then she rolled the window down, just an inch; she sounded like she was warning me off and bidding me on, all at once.

"If you're ready," she said.

15

From South Jersey, it was less than two hours to Philadelphia. Odd, random moments linger from that trip. I came up behind a yellow school bus and tried to pass it for half an hour, nosing out into the middle of the road, always blocked by oncoming traffic. The kids in the bus were singing and laughing, like they were on their way to a class picnic, and some of them made a game out of teasing me: stop, go, hurry up, get back. When I finally edged by, they cheered me, and when I looked up to return their greeting, I saw that they were senior citizens—canes, braces, and all. The youngest person was the bus driver. I drove, without stopping, through Vineland. Eddie's home was three blocks off Landis Avenue, to the left. His grave was behind a church, on the right. I looked for signs that Vineland honored its favorite son—a banner or a marker—but if they were there, I missed them. What I noticed was what Eddie used to say: how the town smelled of vegetables, tomatoes, spinach, or asparagus, every day a different smell in the air, depending on what the canneries were processing. The flavor of the day was celery. Forty-five minutes later, just when the highway lifted up towards the bridge across the Delaware, and with Eddie's *Leaves of Grass* beside me on the seat, I drove over Camden, a vast red sore slowly hardening into an everlasting scar. Strange. Some places, to be born again, all they need is a new mayor, a can-do governor, a concerned president. Other places, it'll take a personal appearance from Jesus Christ himself. That was Camden.

I parked in the long-term lot near the airport, rode the shuttle bus to the terminal, and checked the departure screen. I chose a flight down to Florida. I wanted to hide away in a place that was hot and old and out-of-season. I thought I'd head for Cape Canaveral-Kennedy. With space shots out of fashion, there'd be weeds in motel parking lots, and empty beaches, and an appropriate sense of things-winding-down. But near Melbourne, a gas jockey tipped me to the Golden Years Trailer Court, and I decided that here was where I'd make my last stand. There must be a homing instinct in northerners, that whenever life's warning light starts blinking red, we head down South to a place like this, hoping to delay that last and coldest season.

They may look tacky when you pass them on the highway, but these trailer courts turn out to be little Walden Ponds. You pare life away the way an impatient reader thins out the irrelevant sections of a bloated Sunday newspaper. Out go travel and real estate, sports and classified, current events and business. Gardening, stamp collecting, health: those are the important things.

Still, busy as I've been, news of the outside world does intrude. In California, *The Eddie Wilson Story* rushes in front of cameras. I have this information from watching the first half hour of the Carson show with Ed Riley, while we were waiting for *A Walk in the Sun* on another channel. The hero will be portrayed by Michael Landon, his buxom, omnipresent, and thoroughly supportive wife by Adrienne Barbeau, and Michael Jackson will be featured—obviously

—as Wendell Newton. They didn't mention who'd be me. If anyone. No matter, it's a walk-on. Musical arrangements and "new material" by Johnny's guest, a short, witty man named Paul Williams, who claimed he'd been a fan of Eddie Wilson's since he was this tall.

Another item: Salvatore Amato presented brief remarks when they finally got around to dedicating the Eddie Wilson Memorial Playground down in Vineland last weekend. "He was all New Jersey," Sally said. "He never wanted to leave and he never did." Missing from the newspaper was whether Sally played some tunes. Or hawked his latest album off the back of a truck. Or what they were canning that day.

Two more oddments on the Eddie Wilson front. Relaxing in my trailer the other day, I listened to a radio call-in show —dedications from Louise to Tony—that sort of thing. But when someone requested the memorial song for Elvis and Eddie and Buddy, I lunged for my new tape recorder and switched it on in time to catch the part of the song concerning my late friend. I'm sure you know the basic format for this kind of song. It hasn't changed since "They Needed a Songbird in Heaven So God Took Caruso Away."

> "A terrible crash on a wet foggy night
> Took the king of the Cruisers
> Out of our sight . . ."

They sang that part. Then came a choked-up recitative.

> "Your far-away woman
> That came on so strong
> We hope that you found her
> After searchin' so long
> That you're movin' and groovin'
> Way up in the sky
> That you're high on God's charts
> Up where hits never die . . ."

And more singing:

> "Now he's riding God's highway
> And watching his speed
> But the king of the Cruisers
> Is still in the lead . . ."

There you have it: movie, monument, maudlin lyric. I could be wrong, but I bet that the Eddie Wilson revival has entered its last phase. Soon the backlash will set in, the indifference and forgetting. Returning from the dead is one thing. Remaining permanently in the hearts of the living is quite another.

One last development that didn't make the newspapers. In Elizabeth, New Jersey, at the Union County courthouse, Doris Campbell Ridgeway filed papers for a divorce which I will not contest. We live in different countries. For Doris, today led to tomorrow; for me, it pointed back to yesterday. She hoped for the future. For me, the future was meaningless unless I could come to terms with the past. That's why I'm sitting in Florida—just waiting for the then and the now to connect, as they surely will.

I can't wait for it to happen! Knowing my adversary is more important to me than escaping him. I don't want to spend the rest of my life wondering whether publicity-starved Sally or cunning Kenny butchered Doc Robbins at his turntable. I don't want to keep asking myself who was standing in the shadows at the back of the quonset, or sitting behind the wheel of the '51 Ford that drove into Joann's driveway. Every time I reread these pages, I find another suspect, a new scenario. No one escapes. Susan Foley, Elliot Mannheim, Sally Amato, Kenny Hopkins, Eddie Wilson, and Joann Carlino. Everyone I've met is a possible killer. I want to find that killer—and vindicate the rest.

There's more. I told Joann that all I wanted was the true story. I meant it. But I also had to write it. Even now, I can't shake the memory of Wendell Newton asking me, "How many books you written so far, Wordman?" They all expected more of me. Whatever happened to you, Wordman?

The question haunts me. Wendell looking me up in the card catalog. Joann watching for me on the Academy Awards. Sally figuring I must have taken a pseudonym. Whatever happened to me? I can't ignore that question. These weren't high school seniors voting the most likely to succeed, or jaycee hustlers electing man of the year. These were people I loved, who knew my strengths and weaknesses as well as I did, and I let them down. Well, it seems to me that whatever happened had to do with an excess of caution, a too-measured pace, a low level of expectations, a reluctance to take chances with music, with women, with life itself. There's not much I can do about it now. I can't picture myself picking up a guitar or peddling lyrics; becoming a Cruiser at thirty-seven makes as much sense as renting that '51 Ford. But there is one thing I can do. I can face the man, or ghost, who's been moving through our lives, meet him—or her—head-on. That's what I've been waiting for.

Kindly Herman Biedermann knocked gently on my trailer door, reluctant to interrupt my work. He brought my eviction notice. I'd expected Martha Darmstadter, armed with broomstick and garden hose, heading up a lynch mob. But it was only Herman, blushing and shuffling. I readily agreed to move, of course, and Herman was too polite to press me for the fixed moving date Martha had obviously insisted on.

"These phone calls, Frank. What are they all about? Is someone after you?"

"Yes."

"If it's a matter of money . . ."

"It's not money. At least not in the way you mean . . . "

"Some woman? Your wife? Or somebody else's?"

"It's not that. It's a matter of . . . information."

"Like a trade secret?"

"You could call it that."

"I read about that stuff. Those big corporations, it's terrible the things they'll do to get a leg up. Industrial espionage, they call it. What line of work does this concern?"

"Music."

"They're the worst! I read about them. Payola and drugs and broads. *U.S. News & World Report* had a long article about that racket. I think I saved it. Now these phone calls, what are they supposed to accomplish?"

"Flush me out, I guess."

"Looks like they worked," Herman said, growing angry. "We behaved just the way they wanted us to. Like chickens in a coop. Wait'll I tell that Martha."

"Hold on, Herman . . . I'll be out of here . . ." But Herman was gone before I could stop him, rushing across to Martha Darmstadter's trailer.

"Open up, you dingleberry!" he shouted, pounding on her door. They all came out, everybody but Minnie Schumacher, assembling for a town meeting that lasted all afternoon. That night, when I came back from my evening walk, I found a note under my door.

> *Frank . . .*
> *I fixed it with the rest. You stay as long as*
> *you like.*
>
> > *Your friend,*
> > *Herman*
>
> *P.S. I'm looking for that*
> U.S. News

Reading that note, I thought there was nothing they could do that would move me more . . . until yesterday morning, Al Ferraro told me what they'd planned. They'd get the phone company to route all calls to one phone, at Martha's, which would become their "command post." Women would be in charge of food and coffee, while men took turns at the phone, four hours to a shift, and they'd keep doing it, Al said, "until the son of a bitch who's after you runs out of dimes."

I think they were all up for it. They wanted to transform
Golden Years Trailer Court into Fort Apache. So they felt
cheated when the calls stopped as suddenly as they started.
A hypochondriacal torpor settled over the place this morning, the same feeling I sense when Al finds his mailbox
empty or Ed Riley's son doesn't call.

This morning, though, there was one last call, for me. The
call I've been expecting.

"Frank Ridgeway?"

"Speaking."

"Wow. You took some tracking down. This is Elliot Mannheim. Remember me?"

"Sure I remember you." So it was Mannheim! I'd wondered who the last phone call would come from. I'd hoped it
wouldn't be from Sally, just happening to be in the neighborhood, or Kenny Hopkins, suddenly anxious to talk over old
times, or Joann Carlino, wondering whatever happened to
me. Mannheim. Fine. Let it be Mannheim.

"I was wondering about your article," I said. "You said
you'd send me a clipping."

"It hasn't appeared yet. This story just got bigger and
weirder as it went along. The further I got into it, the more
I came across."

"I can imagine."

"But I've got most of what I need now. Except . . . well
. . . you know."

"I'm not sure I do."

"To put it frankly, you turn out to be a more important
source than I figured. Everywhere I go, they talk about the
Wordman. I really need that second interview with you, to
wrap things up."

"You came all the way down to Florida just to see me?"

"Well, there's another story. The Bee Gees are down in
Miami, of course. You've heard of them?"

"No."

"Anyway, when can I see you?"

"Oh, anytime. I'm not up to much these days. The sooner the better."

"Look, I'm spread all over a room up at The Tides in Cocoa Beach. Would it be asking too much if you came over here? I could pick you up."

"Not necessary. When do you want to see me?"

"How about tonight?"

"Why not this afternoon?"

"Well . . . okay. I'll be ready."

"I'm sure you will." The conversation had gone so well, I bet Mannheim didn't know how to top it off. How could he know that I would be so docile, so easily gulled, so willing to surrender?

"Along the way, I've heard that some interesting Wilson material may have come into your possession since our last interview. If it'll help jog your memory, you can bring it along."

"You have a tape recorder in your room?"

"Oh sure. You know me—I'm lost without one."

"Then there shouldn't be any problem. I'll bet we can finish everything in one session."

"I bet you're right," Mannheim said.

I've borrowed the keys to Herman Biedermann's car, straightened up the trailer, and stacked this manuscript on the dining table, next to a book of airmail stamps and a large manila envelope addressed to Wendell Newton. I hope the Dewey Decimal System leaves room for unpublished manuscripts. Slip this one in among the prison confessionals: my life in crime, my soul on ice.

Wendell: I never played the tapes. Funny about that, hard to explain. Joann might understand; I suggest you talk it over with her the next time she visits. The first thing I bought in Florida was a tape recorder. But I couldn't play them. Some failure of nerve, maybe. I feel that I have to go into this final confrontation not knowing.

See, Wendell, if the tapes were great, I might feel I had

to run to New York, find someone to release them, tell it to the world. If they were awful, or if they were blank, I might not have the heart to keep this appointment that I'm about to keep.

Good, bad, or indifferent, Eddie died for those *Leaves of Grass*. They were his stab at pulling his life together, and the lives of everyone who touched him. He was taking a shot at what the rest of us are too small or cautious or smart to try. He wanted to cover the territory just like Whitman did. You know, Wendell, when you mentioned *Leaves of Grass* back at the prison, I didn't have the faintest idea what you were talking about. Later, when I recalled Eddie's visit to the Whitman house, it made some kind of sense, but I still didn't grasp what he intended. But Joann's account of the Lakehurst sessions, of all those Mr. Blacks and Mr. Whites you and Eddie brought together, completed the picture. Now *Leaves of Grass* sounds to me like a dream remembered, Eddie's dream, and yours.

Does that make any sense at all, old friend? Perhaps not. Yesterday it would have seemed illogical. Tomorrow, too. But today, just now, it's the only way to go.

16

If a couple thousand Midwest truck drivers ever want to find out where their pension money went, they can check out The Tides resort in Cocoa Beach, Florida.

It's a resort for all seasons, with pools and beaches, greens and stables and racetracks. They sponsor tennis classics, celebrity golf tournaments, and telethons that combat the deadliest of maladies.

They can put you up on a houseboat, sell you a condominium, rent you everything from a chalet to a bungalow. You go to bed with the Gideon Bible or the Dallas cheerleaders, it's all the same to them.

It's not the sort of place you'd expect a scuffling young free-lancer to put up at, but I'd long since given up the notion that Elliot Mannheim lived by pen alone. Oh, maybe he could write a scratch, but as soon as he got wind of the Lakehurst tapes, he turned entrepreneur. I bet he made a honey of a deal, with enough money up front to hire all the help he needed.

I'd underestimated him. I'd put him down as one of those dopey enthusiastic kids who turn up in my high school classes from time to time. The oh-wowers who get way into comic-book collecting, *Star Wars,* video games. I give them a C-plus and watch them graduate, wondering how they'll ever survive in the cruel world. But a funny thing about those goofy kids. They grow claws. They find angles. They get into collecting money the same way they collected comic books. And they kill to add to their collection.

Mannheim was staying just off the beach in a secluded bungalow, surrounded by a grove of soft-needled pine.

A '51 Ford was parked in front. Elliot Mannheim was beyond pretending.

I pulled in next to the Ford, slipped Joann Carlino's pistol into my pocket, and picked up the paper bag of tapes. There were five of them, all unlabeled, except for one. It said: *Leaves of Grass.*

Inside the bungalow, Mannheim was warming up for the interview session. I heard Eddie singing "Down on My Knees," pounding through equipment that was so good you'd swear he was in the living room. It was so convincing, I checked myself, waiting for Hopkins' drum break, making sure it was just a record. I don't know what I'd have done if Eddie kept on singing unaccompanied.

With the music blaring, there was no point in knocking on the door. I pushed it open and walked inside, through a kitchen littered with leftover carry-out food. The living room was next—dark, sunken, covered with a whirlwind of transcripts, tapes, manuscripts, and magazines. I moved through, out into the patio–swimming pool area.

Mannheim was lying on the diving board, flat on his back, sunning himself. The sun had already passed over the board, however, and he hadn't followed it. He never would. He'd never move again, unless movement meant the slow drip of blood into the swimming pool below.

I walked closer to the edge. I feared what I would find there, and I found just what I feared. Susan Foley was floating on her stomach, face down, like she'd lost something on the bottom of the pool. And, for a moment, I prayed that she was only floating. I grabbed a lifeguard's hook off the fence and pointed it toward her. I touched her, and I thought she turned, ever so slowly, toward me. I'll never know what it was—a last living movement or an accident of the water. But her face was gone, one whole side of it, cheek and smile just blown away. I gagged, dropped the pole, and backed away.

Eddie's music was still playing, his twenty-year-old voice the only thing of life left in the house. I stepped into the living room, thinking that I'd better call the police. First, though, I had to turn off the tape.

Only it wasn't a tape. It was an l.p. album, our one and only, with the phonograph arm just crossing into the innermost song. That meant that eighteen minutes ago, twenty at the most, someone had put that record on. Was it Mannheim, buck naked, flipping on some sounds before joining his woman on the patio? He knew that I was coming, but perhaps that would be his triumph over me: contemptuously parking the Ford in front, greeting me naked, his woman waiting for him at the pool. Or had they already been out there, sunning and swimming, fellating each other on the diving board, when the music suddenly exploded, loud and strong, "On the Dark Side," and they turned to chase the maid and faced their killer, stepping out onto the patio, the sound of his shots muffled by that old-time rock and roll? Maybe the Ford didn't belong to Mannheim. Maybe it belonged to Mannheim's visitor.

I lifted up the needle and the room turned quiet, and then I guessed I wasn't alone. Suddenly I heard a low, humming sound, and the living room drapes drew over the picture window, casting the room into darkness. From the far side of the room, from the top of a sleeping loft, I heard that voice again.

"Hello, Wordman."

I peered into the darkness. There was someone sitting on

the loft bed. I saw legs dangling in the air near the ladder, but the upper half of his body escaped me.

"Don't strain your eyes, Wordman. Better turn around."

"Eddie?"

"Turn around, Wordman." This time it was a command, which I obeyed.

"You do like I say, old buddy. I'd hate like hell to fuck up the group. You bring my tapes?"

"Yes," I said. And then I muttered, *"Leaves of Grass."*

"What's that, Wordman? Speak up."

"I said ... *Leaves of Grass.*"

A puzzled silence.

"Leaves of ... Just leave them leaves on the table. Then you can leave yourself."

I didn't believe him. I dropped the bag on the table, fell to the floor. By then, the first bullet had smashed into the glass-topped table next to me, and the second scraped the floor.

I fired two shots up at the loft. They both missed, but they made him move. It would take more than a mattress to protect him.

He fired again, and this time the glass table exploded, splinters of glass all around me, at my hands and knees, blood spurting through my hair, across my forehead, but I could still see. I could see his feet reach for the top rung, I could see his first step down, his feet, his knees, and now his waist, and I didn't wait to see the rest of him. I preferred not knowing. I emptied the pistol at the ladder, heard a scream, a falling body, and a pistol that slid toward me like a shuffleboard puck.

I scooped up the pistol and tore open the drapes, first from one side, then the other, and the late-afternoon light came pouring in. And then I walked over to where he lay, a foot still caught in the ladder, hooked and bleeding so it stopped him from turning toward me, but I recognized him and the apologetic smile that flashed behind his pain.

"Jesus Christ, Doc!"

I lifted his leg out of the ladder. He screamed when I did it. The knee looked terrible, and another shot must have found the inside of his thigh. Blood was soaking through his trousers. I ran out to the bathroom, found a towel, wrapped it tightly around his thigh, securing it with my belt. The towel turned red in no time.

"I thought you were dead, Doc."

"Wish to hell I was," he gasped. I could hardly hear him. "I'm sorry. For shooting. Missing. Hitting. All kinds of sorry. Lemme count the ways . . ."

"That was you I talked to when I called the radio station?"

" 'Master of voices, maker of choices,' you remember, don't you? Daddy Toecheese, the all-night black and bluesman, with a voice so dark it leaves a thumbprint on coal. Or Edsel Hickey, with the dawn hog-belly prices."

"And Eddie Wilson?"

"Long as you don't ask me to sing. It goes flat, I try to sing."

"What were you doing at the quonset?"

"I followed you to the prison. After that, I knew where you were headed. I arrived ahead of you. I remembered the studio. And the river. I was gonna take a swim. I parked back in the pines, stripped, and was headed for the river when I saw your car coming."

"You were at Joann's?"

"Yes."

"You could have killed her!"

"Oh hell, no way," he assured me. I'll never know whether he was telling the truth or lying to save my opinion of him. "I'da picked up the tapes and run."

"You rousted Eddie's folks?"

"Not me. That was the competition. America's sweethearts."

"Who?"

"In the pool." He was turning pale and tremulous. The towel wasn't working.

"Doc . . . you blew them away. Why?"

"This morning, I stopped by. I knew Mannheim's game the minute I met him. I knew we were both after the same thing. I wanted to make a deal. Him, you, and me. Everybody would get a cut. But he treated me like . . ."

I knew how Mannheim treated Doc. Like he was small-time and out-of-date, not worth talking to, a radio character in a cheap toupee and a loud suit.

"He had it in the bag, he said. He laughed at me. Who needed me?"

He was crying now, not just because his leg was hurting. All the indignities and slights, the near-misses and might-have-beens piled in on him. So he returned, driving the car that was as dated as he was: a blast from the past.

"Who needed me?" he sobbed.

"I'll call an ambulance," I said.

"No," Doc said. "Ambulance means doctors. And cops. And prison. I want it here."

"You need help."

"Yeah. What would you say . . . if I asked you to leave?"

"Leave you here? Like this?"

"I brought you into this. Now I'm telling you to pull out."

"You'll die!"

"Either way, I die. It's a no-win situation. This is how I want to end it."

He wouldn't have long, without help. Any minute, he'd lose consciousness.

"Get out, Wordman. It's over!" And then, begging me, "*Please!*"

I'll never know if what I did was right. It'll haunt me through the years, the picture of Doc bleeding on the floor and me backing away, shaken and crying. I tell myself I'd have done anything for Doc. And that's just it: I did what he asked.

"Doc . . ." I stood over him. He looked up, but I'll bet he didn't see more than a shadow. "Why'd you bring me in?"

"You were the only one I trusted . . . and the only one who trusted me . . . Wordman."

I left, a step at a time, each step turning life to death, doubt into finality, present into past, a step at a time, dividing yet connecting us forever. The last I saw of Doc, he was reaching for his thigh, to loosen the belt and let his life flow out.

A second time, I mourned him. At fifteen miles per hour, driving out of The Tides, waving pedestrians across, slowing for golf carts, I mourned him. Down corridors of hibiscus, past golf course and nursery, out onto the highway, my speed increasing, the distance between us widening, I mourned him more.

That night, when I finally got finished talking to the police, I played the tapes.

Epilogue

She came down the steps at the Port Authority Bus Terminal, saw me waiting at the newsstand, ran toward me.

"Is it over?"

"The bad part is," I said. "I guess."

At a Greek restaurant in the West Forties, I brought out my machine. And the tape.

"Four of them were blank. Not a sound on them."

"That'll break Wendell's heart."

"He gets out next month. I plan to be there. Will you join me?"

"Yes."

"Listen closely now."

She held my hand. I felt it tighten when we heard Eddie's voice, half speaking, half singing, unaccompanied.

"I bequeath myself to the dirt to grow from under
the grass I love

If you want me again, look for me under your
    boot soles
You will hardly know who I am . . .
Missing me one place search another,
    I stop somewhere waiting for you."

"It's the ending from 'Song of Myself,' " I said. "In *Leaves of Grass*."

"It sounds," she said, "like Eddie was saying good-bye."

"Yes."

"And that's all there was? A scrap of poetry?"

"Yeah," I said. "I'm grateful for that."

She didn't say a word.

"I mean it, Joann. I'm glad you left the poem."

She was something! She still didn't react.

"Four reels of blank tape and twenty seconds of poetry on the fifth. Come on, Joann! Why'd he give you all that tape if so little was on it?"

Now she smiled. I suspect she was grateful I'd figured it out. I don't think she would ever have volunteered it, but she was glad I knew.

"You lied to me about never listening," I said. "I guess you had a reason."

She nodded, reaching for my hand.

"Sure I listened. Right after he died. I wanted to know why Eddie left. I figured he wanted me to know."

"And?"

"It hadn't worked at Lakehurst. You want me to tell you all the different ways it didn't work?"

"No."

"I kept the tapes. But when 'Far-Away Woman' came back and it looked like people would want the tapes—would want anything—I had to ask myself what Eddie would want. We had an acid test, you know. Whether we could close our eyes and hear it playing at Vince's Boardwalk Bar."

"I understand," I said.

"Eddie wouldn't have wanted people picking over bits and pieces, dubbing in new arrangements, violins and voices and all. And he wasn't into being a curiosity. 'Top Forty's where it's at,' he used to say. 'All the rest is stamp collecting.'"

We laughed at that, hearing Eddie say it, remembering his voice and picturing the expression on his face. It felt fine, remembering him that way.

"The night before you came I erased everything but the poem. That I was saving for us."

"Thanks."

"And . . . what now, Wordman?"

"Get on with the music."

The Garden was packed. Thousands of kids.

"I feel old," she said.

"No you don't."

We waited past Bobby Rydell and Jay and the Americans, till Sally Amato and the Original Parkway Cruisers came on.

"They sound good," Joann said. "Never better."

"Want to say hello backstage?"

"No. This is close enough."

Near the end of the set they darkened the houselights. We all lit a candle for Eddie Wilson.

Joann Carlino and I cruised out of the Holland Tunnel and drove once more through that weird, fallen landscape which Eddie had loved. The Pulaski Skyway carried us over the refineries and marshes he celebrated. The turnpike and then the parkway led us south along the tawdry, half-romantic shoreline where his voice still reached the corners of a hundred common bars. Somewhere after the Raritan Bridge at Perth Amboy, we passed the place he died. I reached a hand out to Joann and she took mine, but it was Eddie we loved. I loved him that night. I loved him for his intervention in my life, then and now, for the way the memory of him would encourage and reproach me always. I loved him for the music he wove into my time on earth. I loved him for his dream, too, his *Leaves of Grass*.

It was past one when we reached Toms River.
She never turned on the light in the living room.
"The couch?" I asked.
"Upstairs." She reached for my hand and led me up the steps.
"Wordman?"
"Yes."
"You've been wanting this a long time?"
"Seems like a lifetime."

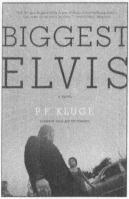
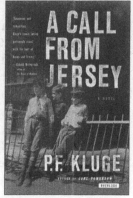
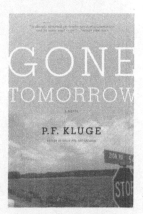